...ffee ... rs
...ul. She has also written two memoirs: ...
School, about her life in Afghanistan, and *The House on* ...
Street, on her experiences following her return to America. She
spent five years teaching and later directing the Kabul Beauty
School, the first modern beauty academy and training salon in
Afghanistan.

Deborah also owned the Oasis Salon and the Cabul Coffee
House, and is the founder of the nonprofit organization Oasis
Rescue, which aims to teach economically disadvantaged
women, and women in post-conflict and disaster-stricken areas,
the art of hairdressing.

She currently lives in Mazatlán, Mexico, where she owns
Tippy Toes salon and spa.

4721800041847 8

Also by Deborah Rodriguez

FICTION
The Little Coffee Shop of Kabul
Return to the Little Coffee Shop of Kabul

NON-FICTION
The Kabul Beauty School
The House on Carnaval Street

The Zanzibar Wife

DEBORAH RODRIGUEZ

sphere

SPHERE

First published in Australia in 2017 by Bantam
an imprint of Penguin Random House Australia Pty Ltd
First published in Great Britain in 2017 by Sphere

1 3 5 7 9 10 8 6 4 2

Copyright © Deborah Rodriguez 2017

Recipes © Vanessa Arena ('The "real" Spice Island spice cake' and
'Ginger beef samosas') and © Jaleela Banu (Omani halwa)

The moral right of the author has been asserted.

*All characters and events in this publication, other than those
clearly in the public domain, are fictitious and any resemblance
to real persons, living or dead, is purely coincidental.*

All rights reserved.
No part of this publication may be reproduced, stored in a
retrieval system, or transmitted, in any form or by any means, without
the prior permission in writing of the publisher, nor be otherwise circulated
in any form of binding or cover other than that in which it is published
and without a similar condition including this condition being
imposed on the subsequent purchaser.

A CIP catalogue record for this book
is available from the British Library.

ISBN 978-0-7515-6148-7

Printed and bound in Great Britain by Clays Ltd, St Ives plc

Papers used by Sphere are from well-managed forests
and other responsible sources.

Sphere
An imprint of
Little, Brown Book Group
Carmelite House
50 Victoria Embankment
London EC4Y 0DZ

An Hachette UK Company
www.hachette.co.uk

www.littlebrown.co.uk.

For James Benjamin Robinton, a tough little guy who was an affirmation of the true magic of life during the making of this book.

*Hauwezi kuvuka ziwa hadi uwe na ujasiri wa kutouona
urefu wa pwani.*

You can never cross the ocean until you have the courage
to lose sight of the shore.

—SWAHILI PROVERB

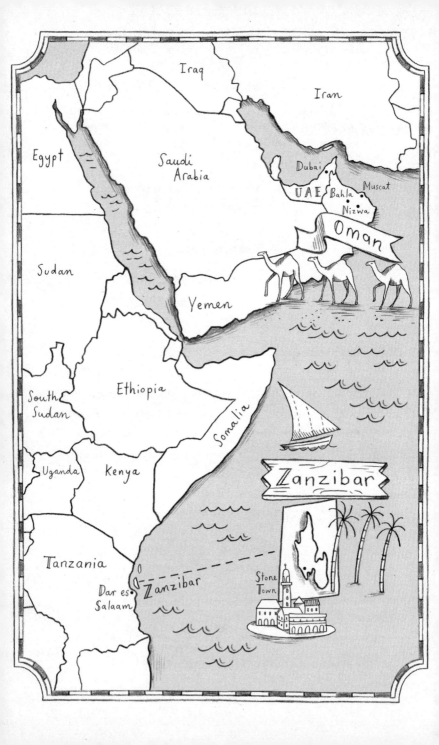

Prologue

Lesbos, November 2015

It was the sounds that first got her attention, the cries and screams loud enough to break through the howling wind and pummeling rain. Everyone had heard them, and now it was a race down to the sea. Who would get there first this time, she wondered as her boots flew over the wet, pebbly ground, her heart pounding from the effort. She willed her legs to run faster as the black dot in the distance became clearly recognizable as a boat. At the water's edge she tossed aside her plastic poncho and pulled the Leica's strap from her neck, securing it around her wrist just as the others arrived behind her. They stood like an army, cameras at the ready as the sagging rubber raft came within wading distance to shore. A young man—the first off—stumbling through the choppy waters. *Click.* A teenager paddling furiously through the surf. *Click click.* A woman climbing over the raft's half-deflated edge, clinging desperately to a tiny sack of belongings. *Click click click.* Soon elbows were flying as the competition heated for the shot, that one gut-wrenching image, the gold prize that would land the front page. She dug in her heels and held her ground, the adrenalin gushing through her veins.

The refugees began to reach the shore. Some stood stunned, some fell to their knees in prayer. Others collapsed with exhaustion. The clicking around her approached a frenzy, a rush to capture the families embracing, the children crying, the faces stamped with mixed fear and relief. The sound of the shutters seemed to reach a deafening roar, drowning out the noise of the chaos and confusion echoing across the beach.

Thirty feet away from land a man teetered among the rocks, the churning water as high as his waist. As he struggled to keep hold with one arm of an old woman staggering behind him, he reached out with his other hand, which held that of the small boy beside him, toward those on shore, his eyes screaming a silent plea for help. She pushed past those standing on either side of her and lumbered into the surf, her camera held high above the waves. As she came nearer, the man released the old woman to devote both arms to the effort of delivering the boy to safety.

Click.

The boy reached out his own tiny arms.

Click click.

Suddenly, just as she was getting close enough to focus on the stubble on the man's chin, she felt a shove from behind her as two hands shot out and grabbed the crying boy.

"What the fuck, Rachel! What the hell is wrong with you?"

*

"*Je prends un verre de vin rouge, s'il vous plaît.*"

The waiter took Rachel's order and pirouetted to retrieve the wine from the bar inside. She was the first to arrive at the café—on purpose—allowing herself time for a glass or two before the others showed up. Her flight from Athens had landed late at Charles de Gaulle, and she'd only had enough time for a quick shower before hopping on the metro to République. Now, as she took her first sip of wine, she struggled to shake the images from the morning in Lesbos from her brain.

Had it only been two days ago? It was hard to imagine, as couples strolled arm in arm through the warm autumn evening, the light from shop windows offering a promising glow to the start of the weekend. It was never easy, trying to reconcile the differences between a world in strife and a world at peace. But Rachel was used to the challenge of working her way back and forth from one to the other. How many times had she tried to grab a quick escape to some tranquil spot between assignments, only to find herself unable to truly enjoy it? And yes, it was often hard for her to relate to people who hadn't been where she'd been, seen what she'd seen. Her impatience with First World problems had lost her more than one old friend.

But what had occurred in Lesbos … that was different. When she'd heard her friend Antonio screaming at her, and watched silently as he let his own camera drop onto his chest to pull the boy to safety, something had snapped. What the fuck *was* wrong with her?

Rachel took pride in her reputation for being tough. It's what made her stand out in a world of men. But it was one thing to be fearless, for being willing to venture where few female photographers dared to go; it was another to be heartless. Sure, she'd been in countless situations before like the one on the beach, an uninvited guest in the midst of other people's most desperate moments. She was used to the necessity of distancing herself, of psyching herself into the zone you needed to be in to get that perfect shot. They all were. But how, and when, did it happen that she became one of the ones who crossed that line between being hardened and being totally callous— no, worse, unfeeling? Because that was what it had been. She had not been able to feel anything beyond her craving for the shot.

Rachel couldn't stop picturing that man as he appeared before them, so desperate for his family's survival, and each time she saw it the image hit her like a rogue wave from the sea, carrying with it a sense of disgust for the vanity of her profession, for who she had become. What good was she, hiding behind her lens as if the cold cylinder of metal and glass were a shield from the real-life suffering she was called upon to document? It was true that there was always the possibility of her photos getting published, and with that the hope of gaining the sympathy of people who had the power and inclination to help. That's how a lot of her colleagues justified their behavior and eased their consciences. Some photographers seemed to cling to the notion of having a calling, serving a noble cause, as if it were their divine destiny. Those were the ones who wore their sense of purpose like a badge. Even Rachel had done that, when it suited her. But deep down she knew she didn't really feel that way.

Of course, who wouldn't hope for their photos to cast some light on the plight of those who had no voice? But if Rachel were honest with herself, her rewards had always felt more personal, especially during those times when the thrill of getting that perfect shot coursed through her blood like a drug. She had questioned her motives more than once. There had been times before when, seeing the compassion coming through in some of her colleagues, she would find herself envious. Her emotions just never seemed to live so close to the skin. Until now.

She gulped the wine as if it were water, hoping that enough of it might help her get some sleep. The last two nights had been rendered sleepless by an endless loop of the horrors she'd witnessed over the past dozen years—every wounded soldier, every burned-out village, every starving child, every lifeless body, every bloody protester, every victim of a deadly earthquake, every desperate refugee, every wailing woman, every stunned survivor of a ruthless tsunami, every trigger-happy, fiery-eyed rebel. Clearly something had happened to her that morning on the beach. She'd felt a breach inside, as if a door were being forced open and she was jammed up against it on the other side, struggling to keep it shut.

A break. Maybe that was all she needed, she thought as she drained the glass and slid the backpack that sat on her lap to the space between her feet. A chance to change the channel and clear her head, to get back to the Rachel she knew she was. She closed her eyes and tried to focus on the smells and sounds of a soft Paris night. Musky leaves newly fallen from the trees. The cartoon beep of a little car. Diesel and espresso. The tinkling of a spoon against a cup. The silky melody of the language of love. *Be here now*, as her mother used to say. And why not enjoy all the beautiful, ignorant bliss around her? After all, the calm and civility of this place was just as real as the turmoil and craziness of another, wasn't it?

"Hey, Lil' Cherry Bomb, how's it hanging?"

Rachel winced. She hated her nickname and all it implied about her gender, her size, her reputation. No man would put up with the amount of teasing and ragging she'd faced as one of the few women in her field. Nevertheless, she greeted Sean with a kiss on each of his smooth, pink cheeks. She hadn't seen him since Darfur—or was it Tahrir Square?

"Lovely evening, isn't it?" he asked, his posh Knightsbridge accent adding a sense of sophistication to the occasion, as if they always came together over cocktails instead of over revolutions or coups.

"Quite," she said with a forced laugh as he pulled up a chair beside her.

"What, you've given up the Jack?" he said, eyeing the last drop of wine in her glass.

"Hardly. But when in France, as they say."

"*Vive la France*, as I say." Sean signaled to the waiter for two more. "There they are." Phil and Tim waved from half a block away, deep in conversation. Sean dragged two more chairs across the sidewalk and held out his arms for a hug from each of the gangly men.

"Long time no see." Phil bent to kiss Rachel on the head.

"Ditto," Tim added as he gave her shoulder a squeeze.

Rachel was happy to reconnect with her old pals, and felt comforted by their familiar presence. It was one of the things she liked most about her world, the way you could pick up with someone at any moment in any city and it was as though you had seen them yesterday. She could feel her limbs soften, her jaw loosen, as she finally started to relax.

After they had each filled in the others on their latest jobs, their recent successes, their next assignments, the inevitable storytelling began. More wine had been ordered. Now Phil was talking. Rachel sat back and half-listened.

"Did I ever tell you guys about that time in Somalia?" His beady eyes narrowed as he recounted the time he was taken captive at gunpoint and had, against all odds, managed to convince the teenage insurgents that all he wanted to do was tell the world of their plight, and how these kids ended up treating him like a god, and how he got the most amazing shots that he, no *anyone*, could have ever gotten down there.

Rachel rolled her eyes. Phil was sort of sweet, but what a bullshit artist. How could she have ever slept with that guy, even if it was just once. Or was it twice? It had been about a year ago by now—she couldn't remember. A rebound fling. Not serious.

Then it was Tim's turn to boast. His story? The one about how he once managed to get inside a Taliban stronghold for an exclusive with a commander who, during the course of the interview, became suspicious and threatened Tim with execution by beheading if he turned out not to be who or what he said he was. Tim claimed his narrow escape was due only to his astoundingly comprehensive knowledge of the Koran, and his awesome ability to charm his way out of any situation. She knew damn well that wasn't quite the way things went down, as she had been paired with him for that assignment. In those days the two of them had been quite a topic of gossip on the conflict trail. Rachel didn't mind, but nothing serious had really ever happened between the two of them.

Back then she was still with Jonathan. That was before he'd walked away from their relationship, after having enough of waiting for her too infrequent returns home, and enough of her restlessness and impatience when she was there with him, as he had put it so succinctly in a letter that she still kept tucked away in a box somewhere. She had bristled at his words, responding with a fury that no doubt served to prove his point more than it helped to make hers. She had insisted that he was threatened by her work. He in turn blamed everything on her addiction to an adrenalin-fueled lifestyle.

She should have seen what was coming. The truth was, for most of her colleagues, their passions were in their profession. Everyone out in the field got divorced, became separated, cheated. *Wheels up, rings off*, the saying went. But the part that really stung—the words that had truly pissed her off that day Jonathan dumped her for good, the words that now came crashing back to her with the force of a hurricane—was his final blow before he walked out the door. *There is something seriously lacking in you, Rach. It's like you have no soul.* Until two days ago she would have defended herself fiercely against his accusation, had he given her the chance. Now, as she sat watching the passing parade on the street before her, she feared he'd been right.

Beside her the game of one-upmanship continued, growing louder with each tip of a glass. Well, at least they're not swapping lies about me, Rachel thought. Then again, perhaps they'd already done that on the way over. Out of the three, Sean was the only one she hadn't ever considered sleeping with—yet. Maybe it was Paris, maybe it was the wine, maybe it was her desire to escape the discomfort of her own thoughts, but he was looking pretty good right now in his crisp khakis and crumpled white shirt, his blond curls turning golden under the light of the streetlamps. She moved in closer to the table and waited for an opening to rejoin the conversation.

The shots rang out before she had a chance to offer a single word. Everything seemed to go silent for a moment, and then

8

more shots. Yelling. Screaming. People scrambling in all directions. *Ç'est une attaque! Fuyez! Run!*

Her three friends grabbed their camera bags and leaped from the table in unison.

"Aren't you coming, Rach?" Sean yelled back as they went rushing into the fray as one, like a pack of dogs who had caught a scent.

But Rachel couldn't move. Instead she inched her backpack under the table with the toe of one boot and closed her eyes against the sweet Parisian breeze, squeezing them tight until everything became as black as the hole she felt opening up inside.

1

"Be safe!"

Maggie's last words from the sidewalk above were buried by the screech of the F train pulling away from the Bergen Street subway station. "*Shit*," Rachel said aloud as she clomped down the remaining stairs to the tracks, alone. It would be well past midnight by the time she got back to her apartment, if she were lucky. She slumped against the tiled wall and shifted her eyes warily along the empty platform. Ugh. Why had she agreed to meet her old friend way out here in Brooklyn in the first place? Maggie had always been the one person with the rare ability to talk her into doing whatever she wanted. And apparently she'd done it once again, Rachel thought with a smile.

The evening had started out innocently enough, with the two of them catching up over a glass of sustainable and organic

Côtes du Rhône and a tiny cup of artisanal olives. "Really. How Brooklyn can you get?" Rachel snorted once the bearded bartender was out of earshot.

Maggie laughed and shifted sideways on her stool. "So what's new with you, Rach?"

Rachel hesitated before answering. Maggie—after giving Rachel unsolicited advice about her outfit and handing her the card of her hair colorist—had already provided the bullet points on the status of her own life. Husband? A love. His bike shop a huge success. Baby? Not so little anymore. "Almost as tall as you," she had joked. Job? Good but tough, with all the cuts and consolidation happening in the magazine world. "What's new with me?" Rachel finally responded in her raspy voice. "Well, let's see. Um, I got a tattoo." She rolled up her sleeve and pointed to the spot where her old shrapnel scar had been covered with a tiny blue compass.

"Lovely." Maggie frowned. "But come on, Rachel. You know what I mean. Been on any dates lately? Met anyone interesting?"

Rachel rolled her eyes.

"So I'll take that as a no. Seen any good movies? Plays? Got any vacations planned?" she asked, sounding as if she were trying to coax a recalcitrant teenager into recounting a day at school.

"No, no, and no again." Rachel popped an oily olive into her mouth and chewed.

"Jesus, Rach," Maggie sighed. "What's happened to you? Don't you miss being out in the world? Aren't you bored? Lonely?"

"I'm fine. I like my life this way," Rachel answered, her words garbled by the pit she held clenched between her front teeth.

"Be serious. You *can't* like your life this way. Nobody would."

"Wow. Thanks." Rachel spat out the pit and placed it in a minuscule ceramic bowl made just for that purpose.

Maggie shrugged her shoulders. "I'm just saying. But really, especially you, after all you've seen and done—how can you stand being holed up in that tiny apartment day after day?"

The fact was that holing up in that tiny apartment was about all Rachel had seemed to be able to manage for a while now. That, and the gym, the bicycle, the shrink. She'd arrived back in New York pretty shut down, and it had been only the order-liness of her little life, the self-imposed routine, that had gotten her by since then. And she just couldn't find it in her to explain all this to Maggie. Instead she simply shrugged.

Maggie sighed again. "Look," she said, "maybe it's none of my business, but I just can't sit back anymore and watch you do this to yourself. And if you *don't* think it's any of my business, just tell me to shut up."

Rachel had just begun to do so when Maggie interrupted.

"Oh, I get it," she said. "Believe me I do. I understand how tough it was on you, going where you went, living like you did, seeing what you saw. But you were really something, Rach. You've always been the one I talked about. *My incredible friend Rachel.*"

Rachel had to laugh. "Oh, so now you talk about your poor, pathetic friend Rachel? Or don't you talk about me at all? Don't pity me, Maggie." She sat back and tucked the choppy ends of her wavy brown hair behind her ears.

"It's not pity. And it's not about me." Maggie placed her manicured hand gently on Rachel's arm. "I worry about you. Don't think I'm not sympathetic to how difficult it all must have been. I've heard the stories, I've read the books."

Rachel signaled to the bartender for another glass of wine. How could her friend, with her tidy little brownstone life, ever truly understand what it was like to wake each morning to the sounds of sirens and shelling, gunfire, the crash of mortar rounds? To hold your breath as you passed through hostile checkpoints and border crossings, your heart nearly bursting from your ribcage with the fear that you'll be discovered for who you are—or worse, suspected of being a terrorist or a spy? To be on constant lookout for an ambush that could end in kidnapping or death? And even if Maggie could, in her wildest dreams, picture those things, she would still never know of Rachel's worst fear. It was the recognition of it that had truly driven her out of the game. Her nightmares weren't of bullets or bombs—they were born from those words flung at her by Jonathan the day of their breakup, and from that morning on the beach at Lesbos. They lived in the coldness that wrapped around her like a boa constrictor, in the distance she kept between herself and others. They echoed in her memories of the attacks on Paris, that instant when she knew she couldn't go on. And they lingered in the waking moments when Rachel sensed just how forceful the return of all those feelings that had been pushed down so adeptly for so long could be, given a chance.

Her gaze wandered to the crowd closing in around them. Bare-armed, pierced girls greeting each other with warm hugs and rippling laughs, men dressed like lumberjacks sipping bubbly out of tall glasses, couples locking eyes as if there were nobody else in the room. Who are these people? Sometimes she felt like a ghost, drifting unseen through a world that she was no longer a part of.

"I'm sorry," Maggie continued. Rachel straightened at the sound of her voice. "But I can't stand to see you giving up on something you're so incredibly talented at. It's a crime." Rachel hadn't mentioned to Maggie that a couple of times lately she'd taken her camera along on her endless bike rides through the city. At first the Leica had felt awkward in her hands, as if she were holding a complete stranger's child. But looking over some of the shots she'd managed to get, she knew she'd keep going back for more. A homeless guy washing up in a water fountain. A Times Square cop screaming at a panhandling Elmo. A pair of pigeons perched on an old man's arm as he shared the scraps of his lunch. "And I know you could use the money."

"Wait, what? Did I miss something?"

"Have you even been listening to me, Rachel?"

"I'm sorry. You mentioned something about money. Which happens to be kind of a trigger for me these days." Just that afternoon Rachel had been looking through apartment listings, dreaming that she'd somehow miraculously unearth something decent on the Upper West Side for less than the $3500 per month she was currently paying for her tiny street-level sublet. Though she'd made a decent living over the years, New York City ate up money like a hungry Pac-Man.

"So then it's settled. I'll send you the details tomorrow." Maggie picked up her phone to set a reminder.

"What *are* you talking about?"

Maggie heaved an exasperated sigh. "The job? In Oman? For my magazine?"

"Come on, Maggie, you know I don't take assignments anymore."

"No, I know that you haven't said yes to one since Lesbos. But that doesn't mean you will never say yes again."

"I won't say yes again. To you, or anyone else." Rachel turned her attention to her wineglass.

"Stop being an idiot, Rachel. I'm handing you several months' rent on a silver platter. And even more importantly, in my opinion—which you obviously don't appear to value, thank you very much—a chance to get out of the box you've put yourself in, to break out of your little life and once again be a part of a world bigger than spin class and takeout Thai."

"But I like takeout Thai."

Maggie growled, sounding a lot like the nasty bulldog Rachel had photographed earlier that day in the park. "Well then do it for me, Rach. It would be a big deal for me, the struggling assistant photo editor, to land you, Ms. big time award-winning world-famous photojournalist, for the gig."

Rachel took a long, slow sip of her wine before answering. "You said Oman? What the fuck is going on in Oman?"

Maggie laughed. "Nothing! That's exactly it. It's the perfect assignment for you."

Rachel bent over to re-lace her boot and to avoid the smug look on her friend's face. Admittedly the money was tempting, and the truth was she was sort of enjoying being behind the lens again. But Oman?

"No, really, Rachel," Maggie chimed in as if reading her mind. "Oman is supposed to be an amazing place. Clean white beaches and turquoise water, windswept deserts and miles of palm trees. And they say the people are lovely, totally welcoming and inviting. And it's peaceful. Safe. Even in the middle of the shitshow happening around it, it's like an oasis of calm in the Arabian Sea."

"No wonder I've never been sent there. And you sound like a fucking travel brochure. So what's the assignment again?"

"It's easy. You'll be able to do it with your eyes closed and one arm tied behind your back. But please don't." Maggie flicked her long blond hair over her shoulders and leaned in toward Rachel. "Now, what we're looking for is a spread on the regional crafts and the people who make them—you know, like pottery, silver jewelry, daggers, swords. Oh, and there are the Bedouin women who make these incredible masks—they call them Omani burqas, and—"

"Sounds thrilling."

"Oh, come on, Rachel. Do you want the job or don't you?"

Even though they had parted ways without Rachel giving her answer, she now found herself boarding the subway car with her mind on the question of what to pack. Why not? It would be a short trip, maybe ten days, two weeks tops. Easy money. And even though she'd never admit it to her face, perhaps Maggie was just a little bit right. A change of scenery might do her good. Nothing else seemed to be doing the trick, not the therapist, not the Prozac or the Ambien, not the meditation, not the miles logged on the treadmill under the spell of her favorite old-school hip-hop playlist.

Rachel's ears popped as the train traveled far beneath the East River. The car was crowded but surprisingly quiet, full of kitchen workers winding down from their shifts, playing endless mindless games on their phones; young men wrapped in headphones, with their legs spread as wide as the river itself, moving to a beat only they could hear; tired moms with strollers and sleeping babies out way too late; transit workers in full uniform heading out to begin overnight repairs. Directly across from her, a dozing redhead nestled up against her boyfriend's shoulder, counting on him to keep a vigilant watch as she slept. Rachel tried to remember if she had ever allowed herself to feel that way, so fully trusting in another's arms. But before her mind could dive too deep into thoughts she did not want to think, she slipped her hand into her backpack and pulled the Leica into her grip.

2

Dubai, April 2017

Ariana Khan exchanged the paper sack in the boy's hand for a generous fistful of dirhams and thanked him, shutting the door with a click as he turned to press the button for the lift. She slapped across the spotless tiled floor in her gold flip-flops, back to the spot on the sofa that was still warm from her bum despite the chill from the humming air conditioner above. This, she thought, is the beauty of Dubai, where you can pick up a phone to save a trip down thirty-nine stories for one measly Starbucks.

Across the way, the lights from the neighboring towers winked back at her as if they knew something she didn't, like the meaning of life or the secret to happiness, or where her spare set of keys had got to, or how she was going to come up with enough money to pay the rent.

The clamor from the busy marina below seeped through the sliding glass doors leading to her balcony, just like it did every night. Music thumping, horns honking, laughter echoing across the concrete canyons. Dubai was a late-night town, with everyone and their cousin emerging from their climate-controlled cocoons as the temperature dropped. Even the children seemed to never sleep, dragged and wheeled by their parents along the glitzy waterfront that had once been only desert, or herded through the gargantuan malls that had sprouted from the sand.

She twisted the black face of her knockoff Rolex toward her. Too late to check in with her parents. Even with the three-hour time difference, she knew they'd both be in bed by now. A call from her would only set off unnecessary panic in the house in St Albans. Ariana sighed loudly. Sooner or later she'd have to come clean about her job. She hated not being truthful with her parents.

They'd been so proud of her when she'd first received the offer in Dubai from the bank, all their hard work and encouragement given credit by her accomplishment. She'd actually done quite well as an analyst, and had earned a more-than-decent salary, but it was clear that her heart truly wasn't into spending her days with a computer as her closest companion. Ariana was a people person. So when her department was downsized and decent severance packages were dangled as an incentive for voluntary departures, Ariana leaped at the chance to jump ship. But then the reality of having to tell her parents hit her, and she just couldn't bring herself to do that. They would never have understood her decision. And they definitely would have wanted her to come home.

On one hand the urge to move back home to England felt as strong as the pull of the moon on the tides. Although still healthy, her mother and father weren't getting any younger, as her sister often reminded her. She knew they missed her terribly, as she did them. But to her, the thought of being driven out of Dubai due to lack of income made her feel like a total failure. If she did move back, she wanted it to be under her own terms. She wanted to return as a big deal, not as a disappointment. And she certainly couldn't bear to add to that disappointment with the truth about her current gig. With the work visa from her bank job expiring, and the severance shrinking faster than the bow of the *Titanic* in the scene where Leonardo DiCaprio begs Kate Winslet not to let go of his hand, she'd started working as a wedding planner. She meant for it to be simply a temporary stopgap before finding something more substantial, more in keeping with her education, more in line with her parents' expectations. But the funny thing was, she immediately found the work to be totally rewarding, and so much fun. Her bosses told her she was a natural. Unfortunately, the demand for lavish weddings seemed to be plummeting along with the price of oil, and her jobs were few and far between.

So here she was. Struggling to survive in a city of skyscraper dreams, where doing everything one did just to keep up with the others—the apartment, the hair, the nails, the clothes, the bags, the gym—was enough to make a person batshit crazy. And for what?

But Ariana was determined to not feel sorry for herself. She knew all too well that her own struggle was a joke compared with that of others, the millions of migrant workers lured away from their homes by false promises of decent wages, who were brokered by sponsors into virtual slavery, condemned to lives of abuse and poverty. These were the desperate men who swept the streets, the ones who built the roads and picked up the trash, the women who cleaned the houses—the people from places like India, the Philippines, Bangladesh, and Pakistan, who she passed every day with a smile on her face and a pang in her heart. Every Ramadan she'd ease her guilt by assembling care packages for those who were relegated to living in the squalid camps. But lately, with so much more time on her hands, she'd become more aware of just how many of those people there actually were, and haunted by the thought that she was living in a city built on the blood and sweat of so many others.

So there was that. And now her rent—collected in advance for the entire year as for every rental in Dubai—was coming due. Sometimes she wondered what the point was.

Deep down, if she were honest with herself, she knew her parents' joy at having her back home would outweigh any disappointment they might feel about her career. That was her baggage, not theirs. Of course they'd prefer to have her home no matter what. And they would, of course, prefer to have her married, like her sister. Ariana was not anxious to deal with that pressure on a daily basis.

It wasn't that she disagreed with them. Ariana was ready to be married again. The trouble was that the only men in her life at the moment were the two ridiculous jokers who had been messaging her for the past three hours, apparently either from the solitude of their own empty apartments or perhaps from under the table across from a hapless date. Ariana had been juggling them both all night. Really, she didn't even know why she bothered. Neither one of them was serious about wanting a real relationship. Nasim was clearly still pining for his ex-wife, and Nasir was simply a player, exactly the type of man she had no time for, except for the fact that he made her laugh. But she'd met both men through mutual friends, and Ariana believed one should always remain polite to friends of friends.

The other guys she'd met over the past year had been banished to the land of blocked contacts. She blamed it all on her sister, who had relentlessly insisted she try meeting someone online. "We're *all* concerned about you," she had said to Ariana during a visit home last year, making her feel like such a loser. It truly pissed her off, imagining them talking about her behind her back. Her sister then claimed that Ariana needed to engage more, spend more time being with people. The irony of that comment seemed to be lost on her, Ariana thought as they sat down together to reach out from behind the screen of her phone. Her sister watched as she composed her Tinder profile. *Not in the least interested in hook-ups, but if you truly want to commit to a likeminded person, then I might be interested, if you look like George Clooney.* "Well, that's bound to get you a ton of responses," her sister said, smirking. In the end Ariana decided to limit her efforts to a Muslim matrimonial website, thinking that the men there were likely to be more serious and ready to commit.

"The time of sociopaths and idiots", she'd later dubbed that experience. Her sister had sent her off on her first date with the advice to "get over herself" and not talk about the things she normally talked about. Not quite sure what was meant by that, she nevertheless tried to keep her mouth shut. She really did. But it didn't seem to help. One guy wanted a traditional brown wife, which she clearly wasn't. One gave himself away with the wall-paper picture on his phone—a stunning blond, which she also clearly wasn't. One date ended with a mysteriously misplaced wallet when the check arrived. Another featured a misogynist who knew nothing about the true meaning of Islam, and who accused her of becoming too anglified. Some disappeared, only to resurface months later in full stalker mode. And all of them offered zero chemistry.

What was even worse was how she became an expert on all the ways guys misrepresented themselves online. She'd even caught a married man from her family's neighborhood—a guy with three teenage children—posing as a childless widower. And that, she felt, was despicable. It was one thing to lie on a dating site, where the other person could be just trying to find a quick hook-up as well. But on a *matrimonial* website? She was tempted to post a comment suggesting he try one of the polygamy websites she'd read about, but thought better of it.

Though the weekly reminders of potential new suitors awaiting her response were still popping up in her inbox, Ariana had fallen into the habit of deleting the messages without even a glance, choosing instead to concentrate more on the weddings of others than on her own.

Now Nasir was saying something about work. Or was it Nasim? She flipped her long, dark hair over her shoulder and scrolled through a thread she'd barely been paying attention to.

. . . *Need to ask you something. Job related.*

. . . *What, you need a bit of arm candy for some chichi work event?*

. . . *Call me if you can. Easier to explain.*

. . . *And interrupt your hot date?*

. . . *Ha ha. I'm alone. At the shisha bar.*

Ariana could practically smell the sickly sweet smoke through the phone as Nasir answered the call. How he could actually enjoy ending his evenings in a cloud of tobacco in a downtown hookah lounge was beyond her.

"Hello, doll," she greeted him with a chuckle.

"Hello doll yourself," he countered. "And why are you at home on this lovely night?"

"Because Brad Pitt has the sniffles, and had to cancel at the last moment."

"Pity. Why don't you come on down and join me? All the other guys will be here soon."

"I don't think so. Too much traffic." And besides, she thought, I am *so* not interested in being one of the guys. "So what was that about your job?"

"I need a fixer. Know anyone?"

"Depends. Just what is it you want fixed?"

Nasir explained. He usually worked as a part-time local journalist, but occasionally also did work with foreign correspondents, filmmakers, corporations and NGOs to get whatever they needed done—interpreting, guiding, finding sources, procuring access, basically helping to pave the way.

"And?" Ariana asked.

"I was supposed to do a job with a photographer next week, but a big story has come up so now I can't do it."

"And?" she asked again.

"And I need to find someone else who can."

"I'll do it."

"*You?* A fixer? You can't even fix your own dinner!"

"Thanks a lot, my friend. You know damn well how good I am at what I do. Remember the Ilyas' wedding? You were there."

"That was a great party. But honestly, Ari, this is different."

"Really? If I can manage to organize a good time for hundreds of people at a pop I can certainly deal with one little journalist."

"It's a photographer."

"Okay. A photographer. How hard can that be?"

"I don't know—"

"Come on, Nasir. If you can do it, I can do it."

"You sure?"

"Of course I'm sure. Don't be such a sexist pig."

"Okay, okay." He laughed. "Just don't blow it. It's my reputation that's at stake here. And actually, it's not all that difficult."

"Speak to me."

"So an American photographer needs to have her hand held over in Oman. You've been to Oman, right?"

"Only on a visa run," she answered, thinking about those monthly pain-in-the-ass five-hour round trips to the border when she'd cram into a van full of other expats all looking to get their passports stamped. "I really don't know much about it."

"So start studying. You'll be needing to book hotels, hire drivers, locate whoever and whatever she wants to see. Google it. I'll forward you the email with the specs of her assignment and her contact info. You'll be fine. I hope."

"Thanks for the vote of confidence." Ariana stood and silenced the chirping alarm on her iPad, and headed down the hall. "I've got to run. I'll ring you tomorrow."

"Yay. A job," she said to the face in the mirror as she stood at the bathroom sink twisting off her rings, one by one, and placing them carefully on the back of the basin. "And money is money, right?"

'*Bismillah*,' she whispered softly before passing her hands slowly under the running faucet three times. She opened her mouth and splashed in a handful of water, swirled, spat and repeated twice again. Then it was three times for the nostrils, the face, the right arm and then the left—like a doctor scrubbing up for surgery—and then a wipe of the head, the ears, the back of the neck, and finally a triple rinse of both her feet, the right, as always, before the left.

She then crossed the hall to her bedroom, where she pulled the black *abaya* and *shayla* from the hook behind the door. The feel of the shiny fabric as it slid down her body and nestled around her head always comforted her, as if all the loose pieces were coming back together, and as if, for the moment, she was part of something bigger and more important than herself.

Ariana took a deep breath and stood up straight, her feet pointed toward the far corner of the room, facing Mecca, her eyes on the rug before her. She raised her hands to the level of her shoulders, her palms facing forward, and began reciting *isha*, the fifth and final prayer of the day.

3

Muscat, April 2017

The knife danced through the glistening onion at lightning speed, Miza's hands transforming the orb into perfect little cubes with machine-like precision before scooping up the pieces from the counter and dropping them into the hot oil to brown. The ginger had been mashed and the garlic chopped ahead of time, just like her mother used to do. She remembered first learning to make *pilau*, standing on a stool in the kitchen of their house in Zanzibar, back when her parents were still alive. She would wonder at her mother's long, dark fingers flinging pinches of cardamom and cumin and ground cloves into the pot, as if she were a sorcerer concocting her magical brew. Then her mother would add the browned potatoes and leave it all to simmer, bringing alive the smells of the Darajani Market they'd visited that morning.

Miza had loved going shopping with her mother, and had treasured the time they would spend wandering through the narrow lanes of the old Stone Town section of Zanzibar City hand in hand, just the two of them, picking through the plantains and cassava and the spiky durian, so stinky it would make water spill from her eyes. The covered halls and twisting alleys would become thick with shoppers as midday approached and they'd hurry to finish their rounds, Miza holding tight to make sure she didn't lose her mother in the crowd, before heading home for lunch. That was before the wonderful and horrible day Miza's baby sister had come into the world, the same day she lost her mother for good.

Miza added cold water to the rice, pouring from a coffee cup until the amount of liquid matched the distance between the tip and first crease of her index finger, and checked the time. Still at least a half-hour before her husband would arrive—plenty of time to start the octopus curry. How odd it felt to call Tariq her husband, even after over a year of marriage. Sometimes she still pictured him as the boy he once was, the spirited child who would come from Oman each year with his younger sister to spend holidays at their great-uncle's house in Stone Town, trading the brutal Muscat heat for the tropical breezes of the Southern Hemisphere. Even though he was a few years older than the two girls, the three of them had been friends back then, until the year Miza turned fourteen and her grieving father had no choice but to move the tiny family to his older brother's house in the village he had grown up in. It would be twelve years before she and Tariq would see each other again.

Miza pushed up the sleeves of her blouse and tore open the package of octopus she'd found at the local grocery. Back home she used to accompany her parents to the beach to find the *pweza*, her father searching the coral during low tide for a glimpse of one of the tentacled creatures stranded among the rocks. Her mother would scrub the ink out into a saltwater pool, kneading the octopus's body into the sand before rinsing and repeating until the water ran clear. Then she'd whip the animal up into the air by one of its eight legs, bringing it down with a thud against the rocks over and over again until it was sure to be tender. This, Miza thought as she ran the sliced white meat under the faucet, was certainly easier.

In fact, everything was easier here in Oman. But that did not mean she wanted to stay. She had heard of plenty of Zanzibaris who were happy living here, among the hundreds of thousands of others who were either born here or came from parents who were. The ties between the two countries were deep—deeper than the ocean they shared—going back to a time centuries before when the island fell under the rule of the Sultan of Oman and became a prized source for the trading of ivory, spices and slaves. It was true that Swahili could be heard on just about every street corner in Muscat. But Oman wasn't for her, even though the apartment Tariq had set up for her here was more than nice, she thought as her eyes scanned the thick white walls and plump armchairs sitting atop soft Persian rugs. Perhaps it was not quite as grand as the large home where he stayed with his other wife—his first wife, Maryam—but Miza didn't care. Though the law said that a man who takes more than one wife must provide for them all equally, her stay in Oman was a temporary one, and she was grateful for what Tariq had already done for her.

The day they had reconnected after so many years was one of those days where the turquoise ocean matched the sky so perfectly you felt like you could dive down far below and soar back up over and over again like a hungry tern in search of dinner, until you burst right through the horizon onto the other side of the world. At least that's what Miza had been dreaming of as she stood knee-deep in the water, her back aching from being bent so long over the *mwana* seedlings, stringing the little seaweed plants one by one onto nylon *tie-ties*, then attaching the thin ropes to the wooden sticks she'd dig into the soft sand in neat rows that seemed to stretch out forever. Harvesting seaweed was hard work that started early with the low tides and often ended late with feet shredded from the sharp shells and stones on the ocean floor, with skin itching and scarring from so many hours under a relentless sun made even more powerful by the glare of the saltwater. Miza feared she'd soon start looking like Bi-Zena, the farmer who'd hired her, a woman who had to be more than twice, or maybe even three times, her age. But worse was her fear of the venomous stings from stonefish and stingrays that lurked innocently in the shallow waters where she worked, until they were stepped on. An encounter with one of those beasts was bound to end in painful tetanus injections and a month of lost wages. Yet, as brutal as it could be, the work was welcome. For most women it was the only way to keep their families alive. *Mwani* was money, they said. A gift from the ocean. For Miza it was the only way to keep her uncle at bay. She'd learned that his lust for money was even greater than his appetite for flesh.

Miza had been approaching the shore, balancing a bundle of leftover wooden sticks on her head, her long yellow dress dragging in the rising tide, when she heard someone call out her name. *Mi-mi, it's me!* But perhaps she had been in the sun too long, as nobody had called her by her childhood name since her parents had gone.

She dropped the sticks onto the dry white sand and stretched her arms high to the sky, her spine creaking like an old, rusty hinge.

Mi-mi!

She turned to see a tall man in a clean white *dishdasha* and with a neatly trimmed beard, who looked more like he belonged in an office than on a beach. Her first instinct was to run. What could this man want from her? But if he were after something, how did he know her name, and why was he smiling so broadly? It wasn't until he was practically on top of her that she recognized Tariq. Those warm eyes as brown as chocolate took her instantly back to the carefree days in Stone Town. Miza smoothed her sand-crusted dress and tucked her scarf tighter around her head.

"What are you doing here? How did you find me?" Miza furrowed her brow.

Tariq laughed. "What, are you not happy to see me? Are you going to tell me to take my things and go home, like you used to?"

Miza had to laugh as well. She remembered being tough on her old friend, who always showed up at her door every day no matter what. "I *am* happy to see you. But what are you doing here, on this beach?"

Tariq then told her about how he took the five-hour flight back and forth from Oman to Zanzibar quite often for his work as an importer. He had inquired about Miza's family a number of times around Stone Town, but it wasn't until this trip that he had come across someone who knew of her situation.

Miza was well aware of how, among her people, gossip spread like blood dripping into water. Tariq would have heard about how her father had died from malaria shortly after their move from Stone Town, leaving Miza and her sister, Sabra, in his brother's hands. How her uncle, the village elder, ruled both the town and his family with an iron fist and a greedy palm. How Miza fought to protect her sister and endure under the brutishness of the man and the abuse from his wife.

"But why would you do this for me?" Miza asked when he offered his help, her eyes narrowing to slits in the afternoon light.

That is when Tariq turned quiet, a flush of pink rising from behind the high collar of his *dishdasha*. "You are my friend," he finally said. "I never forgot that." And Miza, remembering now how he used to look at her with those eyes, suddenly understood what she had been too young to grasp. Her chest swelled with a warmth that rivaled that from the sun above.

But when Tariq, several visits later, suggested marriage as a solution for getting her out from under her uncle's grasp, she had respectfully declined. She treasured the kindness Tariq showed her, and could not deny the feelings growing inside that made her miss him more and more each time he headed back home. But leaving Zanzibar was out of the question. The island was a part of her, as much as the blood that had run through the veins of her grandparents and parents and into her own body. And what about her little sister? Her uncle would never agree to let go of what was considered his property. And there was no way Miza could ever leave Sabra behind.

"Do not worry about your sister," Tariq assured her. "I can take care of your uncle."

And, of course, there was also the matter of Tariq's wife. Miza was not eager to be a *wakewenza*, a co-wife, to share the man she was coming to love. And Tariq was reluctant to walk away from the obligation of his marriage, as broken as that marriage seemed to be.

In the end it was Bi-Zena who came up with the solution. "It does not matter if you are his *twentieth* wife," the old woman said after Miza had confided in her. "You must marry this man and get yourself and your sister away from this place for good." Though Bi-Zena was known to be a quiet, guarded person, one who never engaged in the local gossip, she was keenly aware of everything that happened in the village. She had known enough about the goings-on in the village elder's house to have taken it upon herself to dare approach him one day, the seaweed slung around her neck like a feather boa and her low, heavy breasts swinging freely under her damp cotton dress, to suggest that she take his niece into her employ. To others Bi-Zena showed only her firmness and diligence as a *mama*, a boss. To Miza she showed only care. "You will become Tariq's second wife," she insisted. "And you will stay in Zanzibar, in Stone Town. That way, when he is with you, it will be as if you are his only wife."

Of course, Tariq was thrilled with Bi-Zena's idea. He would spend half his time in Zanzibar. Maryam, his first wife, would barely notice he was gone—as long as she had money to spend and servants to care for her.

Where is that man? Miza pulled the rice off the burner and checked her phone. Tariq had assured her he'd be home by now, that his meetings would be done in plenty of time for dinner. Yet she had not heard from him since he had called to say he was on his way, more than two hours earlier. He had said he was coming straight to her, not stopping at the house across town that he shared with Maryam, hadn't he?

She took off her apron and padded down the hall in her bare feet to the bathroom, with its cool tile and gleaming white porcelain. Even the toilet was decorated in marble. What a ridiculous luxury to have this all to myself, she thought as she checked her reflection in the mirror, the space between her two front teeth gaping back at her like a door someone had forgotten to close. If only her sister had been able to come here with her, to stay until the baby was born. But Miza had decided it was more important that Sabra not interrupt her studies, as she, herself, had been forced to do so long ago, once her uncle had gotten a taste of the money she could bring from the sea. And Sabra had sounded perfectly happy back in their Stone Town flat with Hoda, the maid, when she and Miza had traded messages earlier that afternoon.

She ran her fingers lightly over her smooth cheeks, now fuller and shinier than ever before, and inserted a thick hoop into each earlobe, the gold setting off the darkness of her long neck. With a fresh scarf tied around her hair—the green and purple one with flowers that Tariq had once admired—and a quick swipe of color across her lips, Miza headed back to the kitchen to wait.

Her stomach rumbled, from both her hunger and the life inside. "Soon, little one," she said out loud as she rubbed her churning belly. "Soon you will come into this world as a true Omani baby, just as your father wished. And soon we will be back home in Zanzibar together, where I will teach you to fish and play *mamba*," she promised, recalling the tug-of-war game she'd played as a child. Of course, thought Miza, sighing as she added the turmeric and coriander into the curry, it was cooking she had most been looking forward to teaching her child, as mothers had taught daughters for generations back home. But that was not to be, for now. She couldn't wait to share today's news, from the visit to the doctor, with Tariq. How thrilled he would be to learn that his firstborn child would be a son.

She covered the *pilau* to keep it warm. Why hadn't Tariq called? He probably forgot to charge his phone again, she thought. But then another thought crossed her mind, the thought that perhaps he actually had chosen to stop at his other wife's house instead. She took a deep breath and lowered herself onto a stool, her phone tight in her grip, her eyes glued to the ticking clock above the stove as she watched each minute pass.

4

Rachel had never seen anything like it. It was as if she were the lone car traveling the wrong way on a rush-hour highway, or a rebel fish trying to escape upstream. The best part was the guy stationed by the mall's exit, frantically waving two orange light-up batons in the air in a fruitless effort to control the throngs shoving their way through the doors to catch the next show at the dancing fountain outside at the base of the Burj Khalifa. *Fountain?* To Rachel it looked more like a lake. But then again, from what she already knew and had already seen, along with what she had heard from the taxi driver, everything in Dubai was out of whack. It was a city of superlatives—the biggest, the tallest, the shiniest, the newest.

Right now it just seemed like the crowdedest. In all her years of traveling through Dubai—always on her way to or from one assignment or another—she'd deliberately never set foot outside the airport. And if she had, the mall would definitely not have been at the top of her list of must-sees. Especially on a Friday night, when the entire population of the city seemed to share the same idea of how to spend an evening out. It was more crowded than the week before Christmas at a mall back home. But, for the most part, not many of these shoppers seemed to be actually shopping at all. There were hundreds of stores in the mall, and behind the windows of almost each one she passed all she saw were yawning clerks with folded arms, shifting impatiently from leg to leg. Most would-be customers were just wandering the broad corridors, as if strolling a Paris boulevard on a lazy afternoon.

It's like a parade of nations through a canyon of consumerism, Rachel thought as she followed the signs to the escalator. The men in their crisp, white, ankle-length *dishdashas*: the Emiratis distinguishable by the *keffiyeha* secured to their heads with black cords that dangled down their backs, the Kuwaitis set apart by their sharp and pointy collars, and the Saudis by their red-and-white scarves. And then there were the women: the Palestinians in modern dresses and tight headscarves, and the Pakistanis in their *shalwar kameez*. The Indian women wore saris, and those from the Gulf countries were draped in traditional *abayas*. They were the ones who made the most of their visible body parts, with designer shoes and handbags that would be right at home on upper Madison Avenue or the streets of Tribeca.

Of course there were those in more Western clothes as well. Nobody seemed to give her own khakis and Timberland boots a second look. Or even a first. In fact, she noticed, short of an annoying invasion of personal space—cutting in line, bumping, a little pushing—nobody was really acknowledging anyone else's presence at all. They traveled in packs, like members of street gangs displaying their colors. For her, it actually felt good to once again be blending anonymously into a jumble of cultures. It was almost as if she were invisible. It was true that, as cities went, New York was usually pretty good for that as well, but her own neighborhood had been becoming way too white and wealthy for her taste lately.

Rachel stumbled off the escalator as it reached the second floor. Jet lag, she thought, her limbs feeling as thick and heavy as tree trunks. She ducked into an empty doorway to fetch the water bottle from a pocket of her backpack, the camera around her neck banging against her knees as she bent to dig. Why the fixer had suggested they meet by the 'shoes in the mall' was beyond her, she thought as the stale, warm liquid slithered down her throat. But whatever. She hadn't had the energy to argue after the thirteen-hour journey from JFK. And where the fuck was the shoe department, anyway?

Rachel had no choice other than to once again surrender to the thrust of the crowd, and soon found herself being herded past a scene worthy of the grimmest theme parks back home. Clusters of families stood eight-deep in front of a massive window, straining on tiptoe with their glowing cellphones held high like torches in the air. Behind the thick glass, sharks and rays were circling as they eyed the spectators with contempt, as if laying blame for their sorry predicament. She muscled her way through to where the crowd had thinned slightly, past a bowling alley, an ice rink, and a dinosaur skeleton as big as any in the American Museum of Natural History. There were zip-line rides, a football arena, and three men in red fezzes dancing in unison in front of a Turkish restaurant, spinning tassels in the air as they hopped from foot to foot in time to the music. But still, no shoe department. Rachel sighed out loud and wondered if she looked as much like a zombie as she felt. Finally she spied a sign pointing ahead: *Shoe District*.

It was a shrine to the foot. A ridiculous display of luxury. All marble and glitz, mirrors and gold, glowing lights and soft music. And, all around her, lone shoes resting on columns and pedestals, displayed preciously on glass shelves and showcased in backlit cases. There were plenty of names she recognized: Dolce & Gabbana, Fendi, Louboutin—she never did understand that whole 'red on the bottom' thing—Gucci, Manolo Blahnik, Prada. And then there were the dozens more she didn't. For a moment she fingered the soft suede straps of a Marchesa sandal, straining to understand how someone might get caught up by all this. Then she checked the price and did the math, and dropped the shoe back onto the shelf like a hot potato.

Rachel was still a good half an hour early and way too drained to take another step. I used to be so much better at this, she thought. Maybe it was the adrenalin that had kept her going back in the old days. Or maybe it was just the stupid mall that was exhausting her now. Either way, when an over-stuffed sofa appeared in front of her eyes she thought she was seeing a mirage. She poked at the soft foam and freed her weary shoulders from the heavy backpack, then stretched out across the cushions like a sultan in his den.

The next thing she knew, she was hearing her name repeated over and over with a question mark at the end, in a lovely, gentle voice that sounded like a bell softly chiming at the top of the hour. Above her stood a large-eyed woman with long shiny hair. Her artfully ripped jeans and half-tucked silk blouse were a studied attempt at appearing casual, accented with a flair by the rings on every one of her fingers and the striped espadrilles with the telltale interlocking "C"s on her feet. It must have taken her at least an hour to get all that makeup to look as if she were barely wearing any, thought Rachel. Except for those eyelashes. Those looked as if she had collected the long black legs from dozens of hairy spiders and superglued them to her lids.

The woman held out her hand. "I'm Ariana. Ariana Khan. Your fixer?"

Rachel sat up and attempted to smooth her hair. "Seriously?"

Ariana raised one of her lush eyebrows. "What do you mean, 'seriously'?"

"Nothing." Rachel yawned. "Sorry. Never mind." The truth was that she was more used to big beefy guys who could double as bodyguards if need be, or nerdy wonks who had the where-withal to get access to anyone anywhere. She hadn't been out of the game long enough for things to have changed this much. Rachel turned her eyes to the bags hanging from the woman's arm.

Ariana leaned in conspiratorially. "Tried to return a pair of shoes, as I had second thoughts about spending the money, if you know what I mean. Only wore them once."

Rachel nodded dumbly.

"Well, they wouldn't let me return them. Claimed there was an issue with the tag. Bloody hell. So what's a girl to do?" She shrugged. "I guess they were just meant to be mine after all. Come on." Ariana helped Rachel up from the pillows and picked up her backpack, which Rachel wrestled back from her arms. "Let's go have some tea."

"I see you got in all right," she called over her shoulder as Rachel struggled to keep up.

"I did," Rachel answered to her back.

"Did you get any rest on the plane?"

"Not so much."

"Oh look, a sale!" Rachel barreled into Ariana as she slammed to a halt at a makeup counter. "And they've got my favorite lipstick!" Ariana puckered her lips in front of a little round mirror. "Do you find it too pink?" Rachel shrugged as Ariana stood back and dipped her chin to give her a better look. "You should try it, Rachel. It would look great on you!"

"That's okay," Rachel said, but before the words could even get out of her mouth Ariana was once again ten steps ahead of her, pecking frantically on her phone as she walked. Rachel followed blindly, the promise of caffeine the only thing keeping her from giving in to her fatigue and collapsing in a heap in the middle of the crush, which, to her surprise, didn't seem to be letting up in the slightest, despite the late hour. Rachel could have easily got lost in the crowd, had it not been for Ariana's habit of slowing at every shop window and kiosk on the route.

"Look at this!" Ariana stopped in front of a sprawling 3-D model of one of the most obnoxious high-rise apartment complexes Rachel had ever seen. "This is the new development down by Dubai Creek Harbour, isn't it?" Ariana asked the slickly suited man with an iPad under his arm. She had a million questions for the guy. *What's the size? When will construction be complete? What's the occupancy rate? What are the prices?* Rachel looked around for a chair as Ariana sweetly offered to help enter her contact information into the salesman's device.

"Are you looking for a new apartment?" Rachel asked with a yawn as Ariana finally finished and nodded toward the escalator.

"No." Ariana shrugged. "Not really. The poor guy just looked so bored and lonely standing there."

Next was the Camel Company, across from the restrooms. "You need to take a look in this place. Do you have children? They have some quite adorable gifts," Ariana said as she urged

Rachel toward the shelves of everything camel: mugs and T-shirts and key chains and plush toys and coasters and magnets and—before Rachel knew it, Ariana had excused herself and slipped into the restrooms across the way. Rachel leaned back with her pack against a display rack near the entrance of the shop to wait, ignoring the narrow-eyed glare being cast in her direction by the cashier. She stood there for what felt like forever, struggling to keep her eyes fixed on the ladies' room door as she waited for Ariana's return, the sea of people passing in front of her in a blur. What the hell was the woman doing in there? Redoing her entire faceful of makeup?

Finally she spied Ariana approaching, her eyes glued to her phone. "Thanks so much for waiting." She smiled sweetly as she reached Rachel's side, pointing to the restroom entrances, where just above the little man and woman icons there was another sign with an outline of a mosque flanked by two minarets. "I was praying."

"No problem," Rachel answered, her lips sticking to teeth so thick with travel scum it was as if they were wearing sweaters. "About that tea, or, better yet, coffee?"

"Come." Ariana looped her arm through Rachel's. "It's this way."

But Ariana couldn't seem to go ten steps before she'd become distracted by someone else with something to sell. She'd flash her smile at anyone and everyone who managed to catch her eye, and before Rachel could object they'd be deep in conversation, debating the merits of this phone case over that, or comparing their favorite scents as Ariana held out her wrist for a spritz. She'd ask them where they were from, if they had a family, if they were happy in Dubai. She even stopped to thank a guy emptying trash bins for his hard work. Rachel couldn't tell if Ariana was truly interested, or if she was just being polite. Either way, it was driving her a little nuts. The last straw was the Filipina woman with the "miracle hairbrush". "This is perfect for you," Ariana said as she herded Rachel toward the kiosk.

"No, really, I—"

"Come on, it will be fun. You'll see."

The saleswoman grabbed a clump of Rachel's hair, still snarled from the plane and frizzy from the heat, and began to brush. "This good for you. Make your hair nice and smooth."

"But I—" Rachel could feel an uncomfortably hot steam begin to penetrate her scalp.

"Wow," Ariana said. "That really works well! How much is it?"

The saleswoman continued to brush as she and Ariana talked price. "Okay, I'm good," Rachel interrupted, breaking away from the woman's grip. "Can we *please* just go get our coffee now?" she begged Ariana.

Ariana thanked the salesperson, assuring her they'd be back, and hurried to keep up with Rachel, who'd just caught sight of her own reflection in a shop window. She looked like a walking before and after ad, with one side of her head plastered flat, the other sprouting kinks and curls going every which way. She spied Ariana stifling a laugh.

Finally, as they approached a long escalator leading to the floor below, she heard the rattling of cup against saucer, and smelled the sweet aroma of Turkish coffee floating up toward her. "So even the coffee is designer?" she snorted when she spied the name on the awning beneath them.

Ariana leaned against the railing and laughed. "The Armani Café is one of the most popular spots in the mall. Especially on a Friday night. Look." Rachel followed her finger down to a table with six young men in white robes, each seated behind a small cup with a phone resting at its side. There seemed to be little conversation among them. Across the way was a tableful of women in black *abayas*, eyes lowered to the screens in their hands while they talked to each other in hushed tones.

As she widened her view, Rachel could see the same scene repeated around half the tables in the café below. "I don't get it."

Ariana laughed. "They're all singles. The guys are looking for women."

"I still don't get it."

"They use Bluetooth. For flirting."

"And that works how?"

Ariana took Rachel's elbow and led her down the escalator. "Easy. Think about it. In this culture, unrelated men and women can't be seen talking to each other, right?"

"Right."

"But all they have to do is turn on their Bluetooth to see the names of who else is in range."

"Do they know each other?"

"No. But people will click on IDs they think are sexy or cute, like Poster Boy, Sensitive Girl, Lion Heart, Little Princess."

"That is so weird. Then what?"

"Then they exchange phone numbers and photos. Sometimes the girls even share pictures of themselves uncovered and all dolled up. But, of course, it's better to get someone's attention directly than on the phone. They do that by being really obvious with their phone, like checking or typing, and then if the other person is interested they'll do a Bluetooth search and locate you."

"So then they meet face to face? How do they do that?"

"They don't. At least probably not right then. They still have to be careful."

"Well that kind of sucks. It's hard enough to meet people . . ."

Ariana snorted a little. "You're telling me! Of course, it's better than the old way of doing it."

"What was that?"

Ariana lowered her voice as the host led them to their table. "They'd throw notes at the women through car windows, or drop them at their feet. Sometimes they'd even just drop a phone right in front of them."

Rachel shook her head at the scene around her. "I think it's kind of sad."

"Ah, they're all just a bunch of players and gold diggers." Ariana waved away the menus as big as an atlas and ordered one English breakfast tea with milk on the side and a double espresso. And finally, after a first sip of the espresso that hit Rachel like a jolt from a pair of defib paddles, they got down to the business at hand, though it was difficult for her to compete for attention with the phone in Ariana's hand. She had to wonder if the woman wasn't also playing virtual footsies with some of the robed men around them. She couldn't even seem to get a straight answer when she asked Ariana about what had been booked in Oman, who they'd be seeing, where they'd be staying. By the time the check came, all she knew was that they'd be meeting at Dubai airport at ten the next morning for the flight to Muscat.

"Can I drive you back to your hotel?" Ariana asked as she dabbed at her lips with a napkin and pushed back her chair.

"Thanks. I do need to check in." Rachel felt like she could sleep for days.

Ariana cocked her head. "Where are all your things?"

Rachel swung the pack over her shoulder and adjusted the camera strap around her neck. "Got it all right here," she said as she hurried toward the exit before Ariana could find another reason to delay.

"I thought that was your purse," came the voice from behind her as Ariana scrambled to keep up.

5

The sheer volume of Ariana's luggage when she showed up at Dubai International the next day should have been Rachel's first warning. One oversize, hard-sided, glossy black wheelie bag that could turn on a dime, a duffel stuffed to the max and a large pink leather handbag—no doubt some designer thing that Rachel had no clue about. Rachel was dumbfounded, literally. But what was there to say? After all, it was Ariana who was going to have to schlep all that crap around, not her.

The woman did not stop moving throughout the entire one-hour flight to Muscat. With her phone on airplane mode, Ariana seemed not to know what to do with herself, as was made clear by the way she fiddled with the entertainment system, chatted with the flight attendant, drank two bottles of water and a cup of tea, and climbed over Rachel—who had shut her eyes and was trying to sleep—three times to go to the bathroom. When they finally reached the hotel, Rachel hurried ahead to the reception desk, desperate to check in to her room to have a few moments to herself before they headed to the souk.

The place was nice—a hell of a lot nicer than what she was used to while on assignment. Usually her accommodations had run along the lines of crappy hotels and guesthouses, or she'd find herself crammed into a rental with dozens of other photographers and correspondents, along with their inter-preters and drivers. As an embed she'd stayed in more remote military bases and barracks than she cared to remember. And once she'd spent an entire week sleeping in bunkers and caves. This was a proper hotel, with a marble lobby made bright by the floor-to-ceiling windows overlooking the sea.

As she stood at the reception desk digging for her passport, she spied Ariana across the way, perusing a rack of brochures that was bolted to the wall. Odd, she thought as she watched her fixer slide a handful of tourist literature into her bag. She signed for her room and was handed the keycard. "Meet back here in fifteen?" she suggested as Ariana approached.

"Minutes?"

"What, you need more time?"

Ariana checked her watch. "Would a half-hour do? It's almost prayer time, and, besides, the souk doesn't open again until four. Do you mind?"

Rachel headed to her room, frustrated at wasting practically a whole day right off the bat. When she returned to the lobby after plopping her backpack down on the bed and splashing some water on her face, she was surprised to see Ariana already there, deep in conversation with the concierge. Ariana gestured with one finger for her to wait, which Rachel did until they were led outside to a taxi.

"Did you forget your makeup?" Ariana asked, squinting a little at Rachel as they headed west along the water. Rachel just stared back at her. "Because if you did, we can always make a stop. Or perhaps I have some extra," she added, rooting around in her purse. Rachel turned her head and stared out the window. "Do you want to take a quick look at the Royal Opera House?" Ariana continued. "It's supposed to be spectacular. Oh, and the Grand Mosque. I hear there's a hand-woven rug in the main prayer hall that's seventy meters long. It took four hundred weavers four years to make it." Ariana looked quite proud of herself.

"The craftspeople? My assignment? Remember?" Rachel checked her watch and slumped back into the taxi's lumpy upholstery.

The Muttrah Souk sat across from the harbor in the old commercial center of the city. On this afternoon the port was dotted with cruise ships, bringing the owners of the cafés and juice bars along the corniche out to their sidewalk posts with practiced German greetings shouted in competition for the attention of the camera-toting tourists walking by. "*Guten tag damen. Kaffee?*" they called out to Rachel and Ariana as the pair passed on their way to the market's main entrance.

The first steps into the souk brought immediate relief from the blinding heat outside, but with that came a sweet, sickly smell that filled the air like cheap perfume. Rachel sneezed and shifted the camera around her neck as she waited for her eyes to adjust to the darkness. The main thoroughfare was crowding quickly as the shopkeepers opened up for the afternoon rush. Omani families—the men in robes and embroidered *kumas*, pillbox hats not unlike what Rachel's grandmother used to wear, the women in black *abayas* that swept the ground—were

49

swarming the place, diving into the dance of bargaining over coffeepots and shoes and pots and pans. The tourists were drawn to piles of scarves from Kashmir, to the "I ♥ Oman" T-shirts hanging from the beams above, to lamps from Turkey, brass figurines from Africa, and purses from India. Rachel had seen a lot of this stuff before, in the markets of Morocco and Turkey and Egypt. But nowhere in sight were the handmade local crafts that she had hoped to find, let alone any photogenic craftspeople to go along with them. In her past assignments all she'd had to do was follow the sounds of gunfire or explosives, or head the wrong way into a fleeing mob to find the source of a story. This was something else entirely.

Ariana must have noticed the scowl crossing her face, as Rachel suddenly felt herself being pulled to the right into a dark labyrinth of narrow alleyways, where everything became even darker the deeper they tunneled. I should be leaving a trail of breadcrumbs, she thought as they followed a route that seemed to turn in on itself in an endless coil. Clearly Ariana had no idea where she was going. They wound inward past tiny stalls spilling over with old silver necklaces and strings of beads so heavy it seemed as though even the strongest woman would collapse from their weight. There were antique swords and daggers and ammo belts fully stocked with bullets, dresses so bright they nearly glowed in the dark, and tunics so crisp they looked like they might crack at the touch. And everywhere that cloying smell that stuck in her throat like thick syrup.

And Ariana? She could not resist even the weakest pressure from a shopkeeper to come inside for a look. "Where is this from?" she would ask as she fingered each piece of fine embroidery or soft woven fabric. *India, Kashmir, Turkey*, would be the answer.

As they made yet another right turn deeper into the maze, the musky odor suddenly became more intense. Rachel sneezed again, loudly, as smoke filled her nostrils. "*Gesundheit!*" said a shopkeeper, beaming, as he stood from straightening the heaping piles at the entryway to his stall.

"Oooh," Ariana said as she lifted a clear plastic bag filled with pale yellow pebbles up to the light spilling from the shop's interior. "Frankincense! Like in your bible. The three wise men."

"Not my bible," Rachel muttered.

Ariana cocked her head and blinked, her batwing eyelashes fluttering with confusion.

"Yes, madam," the shopkeeper interrupted. "*In fact*, it is frankincense of the finest quality. From Dhofar." He dug into a bin and offered a chunk, silvery compared with those in the plastic bags, to Rachel, who held it in the palm of her hand. "The frankincense resin is considered a gift from God. Those on whose land the trees grow are extremely blessed. Go ahead. Chew. It is okay."

Ariana reached across Rachel and popped the nugget into her mouth. "They say it's supposed to help with digestion," she said as her rouged cheeks pulsed in and out. "And your skin, and your mind as well. You know, for things like anxiety and depression."

"*In fact*," the man continued, "do you know that in ancient times it was more valued than even gold?"

Rachel sneezed again.

"*In fact*," he repeated, "the trees that give the resin are not planted or watered. They just appear. They are a symbol of immortality. *In fact*, this kind," he said as he picked up a bag of cloudier, greenish chunks, "it is for burning, to bless and uplift your home. In the old times people would burn it throughout the night to keep away the dangerous animals and evil spirits."

In fact, thought Rachel as she dug in her pack for a tissue, it would be enough to keep me away as well.

"The best, it is true, is reserved for our king His Majesty Sultan Qaboos." The man folded his arms and smiled proudly.

Ariana bought three bags for herself and one for Rachel, a transaction that lasted five times longer than it should have. By the time she had tucked her change away in her purse, she knew more about the shopkeeper than Rachel knew about her own uncle.

"What's up with all the questions? What, are you looking for a husband or something?"

Ariana reddened, and then screamed. Rachel looked down to see a wave of murky brown water cresting over Ariana's baby-blue wedges. Her own boots were nearly submerged before she could jump out of the way. Soon a river of crud was rushing down the slanted pathway toward them. "Disgusting!" Ariana lifted the legs of her white linen pants as if she were about to curtsy for the queen. From the look on her face you'd think it was a ninety-foot tidal wave that was about to hit. Rachel couldn't help but laugh as Ariana became increasingly frantic. Then, in the darkness, an army of men with buckets and brooms appeared. Rachel backed up onto the steps of the stall behind her to make way, as did Ariana at the stall across from her. The men passed slowly between them, urging the brown sludge forward with their brooms as they went.

When she looked up, Ariana was gone. Probably making yet another friend, thought Rachel as she crossed the wet walkway and entered the shop. But Ariana was nowhere to be found among the pots and bowls and hookahs and urns. "I give you a very good price," the shopkeeper said, pointing to a bin teeming with antique coins.

"My friend? Did you see my friend?" She held out her hand at the approximate level of the top of Ariana's head and batted her eyelashes. The guy shrugged his shoulders.

Rachel did not like being lost. It was a waste of good time. She quickly tried to backtrack their route, but soon became disoriented. Normally she would have used her camera to record landmarks along the way, but she had been trusting Ariana to keep track. That, apparently, had been a mistake.

Now she peered into every twisted alleyway and narrow doorway in search of the woman, while at the same time struggling to find a ray of natural light or a breath of fresh air—any sign of an exit to the street. The thick smell of frankincense was making things even worse. The cloud of smoke that had closed in on her was becoming intoxicating, making her feel as though her head were lagging three steps behind her body and taking with it any sense of bearing, as if she were walking in a thick fog on a dark night.

She stepped up onto her tiptoes with the hope of spotting Ariana in the growing crowd, but all she managed to find was herself clumsily walking right into the person in front of her.

"*Afwan*. Excuse me," Rachel hastily offered in Arabic as she lowered her heels to the ground, where she found herself face to face with a stooped woman wrapped in a red paisley scarf that seemed to reach all the way down to her ankles, her face hidden behind a black satin mask that reminded Rachel of Darth Vader. Only her eyes were visible through wide slits in the shiny fabric, one of them milky and white, the other clear and sharply focused on Rachel. And by her side? A shaggy white goat with a tail as pink and fluffy as a stick of cotton candy.

"*Ma fi mushkila*, no problem, Lil' Cherry Bomb," the woman replied, her voice muffled by the mask.

Rachel stiffened, her heart racing beneath her T-shirt. "Did you say Cherry Bomb?"

The woman cackled softly as the goat gently butted its head against Rachel's thigh. Rachel took a deep breath and wiped away the droplets of sweat that had formed at her hairline. I must be hearing things, she thought as she nodded politely and backed away. And when she turned, silhouetted by the light from the street outside, there stood Ariana leaning on a wall, pecking away on her phone as if she had been left standing and waiting for hours.

6

Her uncle had been right. She was sure of it now, with the harsh light of day taking over from a sleepless night, Tariq's side of the bed still cold and unrumpled, his phone still unanswered. "You are only a whore to this man!" he had screamed at her the day she left his village for good. "He has no love for you. You will see."

Perhaps it was Tariq's discomfort from having her dropped into his own world, seeing her among his own people. Perhaps it was the pressure of the child that was coming. Perhaps he felt torn between his two wives, having them both suddenly within arm's reach. Perhaps it simply seemed easier to go back to life the way it was before, to stay in his big home with his fancy wife and allow Miza to simply fade into the Zanzibar sunset like a long-ago memory.

The thought made her sick to her stomach, bringing back the pain and doubt she suffered every time Tariq had kissed her goodbye at the door of their flat in Stone Town to fly back to Muscat. While he was with her, she managed to do her best to not think about his other life, to erase Maryam from her mind and pretend that Tariq was all hers. It was like playing house. She would try not to ask questions of Tariq, but sometimes she just could not help herself.

"I don't understand," Miza had said to him more than once back in Zanzibar, when he tried to assure her that his first wife did not object to their relationship. "Why does she not care?"

"I have told you," he explained. "Maryam does not concern herself with something so far away, something that will not shame her in front of her friends. How she looks to other people—that is what she cares about. As long as you are here and she is there, it is okay. I have made her that promise."

"And why," Miza asked, "would she not be jealous?"

Tariq shook his head. "I have told you that as well, my love. You know I am not what makes Maryam happy. It is only what I can give her, the life she has learned to enjoy that is important to her—going to the salon, to tea at the nice hotels, the opera, the fashion shows. It is being able to fly off to Dubai or London with her friends, just to shop, to go wherever she wants at any time. That is what makes her happy."

"And you, are you happy in this relationship?"

"I am happy here with you," was always his answer.

Tariq pointed to similar reasons for not divorcing his wife. He claimed to be too honorable to bring shame upon her, to her family in Saudi Arabia, who would, out of tradition, insist on her return to them. Her father was strict and unforgiving. A life there, he insisted, would be a cruel fate for a woman so used to a more lenient, permissive lifestyle.

Miza would never forget the day, before they were even wed, when Tariq admitted to another reason for Maryam not feeling threatened by the prospect of a second wife.

"And what is that?" Miza asked, her head cocked.

Tariq lowered his eyes. "It is that there will be no children."

Miza tried to hide her surprise. "You have made her that promise, to save her feelings?"

Tariq shook his head. "I have made no promise. And it is not about her feelings. It is that there will be no heirs. That is what Maryam knows, that her future is secure, no matter what."

"What do you mean?"

Tariq answered without looking up. "I cannot father a child, Miza. When Maryam failed to become pregnant, we saw many doctors. The opinion was that the problem is mine."

Miza had taken his hand and quickly assured Tariq that she did not care, that the love and caring he was offering to her and Sabra was a gift worth more than anything. "But," she also added at the time, "*inshallah*, if God wants us to have a child, God will bless us with one."

So now here she was, with Tariq's child in her belly, in a place she was not welcome, with no husband by her side.

She had urged Tariq to think twice about having her come to Muscat for the birth, about what that might do to their delicate situation. But he was adamant. Nevertheless, she had insisted he tell Maryam of her arrival in Oman, and of the reason for it. She did not like the thought of having to stay hidden, buried away like a dirty secret. *Let me speak to Maryam*, she had suggested. *We are now sisters.* But Tariq, worried about Maryam's unpredictable temper, had said no. He would tell her about the child once Miza and the baby were back safe in Zanzibar.

Miza knew first-hand how cruel the woman could be. When she had been introduced to Maryam so many years back—then just Tariq's teenage cousin and not yet his wife—the Saudi girl had treated her like the dirt under her shoes. Maryam had traveled with Tariq's extended family to spend a summer month in Zanzibar—the one and only time she had set foot on the "filthy, backwards island", as she had called it. Miza knew Maryam regarded her as an uneducated fool, and pretended not to hear when the older girl ordered her around like a servant. Tariq could see it, even back then. He'd tease Maryam into dropping her haughty ways, or would distract her with his silliness until she'd forget Miza was even around. When Tariq had shyly confessed to Miza that he and Maryam were promised to be wed—an arrangement made by both sets of parents when the children were still very small—she could not hide the scorn on her face.

"Maryam is not so bad," he tried to convince her. "It is just that sometimes she does not think before she speaks. Or does not hear herself when she does."

But Miza could tell that Tariq was only marrying Maryam out of obligation to tradition. He had no choice. She would sometimes, during that summer, see the look on his face when he thought nobody was watching, the embarrassment at his cousin's behavior causing his cheeks to redden and his eyelids to drop. To Miza, Maryam was simply a mean girl.

After the two cousins were wed, things got worse for Tariq. In her darkest moments, Maryam's insults and blame would be flung directly at him. "What kind of a husband are you, causing others to see me as barren as the naked hills of this wretched country? I should leave you," she would say, "and find myself a real man." But the truth was, Tariq said, that his wife never wanted the bother of a child, just as she never wanted to leave him and his riches, or the "wretched" country that allowed for a life so easy.

Perhaps Maryam had grown used to sharing her husband with another. Even though the law required that a man divide not only his money but also his time equally among all his wives, Maryam did not seem to care how much time Tariq spent in Zanzibar, as long as he kept his "business" there.

So what had happened? Had someone told her of Miza's arrival in Muscat? Had she threatened Tariq, insisting he maintain the appearance of being a husband only to her? Was he worried for Miza's safety, and that of the baby, as he had often expressed when they spoke of Maryam and her tantrums? Why did he not call?

Miza's heart thumped loudly in her chest as she picked up the phone and dialed the number to his other house, the number Tariq had given her to use in case of an emergency. It rang four times before someone answered. "Nobody is home," a maid responded to Miza's shaky inquiry. She quickly hung up.

Miza shuffled to the kitchen to heat water for tea. What a fool I have been, thinking I could live as a man's other wife, allowing myself to become a part of something like this, believing it would all work out fine. How could I have believed that such happiness was to be mine? What was I thinking, leaving my country and my sister behind—concerned only with my own selfish needs? This is what I get. This is what I deserve.

"But no," she said out loud, slamming her palm down on the marble counter. Tariq would not have taken that road. He was a good man, a strong man. A man who would never leave a woman, any woman, in a position like this. So then, Miza thought, what was it that could be keeping him away from her now?

59

7

"Rise and shine!" Ariana offered the driver a fistful of rials with one hand and gently shook Rachel's shoulder with the other. The poor thing had slept the entire way over from the souk and must have still been groggy, judging from the way she was silently and obediently following Ariana through the massive carved doors, under a gold-domed ceiling and across a floor so shiny she could practically use it to check her lipstick. It must be the jetlag, she thought as they descended a lushly carpeted staircase and headed outside.

The resort was stretched out like a rubber band between a range of rocky mountains and the shores of the Arabian Sea, and seemed to go on forever, the white and earth-toned buildings leading one into the next. Almost seven hundred rooms and a five-star rating, she had been told. Ariana paused at the head of a hedge-lined brick path, under the lengthening shadows of the gently blowing palms that were keeping the desert heat at bay. To their right a row of smooth brown rocks seemed to float atop the water's surface, like giant globs of mocha frosting poured straight from the bowl. Further down, the sandy beach was dotted with square white umbrellas and matching lounge chairs, only a few of them occupied by the diehards who remained to soak in the last of the daylight hours. A pair of camels ambled toward them, led by a short man in a flowing white robe holding one rein in each hand, while on the backs of the spindly beasts bounced two small children, their blond hair glowing from the sun low in the sky. Couples strolled lazily down the path in burqas and bikinis, headscarves and Bermuda shorts, turbans and baseball caps. And everywhere it was quiet, with only the early evening birdsong of larks and warblers piercing the calm desert air.

"What the fuck are we here for?"

Ariana jumped at the sound of Rachel's gravelly voice. "For cocktails!" she answered brightly, taking Rachel's arm and leading her briskly down the pathway. "Isn't this lovely? We really should have booked here, don't you think?" In fact, it was the concierge at their hotel who had told Ariana about the Shangri-La, after she had grilled the entire front desk staff about where she might find some craftspeople in the area.

"What about in the fishing villages I've heard of?" she'd asked.

"Fishing villages?" The check-in guy swept his arm toward the sea outside the lobby windows. "We are all fishing villages."

"So how about the masks? There are supposed to be women who make masks?"

"You will see the masks in Nizwa, the old capital," the concierge said. "You are going there also?"

Ariana nodded her head. "And the Bedouins? Where can I find Bedouins?"

"They are in the desert," the bellman answered. So Ariana had booked a trip to Wahiba Sands for the next day, certain that they would be able to find something for Rachel to photograph. Rachel had seemed satisfied with the plan when Ariana told her about it in the taxi, before she fell asleep. Now, as they settled into facing wicker armchairs in a rooftop bar, Rachel didn't look satisfied with anything at all.

"Brilliant! It's two-for-one happy hour." Ariana smiled broadly over the leatherbound menu. Rachel ordered a Scotch and dug into the mixed nuts before the server even had a chance to put the bowl to rest on the glass-top table. "I'll have a virgin margarita, please. On the rocks. With extra lime," Ariana said, "if you don't mind."

With the first few sips of her drink Rachel's mood seemed to improve a little. Who wouldn't be happy sitting under a sky like this, a soft gold gauze morphing into a thick purple carpet draped above the sea. Through the window behind them a throaty lounge singer was clumsily plunking away at a piano. Rachel winced. Ariana laughed. The server returned with an apology for the racket and a fresh bowl of nuts.

"*Ma fi mushkila. Shukran,*" Rachel answered. No problem. Thanks.

"You speak Arabic?" Ariana asked.

"A little. Came in handy sometimes for my job."

"Which job was that?" Ariana realized she hadn't yet learned a thing about this woman, which was quite unusual for her considering they'd been together for almost an entire day already.

"I'm a photojournalist. I *was* a photojournalist. Mostly in conflict zones. Wars. Coups. Revolutions. Sometimes natural disasters."

"Really? How exciting! And now you just do this sort of thing?" Ariana swept her gold-bangled arm across the horizon.

"This, and some other stuff." Rachel looked down at her drink.

"Well *that* must have been frightening, what you used to do. Is that why you stopped? Felt like you'd pushed your luck as far as it would go or something of the sort?" Ariana could see a no turning into a yes before the word left Rachel's mouth. And that was as far as her answer went. Behind them, the piano player was butchering the tall, tan, young, lovely girl from Ipanema, limb by limb.

"So you worked in Arab-speaking countries?" Ariana tried again.

"Arab-speaking, Pashto-speaking, Turkish-speaking, Dari-speaking, you name it. Wherever trouble called."

"Wow. The things you must have seen." Again, Ariana waited for Rachel to share more. Even for a pro like Ariana, Rachel was proving to be a tough nut to crack. "So you've been to Pakistan?" she prompted.

Rachel nodded, her attention diverted by a little lizard scaling the wall beside them.

"Lahore?"

Rachel nodded again.

"That's where my family is from!"

"Really," Rachel responded, her eyes remaining on the tiny reptile. "Have you ever been there yourself?"

"Of course! Maybe once a year with my family. These days it seems to be mainly for weddings, or funerals. But you, how did you become a photographer?"

Rachel shrugged. "I've been into it since high school. You know, school paper, yearbook, that sort of thing. How did you become a fixer?"

Ariana shrugged back. "Oh, you know. The way anybody does." She busily squeezed a fresh lime wedge over the melting ice in her glass. "So how did you go from yearbooks to wars?"

Rachel fastened her short hair into a clip she'd pulled from one of the many pockets of the brown vest she never seemed to take off. "It just kind of happened, I guess."

"Really?"

Rachel yawned. "I started a couple of years after nine-eleven. It was kind of easy to get jobs back then, if you hustled and were willing to go places most people were no longer willing to go. And I did, and I was. What about you? How long have you been doing what you're doing?"

Ariana laughed. "It feels like forever." They sat in silence for a moment, Ariana struggling to find a way out of this game of verbal volleyball before Rachel figured out the truth. She waited until the other woman finished her drink to lob the next question. "So what was it like?"

"Like? What was what like?"

"Living like that. Being in all those dangerous places. It must have been terrifying, am I right?"

Rachel shrugged her shoulders. "At times. But not always." She swatted at a flying insect with her damp cocktail napkin. "Back when I started, it was a crazy time. Lots of partying— drinking, dancing all night long. And sex. Lots of sex."

Ariana's raised eyebrows spoke for her.

"It was different. A different time, different circumstances," Rachel explained. "It was like you'd meet and it was instant family, because you never knew what was going to happen next, to any one of us. Does that make sense?"

Ariana nodded, watching Rachel as she absent-mindedly rubbed at a small tattoo on her forearm. Was it a globe? Some sort of face? "But the things you've seen," she continued, "I can't begin to imagine what that must have been like."

Rachel paused before returning her focus to Ariana. "Sure," she finally answered. "Things could get a little wonky. But . . ." She twisted around in her chair in search of the waiter. "Landing the front page of a newspaper or magazine? Nothing can beat that."

The night sky became thick with stars. From the lounge behind them the singer ended her set to a round of tepid applause. "So you don't drink at all?" Rachel asked before draining her glass and trading it in for a new one.

Ariana shook her head. "No. I was never interested. And honestly? I really hate it on dates when supposedly devout Muslim guys try to get me to take a taste. Happens quite often. That totally pisses me off."

"I hate dating."

"Me too," Ariana agreed.

"You date a lot?"

"I've done my fair share."

"So why haven't you married?"

Ariana choked a little on the cold, tart liquid hitting her throat.

"Shit." Rachel shook her head. "I'm sorry. I didn't mean to offend you, but I'm really not very good at this stuff. I'm not much of a girl's girl. I guess I'm just more used to being around guys."

Ariana shook away the apology with a wiggle of her hand. "Not to worry. It's sort of a long story. But it's not like I don't have *anything* going on."

Rachel laughed. "I can tell that by the way your phone has been dinging and pinging and chirping every time I'm with you."

Ariana felt her face grow warm. "That's nothing serious. Just a couple of clowns back in Dubai. They're not what I'm looking for, and I seriously doubt I'm what they really want either."

"So what *do* you want?"

"Looks, money, smarts, power—you know, the usual things." Ariana laughed.

"Well that shouldn't be too hard to find," Rachel said with a smirk.

"Seriously, what matters most to me is having someone I can trust." She traced a puddle of water pooling around the bottom of her glass with her finger. "I actually was married once." The words seemed to spill out of Ariana's mouth on their own. This wasn't exactly the sort of thing she shared with everyone.

"So what happened?"

Ariana took a deep breath. "Well, there was this boy. From Lahore. The son of good friends of my parents. He was just a year older than me."

"And?"

"You really want to hear all this?"

"Why not?"

"Okay. Well, I guess it was sort of predestined. The relationship was encouraged by both our parents: his because they knew they wanted their son out of Pakistan, mine because it seemed a proper match. And me? I thought he was the love of my life." Ariana sipped at her drink, her eyelids hanging with the weight of her lashes.

"So?"

"So, he came to England as soon as he got his fiancé visa. I should have seen what was coming, but you know what they say about love."

"I do," Rachel said.

"And so, when he dove into the Western world head first—and I mean all the way down to the sub-basement floor—even before the wedding, I turned that blind eye. I simply would not let myself accept what was right in front of me. It wasn't until we'd been married a year that I actually let myself consider the fact that he had become a womanizer and a drunk."

"Ouch. So then what?"

"Well, lucky for me my father had seen it as well. It was my dad who convinced me to dump him and get on with my life."

"And your mom?"

"It was a bit harder on her. She loved him like a son, had known him all his life. And there was the problem of his parents—her friends—back in Pakistan as well."

"Tough."

"Yes, it truly was. But my father was amazingly supportive, and so it was off to university for me."

"So what happened to the boy—I mean, your ex?"

Ariana shrugged. "I'm not sure. I suppose he probably stayed on in London. His family was quite furious with us all. I doubt my parents ever heard from them after that."

Rachel nodded. "So do you still want it? To be married, have kids, the whole thing?"

"Of course I do. Who wouldn't?"

Rachel shrugged. "Me?"

"Oh, please. I don't believe that for one second."

"Okay, you're right. I'm just kidding."

Ariana raised one eyebrow. "Really?"

"No. Yes. I don't know. It's just not where my head is these days."

"Sometimes I wish I felt that way. I swear, I've seen so many weddings you'd think I'd have my fill."

"Always a bridesmaid, right?"

"Sort of."

"Seriously, then why haven't you remarried? You seem to be attractive enough."

This time Ariana tried hard not to overreact to Rachel's awkward approach. "Thanks, I guess." She tossed her hair back over her shoulders.

"So really, what is it?"

Ariana hesitated for a moment before responding. "Well, it seems as though at least part of it is that most guys who share my values, the ones who are not just looking for sex and are sincere about marriage, aren't interested in someone my age."

Rachel tilted her head sideways, confused.

"You know," Ariana explained, "they want someone to start a family with."

"But you're not too old for that, are you? How old are you, anyway?"

"Thirty-five, almost thirty-six. Okay, so maybe I'm not too old to have one kid, or maybe two, if I hurry. But regardless, they are all looking for the young ones." Ariana poked at the ice with her straw and let out a little laugh. "You know, sometimes I wonder if I'm cursed."

"Yeah, don't we all."

"No, I mean literally cursed. A clairvoyant told me so once." Ariana regretted the words as soon as they were out. "Not that I normally choose to get involved with those types of things, just so you know," she quickly added.

Rachel shrugged her shoulders. "To each their own."

"Honest. It was my friends who made me do it." Ariana remembered the day Farrah and Badia dragged her with them to the fortune-teller, giggling and joking around as if they were simply going for manicures or getting their eyebrows done. The veiled woman had zeroed in on a petrified Ariana, handing her a fistful of shells while coaxing her to focus on the parts of her life that needed change, the things she most wanted to understand. Then the shells were tossed. If the woman hadn't been so spot-on about a few non-negotiable, factual elements of Ariana's life—how many nephews she had, where she was from—she would have maybe been able to dismiss the whole thing. After all, the woman was clearly not a holy person. But though she tried everything she could to shake it off, Ariana could never forget what her shells had shown. "Seriously, I truly believe one shouldn't mess with that kind of thing. It goes against everything I believe in."

"Well, I'm with you on that one," Rachel agreed. "The same thing kind of happened to me once with my friends. I ended up at a psychic downtown. You know, one of those little storefront places with neon signs in the window? She read my cards, and told me my aura was full of negative energy. But she promised she could clean it for a mere four hundred dollars. And then she begged me to give her a good review on Yelp."

Ariana forced a laugh, her mind still on that afternoon with the clairvoyant. "You know," she said as she rested her chin on her hands, "sometimes I just get really tired of being single, don't you?"

Rachel nodded, her eyes seeming to focus on something in the distance. Their drinks finished, they sat in silence, Ariana frustrated—and a little impressed—with the realization that Rachel had gotten way more out of her than she had meant to share, that she had actually been able to beat her at her own game.

8

"*Kwhari!*" Sabra shouted a goodbye to her friends as she hurried around the corner toward home, her black-and-white uniform flapping behind her like the feathers of a wind-blown penguin. Her after-school Islamic studies had been a total bore—the same old lessons about what you should say to your future husband, what you should not say to him, what you should do to keep him happy, what you should not do to avoid making him mad. Blah blah blah. She thanked her lucky stars that she and her sister had moved back to the city, where girls did not marry so young. And she thanked them even more for giving her a sister like Miza, who told her practically each day, including when they spoke that very morning, how Sabra would someday go to the university, how she would someday become a very important woman who would help others who had no voice, and how she would someday make Miza even more proud of her than she already was.

"*Jambo!*" She waved hello to the same three gossiping old men she passed every day, slouched back against the painted mural of the giant shark with its mouth wide open, looking as though it were about to swallow them whole. Jaws Corner, as it was called, was busy as usual, the motorbikes weaving in and out as the neighborhood took care of its errands, the street lined with fruit sellers perched behind buckets of mangoes and papayas and jackfruit, the yellow bananas still bright in the afternoon shade. Sabra's stomach protested loudly, anticipating the savory *chapati* Hoda would have waiting on the kitchen table, the soft flat bread still warm from the pan.

From the end of the narrow street their home welcomed her like a beacon, its clean white facade standing out in sharp contrast to the peeling buildings on either side, their balconies cluttered with clotheslines and their railings draped with armfuls of laundry optimistically left to dry in the moist sea air. Looking up, she could see the windows of her own room already shuttered behind brown wooden slats that Hoda had closed against the swarms of mosquitos the setting sun would bring.

Sabra hopped up the two stone steps and heaved her shoulder into the massive arched door, its brass studs pressing against her spindly arms, its carved teak reluctantly giving way to her forty-three kilos of force. Taking the worn wooden stairs two at a time, she sprinted the three stories to the flat, flinging open the apartment door with the last of the pent-up energy left by a long day in classes. She was about to shout out a *hallo* to Hoda when she heard a familiar voice, one that made her stop silently in her tracks.

"What do you mean she is not here?" her uncle was saying, his tone the one that usually meant a tirade was on its way.

"Like I have told you, Uncle, the lady of the house is out of the country. I do not know exactly when she will return."

"So she went to Oman, am I right?"

Sabra could not hear the maid's response.

"What, marrying that rich, lazy Arab and moving to this big home in the big city wasn't enough for her? She thinks she is now so important, so much better than the rest of us? How I would welcome the chance to remind her of who is important."

At the sharp crack of her uncle's words, Sabra stepped noiselessly back into the entryway, leaving the front door open a slice. Though she hadn't seen the man for more than a year, since that day Tariq moved the sisters away from the village and into the flat in Stone Town, she wasn't too anxious to greet him now. Her life under his roof had been tolerable, thanks to Miza, but Sabra had resented being treated like a servant. Her aunt expected an exhausting amount of work from her—sweeping, washing, helping with her younger cousins—leaving precious little time for anything fun, let alone the energy to tackle even the simple lessons the village school offered. But it was the way her sister behaved around the man that made her own skin squirm whenever he was within earshot. She could almost picture the way Miza's back would stiffen, her muscles becoming firm and unyielding, her mouth setting into a stark slash crossing her broad face. It was as if she were a wild horse being backed into a barn.

"But surely she must have left money in the house," her uncle continued.

"Of course she left us with grocery money. However, that is all." Sabra could hear the fear gathering in Hoda's voice.

"Don't lie to me!"

"But Uncle, I am not lying. Come and see for yourself." Sabra heard the kitchen drawer opening, the sounds of utensils being rattled around.

"This?" her uncle roared. "This is not even a half of the amount that is owed to me. You must call my niece immediately and ask her where it is, the month's payment for that useless girl. That was our deal."

"But I have no phone!" Hoda protested. "The phone is with the child, Sabra."

Her uncle seemed to hesitate for a moment. "And where is she, our little Sabra?"

"She is at school, of course!"

Sabra pushed the door closed with a hush, but her uncle must have heard, for the next thing she knew the door was flying back open and her uncle was towering over her, the shillings from the kitchen drawer still clutched in his hand.

"What's the matter, *toto*? Aren't you happy to see your *baba*?"

Sabra nodded shyly.

"Your *baba*, who came so far just to check to see how you are doing here, left alone by your selfish sister?"

The girl lowered her eyes to the ground.

"Well don't just stand there." He pulled her inside and pointed to a chair. "Tell me, how *are* you doing here in the city? Are you happy?"

"Yes," she said in a whisper as she sat, her thighs tense against the edge of the seat.

"What was that? I did not hear you."

"Yes, I am happy," she repeated, louder this time.

"That is good." Her uncle paced as he spoke, his fingers drumming against one another in a rhythm only he could hear. "But tell me, *toto*, how is it that you can be happy when your

73

dear sister has left you behind to go off to another country? How is that?"

"I'm fine here. Hoda takes good care of me."

"Yes, I'm sure she does. But what happens when Miza does not come back? Hoda cannot stay with you forever, you know."

"But she *is* coming back. She is coming back as soon as the baby comes."

"Baby?" Her uncle stopped directly in front of her. "Oh, I see. So Miza has gone to Oman to have a new family. Now I understand. That is what they all do, you know, those who get the money. They leave our country and they go to Oman, and they do not come back."

"Miza will be back!" Sabra spat out defiantly, ready to accept whatever rage her uncle might deliver. But he simply nodded his head and began to turn slowly, taking in the room around him, his eyes circling from the high-beamed ceilings above to the soft rugs blanketing the floors below.

"She promised me!"

Now her uncle laughed, a harsh bark that stung even more than his shouting.

"Please don't laugh," Sabra protested with tears pooling in her eyes. Through the blur she could see Hoda nervously twisting her hands.

"Okay, so there is nothing funny. You are right, Sabra. It is not funny at all that your sister left you here like this. So, in fact, you are coming with me."

Sabra leaped from the chair.

"What, you don't want to come for a visit with your *baba*? And your poor auntie, who misses you so? Go get your things." He clapped his thick hands together twice. "*Harakaka, harakaka! Hurry, hurry!*"

74

But Sabra refused to move. It wasn't until her uncle grabbed her bony wrist between his lumpy fingers that Hoda stepped in. "Let her be," she insisted in a voice that shook like jelly. "I have been told to watch over her, and it is my job to do so."

Her uncle dropped Sabra's arm and whirled around toward the cowering maid, the back of his hand poised to strike. "You keep your mouth shut, woman! This child is my property. It is the law. And now I am taking back what is rightfully mine. No money?" His arms and his eyebrows lifted in unison. "No deal. Do you understand how that works?"

"But we must talk to the *mama*. We must tell Sabra's sister."

"You will tell her nothing!" he shouted in a voice so loud it seemed to echo across the room.

"But I am responsible—"

"This is family business, and you are not family. In fact, why don't you just get your belongings and get out of this house now. And if I hear of you saying even one word about this to anyone, trust me, I will do everything in my power to bring bad fortune to you and all your family. An ocean of bad fortune, worse than you can ever imagine."

Sabra watched Hoda retreat from the force of the man, just as she had seen so many others do in the village where he ruled. She backed down the hallway and returned with a satchel, and was out the door before Sabra could even say goodbye.

"And now you." Her uncle pushed Sabra gently toward her bedroom. "Gather your things, and we will be off." Sabra's eyes darted to the still open front door. Perhaps she could outrun the man if she tried. She slowly turned as if heading toward her room, and then lunged for the door. In a flash she felt both feet lifting from the ground, her uncle's arm circling her waist like a cobra, his hold so tight she could barely breathe.

"I said gather your things!" he shouted, dropping her onto the bedroom floor as her phone fell from her uniform pocket and skidded across the floor. "I will take that," he said, scooping the device into his hand. "And not one word out of you, or I will show you exactly what happens to those who dare disobey my wishes."

Sabra clawed through the clothes in her armoire as he stood guard in the doorway, searching through her tears for the one thing she knew she could not leave behind. She could hear her uncle behind her, his breath hissing through the gaps between his scattered yellow teeth. Finally, beneath a pile of scarves, she spied the blue border of the *kanga*, her half of the special square of fabric she shared with her sister, a thin piece of cloth that Miza had promised would bind them together forever.

9

"It is five hundred rials that must be paid if you hit one." Adil slowed as a bedraggled camel teetered on the side of the two-lane highway. "For the owner," he explained. "To make up for his loss. But actually? We have insurance for that." The camel safely behind them, Adil stepped hard on the gas to pass a slow-moving truck. Rachel reached for the plastic bottle nestled in the pouch behind the seat in front of her, the water inside already hot as tea from the midday sun. She had been hoping to get an early start, but apparently Ariana didn't do mornings so well. When she had finally appeared in the lobby, in full makeup and a freshly ironed floral print blouse with perfectly matching coral-colored palazzo pants, Rachel wanted to laugh. Ariana looked as if she had stepped off the cover of *Hamptons* magazine. "We *are* going to the desert today, correct? For a shoot with the Bedouin women?"

"Of course we are!" Ariana smiled and took Rachel's arm. "Our driver should be waiting right outside."

And he had been. "Hello, my friends," Adil had greeted them. "Welcome to my car." Rachel had wondered at the Desert Adventures logo on the front door of the 4x4, but Adil spoke decent English and seemed pretty knowledgeable about the area. Now he honked and waved as he passed the rickety truck. "We say *Salaam alaikum* to make peace to each other," he explained to Rachel, who had to smile. Everyone was so damn nice in this country. Adil had already told her how it was against the law to show anger or frustration, to even gesture with impatience. Rachel wouldn't last here a day if she were left on her own. And clean! She marveled at the spotless roadside, at the freshly painted white houses dotting the brown hills in the distance. And not a dirt-streaked car in sight because, of course, there was a law against that as well.

"*Achoo!*" she sneezed loudly, the powerful brew of car air freshener and Adil's cologne prickling the inside of her nose.

"Blessed you," he said as he veered off onto the tight curl of an exit ramp. "Actually? In our country it is the person who sneezes who says *Alhamdulillah*, praise be to Allah. Then the others respond *Yarhamuk Allah*, may Allah have mercy on you. You see, it is believed that sneezing lightens the mind and gives comfort. So it is something good, and one should glorify Allah for it."

"Perfume allergy," Rachel explained.

"But if you yawn," Adil continued without missing a beat, "that is different. That is a sign of sloth and heaviness, and is considered an act that pleases only the *shaytan*, the devil. That is why the Prophet commanded us to stop a yawn either by closing our mouth or by putting our hand over it."

Ariana looked up from her texting. "Are we going the right way?"

78

"All the roads take us to Rome," Adil assured her, his eyes reflected in the rear-view mirror. "Actually? I think you will be hungry now. My friends. I will take us to have lunch, if that is what you want."

Rachel sighed, but Ariana chimed in before she could object. "Oh, that would be lovely, wouldn't it, Rachel?"

The restaurant was empty save for Rachel, who sat down alone to peruse the plastic menu with its pictures of platters piled high with hummus and kebabs and rice and tomatoes. Her stomach growled as she waited for both Adil and Ariana to return from the little mosque attached to the restaurant's restrooms, where she had seen the row of faucets lined up below illustrated instructions on the proper way to wash before prayer. Her mother would have had no patience with this "BS" (as she would have put it), thought Rachel, as she remembered the day her mother told her she'd joined the atheist club at her retirement community. "What do you talk about?" Rachel had asked at the time. "Everything you *don't* believe in?" Rachel liked to think she had a bit more tolerance than her mother, though her own tendencies leaned toward not believing as well. After all the suffering and injustice she had witnessed in the world, how could she think otherwise?

Ariana and Adil took their places at the table, each, like Rachel, seated high atop two chairs stacked one upon the other, as if that made the plastic dining furniture appear more classy. The food came quickly, and after checking to make sure everyone got what they wanted, Adil rolled the sleeves of his *dishdasha* up to his elbows and popped a cube of chicken into his mouth.

"Delicious," Ariana said as she swallowed a forkful of salad. Rachel dug into her hummus platter, scooping the thick, smooth paste up from the plate and into her mouth with a triangle of crisp pita. She felt Adil's eyes upon her as she started for more.

"What?" she asked, her hand halting midway as she looked back and forth between her two dining companions. Adil lowered his eyes sheepishly. "What's the matter?" Rachel repeated.

"You're a leftie," Ariana explained.

"Ah, right. Shit. I'm sorry. I knew about the whole left-handed thing in Islam. But nobody's actually ever explained the rationale to me." She crunched down on the pita and waited for an answer.

"Well," Ariana offered, "traditionally you never use your left hand to eat or drink, as that is what the *shaytan* does."

Rachel continued to dip. "Seriously? So what if someone's born left-handed?"

Adil paused before answering. "Usually? We try to change them." He paused to pull another piece of chicken off the thin stick on his plate.

"So you know there are all sorts of actions that you're supposed to start on the right," Ariana added. "Like putting on your pants and shoes or clipping your nails? And there are some things as well for which you are only supposed to use your left hand. Like blowing your nose or cleaning yourself."

"Actually, most things are started from right to left, just like the way we read the Koran," Adil added. "There is a system. For example in the mosque, we enter with the right foot, to show respect. In houses, too. In any good and clean place. The left is considered dirty." He sat back and rested his forearms on the table. "But the restrooms, they are places of *jinn*. So we enter with the left foot first, and exit with the right foot. With the left, it is an insult to the *jinn*."

"*Jinn*?" Rachel asked.

"You know," Ariana said, "as in genies. Aladdin and his magic lamp? Genie in a bottle? Spirits."

"You guys believe in those things?"

Ariana and Adil looked at each other and then turned back to Rachel. "Doesn't everybody?" Adil asked.

"Not me." Rachel shrugged.

"Adil means that in Islam, it's a part of our culture," Ariana explained. "From the stories we've heard from our parents and grandparents, and from the things we've seen ourselves."

"Everyone has had some experience with the *jinn*," Adil added.

"You?" Rachel asked.

"I think maybe I have a good *jinn*." Adil laughed. "He makes sure I wake up on time for morning prayers when I am sleepy."

"So there are good and bad ones?"

"Of course there are," Ariana said. "But you never know who's who or what's what, so it's best just to keep your distance. Would you like some of my salad, Rachel?"

Once back in the car, Rachel pressed them to hurry to the desert. She had already missed the morning light, and was anxious to get her shots of the mask-makers before the shadows became too harsh. Adil stepped on the gas, the car beeping relentlessly like a hospital monitor. "What is that god-awful noise?" she asked.

"Actually? It is when I am going more than the speed limit. In fact, all of our automobiles do this." Adil slowed until the dashboard showed 119, and the car became quiet.

Rachel stared out the window as they whipped by clusters of new housing developments, uniform two-story white homes shining like neon cubes against the dull brown rock that stretched out in all directions around them. Not a soul stirred in the blasting afternoon heat. Even the roadside flagmen there to warn of construction ahead stood as still as statues, which in fact they kind of were, as Rachel saw when she took a closer look. Work clothes stiff with stuffing, like scarecrows. The only living things brave—or stupid—enough to be out were the goats that seemed to have taken over the land as their own. They were everywhere: standing like hood ornaments on parked cars, grazing on impossibly vertical surfaces, and coming way too close to the edge of the highway, she realized as Adil swerved and flipped on his hazard lights—too late—as a warning to the driver behind them. Rachel squeezed her eyes shut as she heard the thud of goat against bumper.

"It is fine," Adil assured her. "The goat has run away."

When they finally pulled off the highway, Rachel was relieved, until Adil turned into the driveway of an auto repair shop. *Sale of Tire & Repairing*, the sign read in English underneath some blue Arabic letters. "Is there something wrong with the car?" she asked, truly not wanting to believe her luck could be so bad.

"Nothing wrong, *inshallah*."

Rachel looked out at the lineup of white 4x4s, identical to theirs right down to the company logos displayed on the front doors.

"Actually, we must get out some air from our tires to drive in the sand." Adil jumped out of the car and greeted the attendant, their arms touching gently above the wrists.

Rachel turned to Ariana, who was busy with her phone. "You have got to be fucking kidding me. We are literally going to drive *through* the desert to look for the Bedouins? I thought we had something set up. I thought you told me this guy knew what he was doing."

"He came highly recommended as a desert guide." Ariana smiled apologetically.

Their tires half-flattened, Adil was back behind the wheel, peeling out of the parking lot toward the distant sands ahead. When the asphalt suddenly came to an end, he stopped the car, gave a two-thumbs-up and flashed a smile into the rear-view. "It is okay, my friends? Seatbelts are tight?" And they were off, bouncing across the copper sand toward the dunes looming ominously before them, the soft wavy surface interrupted only by tire tracks left by the dozens of other 4x4s corkscrewing around like little kids on a giant water slide.

The engine roared as Adil veered sharply to the left and surged straight up a vertical wall of sand, the tires fighting to keep their grip on the fickle terrain. Suddenly, with a spin of the steering wheel, they were skidding sideways back down again, the light outside obliterated by the thick spray of sand kicked up by the tires, the 4x4 teetering at a perilous angle. And then he did it again, sending the car hurtling and plunging through the deep craters as if he were trying to tame a bucking bronco. Ariana squealed with delight. Rachel's left hand braced the camera against her chest while the right gripped the plastic strap above the window, her knuckles yellow from lack of blood. She could feel her lunch coming back up to greet her as the car tossed and pivoted through the sand.

When Adil finally turned off the engine on the top of a sharp slope, Rachel stumbled from the car, her boots sliding diagonally beneath her before coming to a stop. "What the hell was that all about?" she asked as she desperately gulped in the hot desert air.

Adil's smile melted to a frown. "You don't like the dune bashing? It is what all the tourists want."

"Tourist? Who said I was a tourist?" She shifted her eyes to Ariana, who was sheepishly avoiding her look by pretending to brush some invisible sand from her sleeves. Around them, valleys of brown and black began to appear among the red and yellow dunes as the shadows lengthened with the dropping sun. Rachel sighed. "So much for getting my shots today," she said loudly before stomping back to the car.

Rachel remained silent the entire way back to Muscat. Not that it mattered, as Ariana and Adil were so deep in conversation they wouldn't have even noticed. By the time they reached the outskirts of the city, Ariana had managed to extract more personal information about Adil from the back seat than one of Rachel's old journalist pals would have been able to get in twice the time. Origin? Pure Omani, and proud of it. Born and raised in Muscat. A family man. Education? Studied to be an accountant at the university in Dubai, as his mother wished, but switched to studying English instead. His father was disappointed, convinced he'd amount to nothing. Now, with his English degree, he could work as a translator, or have a job in insurance or education. Or be a tour guide. He liked being a tour guide, liked to move around, liked meeting people from around the world. Yeah, Rachel thought, and scaring the shit out of them.

"And your name?" Ariana had asked him. "Where did that come from?"

"To be honest with you?" Adil answered. "Many people, they are named from prophets. Unfortunately my name is not the name of a prophet. But Adil in Arabic, it means fair. To be fair. So I try my best in my life to be fair. To do things fair."

"That's lovely, Adil." Ariana smiled as she looked out the window.

"And you, what is the meaning of the name Ariana?"

"Mine comes from the Greek. There it means 'holy one'," Ariana said with pride. "But in Arabic, it means 'vivacious'."

"Perfect," Rachel muttered.

"And you?" Adil asked with a glance over his shoulder.

"I have no idea," Rachel answered.

"Wait, I'll find it." Ariana pecked at her phone. "Here it is. It's a Hebrew name. Meaning ewe."

"You? Like you and me?" Adil asked.

"No, ewe." Ariana laughed. "As in female sheep."

Rachel wished she had remembered her earbuds. She curled up against the side of the car and did her best to ignore the incessant chatter.

"And tomorrow?" Adil asked Ariana. "What will you do tomorrow?"

"Tomorrow we really must find some of the handicrafts Rachel is looking for. I thought we'd try Nizwa for the masks and silver and pottery. Say, do you think you might be able to take us there?"

Rachel resisted the urge to kick her in the shins.

"Ah, Nizwa, it is a good city. I would like to take you very much, but tomorrow I cannot. I am taking my children to the waterpark. You will ask at the hotel for another driver." Adil pulled up under the hotel's awning and stopped, opening the doors to help them out. "Thank you. I like meeting you very much." He accepted Ariana's wad of cash with a nod of the head. "And good luck finding the hand jobs you are looking for!" he called out to Rachel as the car door slammed shut behind her.

10

Hani spotted them immediately across the hotel lobby, the two clients who had arranged for a ride to Nizwa with his cousin Omar. "An American photographer and a Dubai expat," Omar had told him when he called early in the morning to ask a favor of Hani, his car unable to start and his reputation with the hotel at stake. Hani was glad to help his cousin out and, as he had meetings scheduled in Nizwa anyway, it wasn't a problem in the least. Now he smiled at the short, sturdy woman with the camera around her neck and nodded to her companion, who stood there teetering on shoes so high while carrying a pink handbag so huge it looked as if she were about to tip over. Instead she came barreling toward him, one finger pointing to a pile of luggage sitting by the glass doors. "You're our driver, I presume?"

"My name is Hani. It is my cousin who—"

"Brilliant. Pleased to meet you. I'm Ariana, that's Rachel.

Those are ours." Her eyelashes batted against each other like two hands clapping.

"Hi, Hani," Rachel said as she followed Ariana out to the Lexus.

"Lovely car," Ariana said as Hani closed the trunk.

Hani was speechless as he opened the back door and gestured for Ariana, and her handbag, to enter. As Rachel followed, Hani noticed a look pass between the two women upon spying the passenger in the front seat.

"Please, let me introduce you. This is Miza." He gently shut the door and climbed behind the wheel. "Miza, this is Ariana and Rachel."

"Very pleased to meet you, Miza," Ariana responded with a precise British politeness.

"Hello," Miza said, and nodded.

"Are you going to Nizwa as well?" Ariana asked.

"Miza is the wife of someone I work with," Hani explained. He looked over at the solemn woman, her swollen eyes hidden behind dark glasses, the bright colors of her head wrap belying the heaviness of her heart. "It is for him that I am taking her to Nizwa." He stopped short of saying more, as the story was Miza's to tell, if she chose to. But for now the woman sat silently beside him, her hands resting on top of the woven satchel on her lap.

Hani drove them through the outskirts of the city and onto the new highway leaving town. At first the car was silent, save for an incessant tapping from the lacquered nails of the one with the eyelashes. Ariana. The woman never seemed to look up from that phone. Texting with her husband? More likely gossiping with her girlfriends. Just look at her, he thought as he shifted his eyes to the rear-view mirror, with her face all painted

87

up and her hair made to look as smooth as gentle waves on a lake. Yet another one who seemed to have more love for her handbags than for her faith. He'd seen it before, at university, with the girls who cared only about what car you drove, how much money your family had. It was a pity.

A giggle bubbled up from the seat behind him. And listen to her, he thought. Acting as if she hadn't a care in the world. She probably didn't. He gave a worried glance over to a somber Miza. At least the other one, Rachel, was quiet, there in the back with music playing in her ears.

But after a while Ariana seemed to have tired of the life in her phone, and turned her attention instead to Miza. "Your earrings, they're gorgeous." Miza nodded politely at the compliment. "So are you from Oman as well?"

"Zanzibar," Miza answered sleepily, without turning around.

"Wow. I've always wanted to go to Africa. Were you born there?"

"Yes."

"And you live here now?"

Miza hesitated. "I have a place in Muscat."

"Oh. That must be nice. Muscat seems like a lovely place to live." Ariana waited only briefly for a response, then continued. "I love your scarf. Did it come from Zanzibar?"

Miza nodded again.

"So have you been to Nizwa before?"

"Miza is new to our country," Hani answered for her. Although it was clear she meant no harm, couldn't Ariana tell that the poor woman was exhausted, and not interested in her chatter?

"So your husband, he is a driver too, like Hani?"

Hani was tempted to set things straight, to tell her of Tariq's successful importing business, of some of the projects they had

88

been working on together, about his own meetings in Nizwa with the municipal officials for approval of his plans for the new sports complex. But instead he decided to have a little fun with her. "Miza's husband and I do share a similar profession," he said with a sideways look at the woman beside him, whose mind understandably seemed a million miles away.

"That's nice," Ariana said. "So how does it work? Do you own your own car?"

"Yes." Hani nodded. "This is my car."

"And do you get a lot of work?"

"Oh yes, I am always working. Sometimes, I think, too much."

"Well, I certainly hope you are compensated adequately."

"I do okay."

"Do you like your job?"

"Sure. I find the work to be very challenging."

"Really? You do? I think that's great. Trust me, I know how important it is to have a passion for your work. But don't you ever wish to do more?"

"More? I am doing quite enough, thank you."

Ariana turned her line of fire back toward Miza. "And how do you like Oman, Miza?"

"Everyone finds Oman a wonderful country," Hani jumped in again, anxious to save the poor woman from Ariana's relentless questioning. "You have been here before, am I right?"

Ariana laughed, checking to make sure Rachel still had her music going before she continued. "Actually, I'm not all that familiar with it," she answered in a loud whisper. "But please don't let on to my friend. And so far so good. We've only been here two days. But I will say that the people seem extremely friendly. And thank goodness they all seem to speak English so well."

"Yes, this is true," Hani answered, relieved to have successfully diverted the conversation away from Miza. "In my family it is my mother who insists that we always speak English together, so that we are comfortable with the language." He smiled at her through the rear-view mirror. "And the friendliness? It is in our blood. Even the Prophet Mohammed, peace be upon him, mentioned the Omanis, saying we are a different people—friendly, good, hospitable. We were used as a good example to others. It is in one of his speeches from the holy book."

"My goodness. That's quite an endorsement."

"Yes, it is. Because it is our faith that is most important to us. That, and family and personal honor. These are our values."

"Well I can certainly get behind that," Ariana said.

"Yes?" Hani asked, raising one eyebrow. "And you, you and your husband have children?"

"No husband," Ariana answered. "Not anymore."

"I'm sorry," Hani answered softly, regretting passing judgment over a woman who was a widow. "But you have your parents? And sisters and brothers perhaps? A big family?"

"Well, we're not big, but we are close. Although my mum and dad live far from me."

"The Koran teaches us that a person has responsibility toward his family, not just to their spouse and children, but to their siblings and parents as well."

"I know that," Ariana answered with a bit of defensiveness in her voice. "And I hope that someday I will live closer to them."

"Then that is my hope for you as well, *Alhamdulillah*." Hani felt like kicking himself. What was the matter with him, lecturing her in that way? But for some reason the words just kept tripping their way out of his mouth. "Me, I cannot imagine leaving my country," he continued. "Our country, it is a special place. It is thanks to our king His Majesty Sultan Qaboos. He is much beloved by our people."

"I can certainly see that," Ariana said, her eyes turning to the windshield sticker bearing the ruler's unmistakable likeness, with its manicured white beard and thick dark brows. "His face seems to be everywhere I look. So far I've seen posters, banners, even coffee mugs. Not to mention every denomination of rial. How on earth can you tell your bills apart? I'd be a disaster shopping over here."

"I doubt that very much. I'm sure you would be a most welcome sight for our shopkeepers in Oman." Hani laughed, glad to find himself back on safe ground. "Now, His Majesty," he continued, "he has done much for our country since he took over from his father. He has brought us into more modern times, yet has also managed to preserve our religious and cultural roots. You can see why we love our ruler. His birthday is a national holiday much celebrated by everyone. And every year he makes a tour of the entire country—our cities, towns and villages—taking with him ministers and other important government members, to meet and talk with the people."

"Wow, that is impressive," Ariana said.

"Isn't it?" Hani embraced the opportunity to share his pride for his country. "And what he has done for our healthcare and infrastructure, it is unbelievable. Look at this nice new highway, for example."

"I wish I could say that about my own government." Rachel had abandoned her earbuds. "Maybe there's something to the whole 'absolute monarchy' thing. No senate standstills, no deadlocked congress. No idiotic elections where the person who actually wins the most votes doesn't win at all. Imagine."

"This is true," Hani agreed, happy to have engaged both women in the conversation. "Also our tourism. Did you know that not that long ago you two would not have been allowed to be here, in my car, enjoying our beautiful mountains and our endless skies? Oman was almost completely closed to visitors. It was our king, His Majesty Sultan Qaboos, who made this possible, who made the decision to open up our country for others to see."

"So what happens when he dies?" Rachel asked. "I've read that he's not been well. And he has no heirs, right?"

Hani shook his head. "We are not worried about that. Our king His Majesty Sultan Qaboos has prepared everything for our future."

"Rainbows and puppy dogs," Rachel muttered from the back seat.

"I'm sorry?" Hani asked.

"Nothing. I'm just remarking on the particularly optimistic nature of your country. Even your newspaper seems to have no bad news in it."

Hani laughed. "It is true that we are positive. And why not? And I will tell you another thing, a thing that is most important to me. Did you know that when our king His Majesty Sultan Qaboos came into power, Oman had only two schools, and not one of them for girls? Today, the university has to have a quota, so that it remains half and half men and women, because there are so many more women who qualify than men! It is a beautiful thing."

"Why is it the only decent guys I meet seem to be taxi drivers and shopkeepers?" Ariana's voice remained low, her muttered comment meant only for Rachel's ears.

"And did you know that in my country only Omanis are allowed to have the job of driver?" Hani snapped back, suddenly fed up with this woman's small-mindedness. "It is a protected profession, and not an easy one. Drivers should be respected for the long hours they work to put food on the table for their families."

"I'm so sorry, Hani," Ariana gushed. "I truly didn't mean to insult you. It's just that I really do wish there were more men like you."

"There are probably many men like me. You just need to keep your eyes, and your heart, open." Hani was sure this woman must have no trouble attracting men, as long as they were interested in her kind of woman.

"Oh, my heart is open, trust me. Sometimes I even wear it on my sleeve like a shoulder bag."

"Well if it is as heavy as the bag you are carrying today it must be a big heart," Hani teased.

"Big, and sometimes stupid."

"Poor heart. Being insulted like that."

"Yes, poor thing." Ariana laughed. "Maybe I should send it on holiday, to a spa for a rest. Perhaps we just need some time apart."

"But then you will be a heartless person."

"True, but imagine how easy life would be."

"Imagine how dark life would be."

"So what is the answer, Hani? Do I just sit back and leave everything up to fate?"

"Of course that is the answer. Destiny and fate, whatever Allah wills happens, and whatever he does not will does not happen."

"I know that. It was more of a rhetorical question. But do you think that sometimes we need to help fate along a little? Give it a nudge?"

"Perhaps. Even with our destinies, I think it is also important to listen to our hearts. Even if they are big and stupid. But then again, what do I know? I am only a driver." Hani smiled to himself. "I think it is time to stop for some tea, yes?"

At the next exit Hani pulled into a gas station, reached over to gently wake Miza, and pointed the way across the pavement to a coffee shop as the attendant approached. As the three women closed the car doors behind them, Hani couldn't help but notice the other two's surprise at the roundness of Miza's belly under her *abaya*. "Please go and have some *chai*. The *karak*, cardamom tea, is the best. You will like it," he urged, anxious to shift the attention from the aching woman. "I will join you in a minute."

As he waited for the tank to fill, Hani took the opportunity to check his phone and catch up on some business. His first meeting in Nizwa was still on schedule, and he would, *inshallah*, arrive on time, more or less. "Omani time", as the foreigners called it. It was sometimes hard for them to understand that, in this country, time was not money, and that personal matters often took precedence over business.

Only Rachel and Miza were seated inside the tiny shop, their conversation coming to a halt as he entered. "Where is Ariana?" he asked.

Rachel shrugged. "Ladies' room?"

Hani ordered his *karak* to go, and took the little paper cup in his hand as he crossed to the edge of the parking lot to return one more call before they got back on the road. As he stood on the pavement, his *dishdasha* fluttering in the breeze, he spotted someone in the distance, kneeling beneath the shade of a small grove of palms. On closer examination he recognized the large pink lump resting on the ground beside the figure. Ariana's handbag. He narrowed his eyes against the midday sun. Yes, it was Ariana, her long, soft hair covered by a silky scarf that draped gently down her slender side. He silently watched as she completed her prayers, his mind struggling to make sense of this pile of contradiction that was the woman before him.

11

"*Allah ma'ik*, God be with you," Hani called out as Miza rushed through the hospital's glass doors as quickly as her extra burden would allow.

It had been four days since the accident that put her husband behind the thick walls of this grim fortress, four days filled with the kind of worry and fear that devours a person from the inside out.

In the elevator she paused to catch her breath, leaning against the cold metal railing behind her for support. Fifth floor, they had told her when she called the hospital in Nizwa, after finally getting word from Hani about the accident that had sent Tariq and his little Toyota spinning across the center divider and into the oncoming traffic. Until Hani's unexpected visit to bring the news, Miza had been left to the torments of her own imagination, her mind flooded with endless loops of dreadful possibilities that became even more horrendous the longer she remained alone. And she did not dare to go to his house, the one he shared with Maryam. The only thing she could think to do was to check all the hospitals in Muscat. But she found no one matching his name.

The longer Tariq's absence remained a mystery, the deeper Miza sunk. It wasn't until Hani had knocked on the door of her apartment—the apartment he'd apparently loaned to his friend Tariq for his new wife—that her thoughts snapped back into focus, and all her energy turned to the fight for Tariq's life.

Of course, Miza thought as the elevator rose, Maryam would have been notified immediately. Perhaps she was even there by his side at this very moment. Miza was worried, but now—knowing the state he was in, knowing that he needed her—there was nothing that would keep her away. All she could hope for was that the other woman would not be interested in keeping a bedside vigil for the man she seemed to care so little about.

The fifth floor corridor, with its shiny waxed floors and ammonia stink, was as still as a graveyard, with only the sounds of beeping machines and stray coughs to disturb the uneasy silence of the sick and dying. Miza slowed her pace at each doorway, eager—yet not—to recognize the form beneath the sheets as her husband's. So much illness and pain, so many sad stories. Her dread rose as the baby stirred inside her, reminding her of the hazy uncertainty of the future, as well as the stark reality of the past, that morning when she watched her mother's eyes close for the last time in a blinding white room of the hospital that was unable to keep her from leaving this world. Even today so many women were still dying while giving birth in Zanzibar and all over Tanzania. That was one of the arguments Tariq had given to convince her to come to Oman for the birth of their child. And now here she was, so near to bringing a new life into the world in a country where she knew no one. Tariq *had* to get better. He *had* to survive. She would make sure of that. And then she would return to Zanzibar, and leave this life for one where her love for her husband and her status as his wife were things she could wear with pride and dignity.

Miza nodded at the polite smiles of two women in green scrubs and blue headscarves. Perhaps doctors, she thought, sighing. There had been a time when she had dreamed of doing this herself, of becoming one who had the power to heal, one who might keep women like her mother from having their lives slip away just as a new one began. To prevent them from being robbed of the gift of the warmth of their newborn child against their breast, of seeing their baby's first steps, of hearing their voice or drying their tears. To be that person who could make that difference—that is what she had once hoped for. But, she thought now as she rubbed her rounded middle, that's what it had been. Just a dream, one that came to a halt the minute she traded her books for a life in the sea. But Sabra's would be a different story, hopefully one that would end happily ever after with a university degree and an important place in the world.

Miza slowed her pace and clutched at the satchel slung over her shoulder as she neared the end of the long hallway. She stopped at the door second to the last, her legs shaking, her eyes adjusting to the dimness of the room. But Tariq looked so peaceful, as if he were simply resting from a long day at work. Only the bandage wrapped around his head and the tube in his mouth told of the trauma his body had suffered. She allowed herself to relax a bit, and approached the bed on tiptoes.

"Tariq, my love," she whispered softly in his ear. "It's me. I am here. Mi-mi is here."

His face remained as still as a plaster mask. Under the blankets his chest rose and fell in a calm, even rhythm. She pulled a metal chair close to the bed and took his cool hand in her own, fighting the return of those same types of dark thoughts that had plagued her during the past few days. Tariq, she thought as she stroked the back of his hand, was nothing but goodness. That he had put up with Maryam's insults and abuse for so many years was a tribute to his patience. He did nothing to deserve a misfortune like this. And what about their child, not even born, who had done nothing to deserve a life without a father? She shook her head, as if to knock the dark thoughts away. Tariq had to get better, he had to survive. And she must stay positive. She must stay strong.

Miza jumped at the sounds of footsteps approaching. But it was just a nurse, her rubber soles squeaking on the polished floors like an army of mice. "*Salaam alaikum*," she greeted Miza with a question mark in her eyes.

'*Wa alaikum a'salaam.* And peace be upon you also. I am his wife," Miza responded to the unasked question.

The dark woman looked her over. "You are from Zanzibar?" she asked.

Miza nodded.

"I am as well," she answered with a smile. "My name is Neema. I have been watching over your husband."

"And I am Miza." She watched as the woman tapped at the thin tube attached to Tariq's arm, adjusted the numbers displayed in red on the screen hanging above his shoulder, listened to his heartbeat and put down the stethoscope to gently plump the pillows under his head.

"*Asante sana*," Miza whispered in Swahili. Thank you very much.

The nurse nodded and left through the door, leaving Miza alone with the motionless Tariq. She scooted closer to the bed and placed his hand on top of her taut belly, hoping that perhaps the movement inside might awaken his spirit, his desire to live. She fingered the cold copper coin hanging from the chain on her neck, worn to protect against evil, and then remembered the vial she kept buried in her bag.

Miza poured a dribble of water from the vial onto her palm and rubbed it gently onto her husband's forehead, willing the liquid—said to hold the power of healing in each drop—to do its magic.

Tariq's eyelids remained fixed; his hands stayed limp at his sides. She would come back tomorrow and do it again, Miza thought as she eased herself back in the chair and pulled out her phone.

No answer from Sabra yet. Perhaps she had been too busy with her schoolwork to notice that Miza was trying to check in. More likely she was running around with her friends. Miza stiffened at the guilt of leaving her behind in Stone Town, where she feared her sister was becoming more focused on the local boys than on her lessons.

She turned her attention once again to Tariq, desperately willing his leaden eyelids to flutter, his listless fingertips to move. Her own eyes brimmed with tears at the thought of a future without this man she had grown to love more than life itself.

The nurses in their white headscarves revolved through the door like sentries on watch as she sat by her husband's side with her thoughts, their arrival announced in advance by the squeak of their shoes. Miza soon grew used to the sound, reassured by the signal of caring and attention the footsteps sent. After a while she found herself struggling to keep her eyes open, and there in the chair with her husband's hand placed once again against her belly, she fell into a sleep.

Her dreams were of Zanzibar—white dhows sailing across the horizon at sunset, the cool sea breeze on her face, the odors of cinnamon and cloves and nutmeg in the air. They were dreams of her past, but, then again, they also seemed to be of a future, in that mixed-up way dreams can be. Bi-Zena was there, draped in seaweed, her arms held out in invitation for a warm embrace against her soft breast. And Miza's sister was there too, but younger, as she had been before they had moved from the city with their father to the village. But there was also Tariq, holding their baby boy proudly in his arms as Miza's mother leaned in with a wicker rattle in her hand, gently shaking it back and forth to soothe the baby with the rhythm of the clacking beads inside.

Miza woke abruptly to the harshness of the real world. Yet the noise from her dream continued, the clatter growing louder, now clearly recognizable as a pair of high heels tromping purposefully down the hall. Her eyes darted frantically across the room. Spying a pile of linens, she grabbed a white pillowcase and tied it over her own bright scarf and slid the woven bag under her dress. Around her shoulders she flung the forgotten stethoscope, wearing it in the way the nurse had been when she first came into the room. Miza hurried out the door with her head bowed and her eyes glued to the floor until Maryam passed, the jewels on her fingers flickering like fireflies under the hallway's fluorescent lights as she turned to enter Tariq's room.

12

"The look on your face! I only wish I'd gotten a picture." Rachel shook the water from her ear and smoothed back her short hair, still wet from the endless laps she'd swum in the hotel pool.

How anyone would actually want to swim was a mystery to Ariana, the way it got your hair all wet and ruined your makeup. But then again, this was as close to relaxed as she'd seen Rachel get. "Laugh all you want. How was I supposed to know?" Ariana cringed inside thinking of what had happened earlier when they pulled up to the entryway of the hotel in Nizwa. The porter, rushing to open Hani's door. The receptionist, clearly impressed by his presence. The manager, scurrying across the lobby to shake his hand. "*Márhaba sayed.* Welcome back, sir. It is an honor to have you here again. How is your father? And the rest of your family is well, I trust? Will you be taking your usual suite?" the man had said, all the while practically scraping the floor with his chin as he bowed down.

"I don't know what I enjoyed more, his reaction or yours." Rachel stretched back in her chair, clearly enjoying herself at Ariana's expense. *I am their very favorite driver*, Hani had said to Ariana with a wink, before saying his goodbyes and returning to the car, where Miza sat waiting. Ariana had wanted to die right there right then, standing on that gleaming marble floor. What an idiot she had been, expressing such a stupid snobbish attitude with her careless comments. She knew better. Her parents did not bring her up to be judgmental of others, to think any less of a person because of how they earned their salary. And now, what Hani must think of her. She could feel her face redden at the mere thought of it.

"What do you suppose he actually does for a living?" Rachel asked as she perused the menu.

"Please, I don't even want to think about him."

"From the way you've been acting, I'd venture to say he's just about all you want to think about."

"Don't be ridiculous." Ariana signaled for the waiter. "Why don't you order yourself a drink?"

The patio before them had filled quickly with other guests, the lounge chairs occupied by veiled women chatting among themselves while keeping one eye on their splashing children. The men were loud, squaring off against each other over a sagging volleyball net they'd strung across the pool's surface. Some sort of family party, Ariana thought.

"Shame the women can't join in," Rachel said. "I've always felt sorry for women who have to cover in weather like this. Must be miserable."

Ariana shrugged her shoulders. "Personally, I've always felt sorry for the women who feel the need to let everything hang out." She pointed with her chin to a blond foreigner prancing around in a tiny bikini, her butt cheeks bouncing with every step. "It's like they're trying way too hard."

"So you don't think those other women ever have the urge to just yank it all off and dive in?"

"Doubtful. They're comfortable with the way they are."

"Well blondie looks like she feels kind of comfortable with herself as well."

"Maybe she is. But to us, modesty is part of faith."

"So why don't you cover, Ariana?"

"Because it really goes beyond what one wears or doesn't wear. There are actually very few dress guidelines in the Koran. Modesty is more about how you act, about what lies in the heart. What matters most is to be a true believer. The rest I leave up to God."

Rachel simply nodded, her eyebrows lifting ever so slightly.

"And you, what do you believe in?" Ariana asked, noting the obvious skepticism.

Rachel thought for a moment. "I don't know. Luck? Science? The brutality of nature? The fallibility of man?"

"That's cheery."

"Sorry. It's just who I am."

The waiter returned with a large bottle of San Pellegrino for Ariana and a vodka tonic for Rachel, who stretched out her muscled legs and rested her bare feet on the seat of an empty chair before taking a long sip through the straw.

"And your family, they go to church?"

Rachel laughed a little. "No. No church. Technically we're Jewish. But my mom put her foot down when Dad wanted to send me to Hebrew School."

"You mean she's an atheist?" Ariana asked in a lowered voice.

"Pretty much. I am too, more or less."

Ariana tried her best to hide her surprise. "You know, you really should be careful with that around here. People have a hard time understanding that way of thinking."

"I'm well aware of that."

"In many Muslim countries atheists are denied the right to marriage or citizenship, and might even be executed for being open about their beliefs."

"Or disbeliefs," Rachel joked.

"True." Ariana poured a second glass of sparkling water for herself from the large green bottle. "So what is it that gets you out of bed each morning, gets you jazzed about life? Is it your work?" she asked, determined to pry open any tiny cracks to be found in Rachel's armor.

But Rachel didn't answer, her eyes shifting their focus to something behind Ariana's back. "Hey, Hani," she said with a little smile.

Ariana pulled her caftan over her knees and smoothed her hair. "Shit," she said in a whisper. "He's back?"

Rachel removed her feet from the chair and gestured for Hani to join them. Ariana wished she could disappear, her body disintegrating into a million little pieces of dust that would blow away in the warm breeze that had suddenly kicked up around them. But there he was, looking quite different out of his *dishdasha* and in a T-shirt and jeans, his plump lips smiling from under the brim of a baseball cap. Hani slipped a room key into his pocket and tossed down his phone before easing himself into the chair and pulling up to the table as if he were settling in for a long business negotiation.

"Back so soon?" Ariana asked, her voice rising an octave with each word.

"Yes. My meetings were postponed."

"What kind of meetings?" Rachel asked with a sideways glance at Ariana.

"Oh, some of this, some of that. I am working on some ideas for the city, to bring more visitors." Hani signaled to the waiter to bring another glass.

"So you're a planner?" Rachel asked.

"In a way."

"Or a developer?"

"Yes, that too."

"An architect?"

"More like a designer."

"Hmm. So an entrepreneur."

Hani smiled. "I suppose that is what it is called."

"Tell Hani about *your* job, Ariana," Rachel urged. "I'll bet he'd find it pretty interesting."

"Oh, I'm sure he doesn't want to hear about that," Ariana answered, burying her face in the menu.

"But I do," Hani insisted. "What is it you call what you do?"

"A fixer," she answered in a quiet voice.

"You fix things?"

"Well, um, in a way. I make arrangements."

"Like a travel agent?"

"Sort of."

"A travel agent who travels with their client?"

"I guess."

"A fixer's job," Rachel interrupted, her eyes boring into Ariana as she spoke, "is to help arrange a story, to find the sources. To make things *easier* for the correspondent or photographer."

"You must be very good at that," Hani said.

"Usually they speak the local language, have some local contacts, that sort of thing," Rachel explained. "But Ariana's approach seems to be a little more seat-of-the-pants, if you know what I mean."

Ariana squirmed a little in her chair.

"But don't get me wrong," Rachel added with a smirk, "she seems to connect *very* well with people."

"It is easy to understand why," Hani said with a smile that made Ariana melt a little.

"My sister calls me 'crazy bait'. I do seem to attract all kinds," she said, feeling like an idiot the minute the words left her mouth.

"And you, Hani," Rachel asked, her eyes still fixed on Ariana. "Do you come from a big family?"

"I do. My mother has five daughters, and me."

"That must be nice for your wife, to have so many women around."

"Oh no, I have no wife. You did not think that, did you?" Hani turned his head from Rachel to Ariana and back again.

Rachel shrugged. "You never know."

"Do not get me wrong. It's not that I don't want a wife; it's just that my work has kept me so busy all of the time. But someday, I hope, *inshallah*. God willing."

"Well I'm sure your god is willing. Why wouldn't he be?"

Ariana shot Rachel a warning with two narrowed eyes, but thankfully Hani just laughed. "Yes, of course. This is true. Why wouldn't he be? Perhaps I should be spending less time thinking about what is in the future and pay more attention to what is in front of my eyes today."

"Always good advice," Rachel responded. "Sounds like something my mother would say." Again Ariana steeled herself for a conversation about religion that could very well head in the wrong direction.

"And my mother, too," Hani added. "She is always telling me to not work so hard, to enjoy life more. Not to mention that she is anxious for more grandchildren. What, twelve is not enough?" He smiled and shook his head.

Ariana breathed a sigh of relief. How different this guy was from Nasim, and Nasir, and just about every other idiotic player she knew. He was like the anti-player.

But Rachel wasn't done. "Ariana and I were just talking the other day about kids, weren't we, Ariana?"

"We were?" Ariana's words came out in a croak. She twisted in her chair to search for the waiter.

"Ariana would be great with kids. She's just so . . . you know, so damn enthusiastic."

Why couldn't the woman shut up already? What was the matter with her? This was just about the most Ariana had heard coming from her mouth since they had met in Dubai four days before.

"See that little guy over there?" Rachel continued, pointing to a dark-haired boy of about four years old who was chatting away nonstop while his father remained prone under a striped umbrella, his eyes half-closed. "That would be Ariana's kid, right?" She turned to Hani. "Am I right?"

Hani's response was interrupted by the buzzing of his phone against the glass tabletop. "Please excuse me for a minute," he said as he stood and walked away to take the call.

"Bloody hell!" Ariana threw her arms in the air. "What was that all about?"

"Oh, come on. You know you're attracted to him."

"I am not!"

"I think you are."

"He's too short!"

"What do you want? He's just your height. Tall enough."

"And he's too young."

"Give me a break. You have no idea how old the man is."

"Well, he probably still lives with his mother. And you know how that goes."

"Come on. You said yourself you wished you knew more men like him."

"I was just talking."

"I saw the way your eyes followed him just now as he left the table."

"But I don't know anything about the guy."

"He's not married. He wants kids. He has a job." Rachel ticked off the facts on her fingers, as if tallying a score.

"Oh, bugger off, Rachel. That's not knowing a person."

"So find out more. You seem to be pretty good at that."

The conversation came to a halt as Hani returned to the table. "Please, you will have to excuse me," he said. "That was Miza, calling from the hospital."

"Hospital? Is she all right?" Ariana stood. "Can I do anything?"

"No, no. It is not her. It is her husband. He had an accident. That is why she is there, at the hospital. But she needs my help. I must go get her now."

Ariana watched as he hurried toward the door leading to the lobby, his broad shoulders and firm triceps straining the sleeves of his shirt.

"Sit," said Rachel, "before your eyes bug out of your head and your tongue falls out of your mouth."

13

"Damn it, Ariana!" Rachel grabbed her throbbing toe and hopped around the suitcase lying wide open in the middle of the floor, its contents spilling out as if the bag had been blown up by suspicious TSA agents. A glance at the other bed showed it vacated, the smooth covers in sharp contrast to the twisted sheets and tossed pillows of her own bed. Yellow light seeped through the cracks around the closed bathroom door, and from inside came the sound of running water.

"I'll be right out!"

Rachel sighed and pulled on her khakis and T-shirt and vest.

"Good morning!" Ariana chirped from the bathroom doorway as she rubbed her wet hair with a towel. "Did you sleep well?"

Rachel didn't answer. She never slept well. And last night was no different, only made slightly worse by the fact that Ariana had made the unilateral decision to move in with her. "It'll be fun! Sort of like a mini slumber party!" she'd claimed as she handed over her own key card to Miza. Of course Rachel couldn't object. The poor Zanzibari woman had arrived back at the hotel looking so distraught—her hands shaking, her eyes red and swollen from crying—that not to take pity on her would have seemed totally heartless.

She and Ariana had moved to the hotel bar after the breeze at the pool turned into a fierce wind, taking menus and towels and beach umbrellas and anything else that wasn't nailed down along with it as it swept across the patio. At the entry to the dark lounge they were greeted by a sign: *DANCING STRICTLY PROHIBITED*. Rachel resisted the urge to break into a little jig, just to see what would happen. It wasn't until they were seated at a corner banquette that she realized they were the only two women in the bar, surrounded by robed men sitting alone or in pairs, sipping drinks as their eyes remained fixed on a television mounted high on the wall, where MTV's finest twerked and grinded their half-naked bodies across the screen.

It was there that Hani found them. And before he could even explain what was going on, Ariana had given up her room.

Now Rachel checked the time and sighed out loud. She took the toothbrush from her backpack and brushed in the sink by the minibar, then headed out to find coffee.

In the breakfast room she filled a mug with three shots of espresso from the machine, then dug the phone from her backpack and began to type.

Maggie: Having a bitch of a time finding what I need. Fixer is worthless. Caught her looking at travel brochures. WTF? Can't we do any better than this? I'd be better off on my own. Tempted.

"Well, come on. What are you waiting for?" Ariana stood before her, her shiny hair cascading in loose curls over her shoulders, her lipstick and handbag a matching salmon. "That's ours." She pointed and led Rachel toward a white 4x4 idling in the driveway.

"My friends!" The driver turned from the rear-view mirror to face the women sliding into the back seat behind him. "Welcome back to my car."

Rachel narrowed her eyes at Ariana.

"What?" she whispered defensively. "It was Hani who arranged the ride, with the hotel. How was I supposed to know?"

Adil beamed at them from the front seat. "Today? Today we visit the Bedu, *inshallah*. God willing."

"No *inshallah*!" Rachel snapped back. "This *has* to happen today."

"Calm down!" Ariana patted her arm. "It's just a saying. A habit."

"It is okay, my friends," Adil said as he turned the key in the ignition. "They are waiting for us. In their home in the desert."

"What? More dune bashing?" Rachel turned to Ariana. "Please tell me this isn't happening."

"Actually?" Adil said. "No dune bashing today."

"That's a relief."

"No sand today. Maybe just a little."

Rachel sighed and pulled the seatbelt across her torso.

In truth, Adil had been accurate. The dirt road leading from the highway wasn't too bad. They drove across the sand and past a barbed-wire pen holding a pair of raggedy camels with tightly rolled blankets strapped onto their single humps, until the car came to a stop outside a metal gate.

A blast of hot air greeted them when they opened the car doors. "Come, my friends," Adil urged. "It will be cool inside.

The house? It is made of palm," he explained as they followed him through a small courtyard. "So that the breezes can come through."

"What breeze?" Rachel wiped the dampness from her cheeks. And things seemed no better on the other side of the low doorway. Adil removed his sandals and gestured for Rachel and Ariana to do the same. He nodded respectfully to the old woman in a long blue dress who sat kneeling next to a pillar in the center of the square room, her fingers flying as she knotted colored threads into a flat, broad band. She, in turn, pointed with her chin to one of the dozen rugs covering the sand below, each topped with a silver tray holding cups, a plastic bowl, and a covered dish.

"What is this place?" Rachel whispered to Ariana. "I'm not here for a fucking tea party you know."

"*Shhh.*" Ariana took Rachel's elbow and turned her away from Adil and the woman. "Don't worry. Just look at all these beautiful things. We'll get you what you need. I promise." She gestured with her arm around the stuffy hut, its corners piled high with shiny pillows, its walls sagging with bright fabrics and straw bags and beaded jewelry.

"And now?" Adil called out to them. "First we sit. For coffee." He smoothed his pale yellow *dishdasha* and lowered his knees to the floor, carefully tucking his feet underneath him. Slivers of sunlight slipped through the palm branches above, landing on his long sleeves in thin white stripes. Ariana kneeled down across from him and patted the floor beside her. Rachel dropped down with a groan.

Adil dipped his fingertips into the water in the plastic bowl and passed it to Rachel, then uncovered the silver dish and offered dates.

"Thanks. Not hungry." She shook her head.

"Please," he urged. "It is a custom."

Rachel's hand emerged from the dish with two brown lumps stuck together like glue.

"Actually? At first you should only take one date. But that is okay." He then passed the dish to Ariana, who took care to extract only one. The two women watched as Adil deftly pinched the seed from the center of the sticky fruit and popped the flesh into his mouth. He turned back to Rachel. "Now you must take one more. Usually it is customary to take an odd number, like one or three. But for women it is considered rude to take more than three."

Next he poured a thick black brew into three tiny cups, the smell of cardamom rising with the steam. Rachel threw back the coffee in one shot, anxious to get up for a closer look at the woman and her wares, to ask where the people who designed and wove and stitched all this stuff were. But no sooner had she swallowed than the cup was filled again.

"Let me tell you about how we drink our coffee," Adil offered. "Usually? We only fill the cup halfway. This is an invitation to drink slowly, and enjoy your time visiting. If the cup is full to the top, it means that the heart of the host is full of hate toward the one visiting, and that they should drink their coffee and leave."

Again Rachel swallowed and rested her cup on the rug. Again Adil picked up the thermos.

"No, I'm good," she protested, the sweat rolling down the front of her chest.

"Actually?" he said as he continued to pour. "When you are finished, you must signal to your host that you are done by moving your cup, like this." He shook his cup back and forth, as if readying a pair of dice for a throw.

Rachel drained the cup and shook it wildly at Adil, then stood and stretched, her legs tingling from the lack of circulation. She circled the hut in her socks, picking at the piles of goods on display until she caught sight of the professionally printed price tags attached with a plastic fastener. Shit.

She turned to see a group entering through the doorway, their T-shirts damp with perspiration and their voices ringing with laughter. A tour guide followed behind, greeting the old woman with a familiar smile.

"Look, Rachel! Aren't these adorable?" Across the room Ariana was crouched over a row of straw bowls resting by the old woman's side. She held out a fistful of bracelets and key chains made from the string in the old woman's hands. "Good gifts for the nieces," she said as she continued to comb through the bowls. "Would you like me to buy you one? Oh, and here, Rachel, here are your masks!"

At the bottom of a bowl sat a pair of flimsy satin masks like the one the old woman in the souk had worn only smaller, plain black, nothing more than the kind of blindfold you'd find in one of those sex shops in the Village. "Photo?" Ariana pleaded eagerly to the old woman, who nodded and slipped on the mask. "Come on, Rachel, here's your chance."

"It is okay," Adil urged from behind. "She will allow this, with the mask on, for the tourists."

Rachel sighed and lifted the viewfinder toward her eye. As she pressed the shutter, the old woman shot her a two-fingered peace sign. Rachel could only imagine how many times that exact pose showed up in a batch of "My Omani Vacation" snapshots.

Outside the heat seemed even worse than before. Yet another group of tourists had gathered, haggling with a tall skinny man over the cost of a camel ride.

"I'm so sorry. I truly thought we might have been in luck with that place," Ariana said as they headed back to the car. "But as long as we're here we really should do a camel ride, shouldn't we, Rachel?" Ariana approached the pen, snapping photos with her phone as she walked.

Rachel shook her head.

"Come on, it'll be fun!"

"Absolutely not," Rachel growled back. One of the camels stood stock still under the sun, his front legs manacled together by a thick metal chain. The other, resting on the dirt with his long legs bent under him as if he were a collapsible table, let out a loud moan as Ariana neared.

"I've never heard them make a noise quite like that!" Ariana laughed. "What do you say, Rachel? Let's at least get some camel selfies."

"Jesus," Rachel muttered to herself. "Doesn't she ever know when to stop?" She stood and watched with Adil as Ariana cocked her head and pursed her lips at the phone she held high on a stick in the air, the standing beast obliging her by lowering its own head toward her shoulder.

"Seriously, Adil," Rachel pleaded, "do you have *any* clue about where the real artists are? The ones who do the silver, who make the cloths and blankets? Anything?" Rachel could feel her spirits plunging to a new low, and sinking along with them any hint of energy and enthusiasm she'd managed to drum up to get this damn job done.

Adil seemed to be pondering her question, his brow furrowing into a deep V. "Actually, my friend?" he finally answered. "If you are looking for the art, I can take you somewhere where the most beautiful thing in the world has been made. Yes."

"And what would that be?" Rachel asked, her faith in Adil only slightly greater than her faith in Ariana.

"It is okay," Adil assured her. "We will go."

They drove in silence, Adil concentrating on the road and Ariana busy on her phone, no doubt sharing her stupid camel selfies with the rest of the world.

Rachel had almost nodded off when she was suddenly bounced up into the air and back down again, as if she'd just dropped over the apex of a roller coaster. The 4x4 began to vibrate in an uneven rumble as the tires passed over rock and stone.

Ariana gripped the looped strap above the window beside her and shot an apologetic look toward Rachel, whose teeth had begun to clatter like one of those wind-up toys as the road became even bumpier.

"It is okay." Adil grinned into the rear-view. "It is only until the other road."

"How far?" Rachel asked, her voice coming out in a stutter.

"In fact, it is about seven kilometers."

Rachel did the math. Over four miles. She closed her eyes as Adil steered around a steep curve, but still couldn't keep herself from seeing the cartoon image of the four wheels clinging to the road as the rest of the car swung out over the deep ravine below. Fuck this, she thought, reaching for the water bottle that was rolling endlessly around under the seat. It was clearly time to call it quits, pack up her camera, and go. Which she would do as soon as they got back to the hotel. She'd book the first flight out. It had been a rookie mistake to let herself get talked into this stupid assignment in the first place. What had she been thinking? In this nowhere of a place where nothing ever happened, this fantasyland of relentlessly cheery people who got their kicks from driving cars where no car was meant to be driven. And with Ariana, who was no more of a fixer than that groaning camel back there in the desert. No. She would go home. And she'd get a job. A normal job. Any job. And she would just keep on keeping on, as her mother always said.

They continued straight up the twisting road with no end in sight, Rachel's resolve stiffening with every gut-churning turn. A few minutes after the car leveled out, they came to a stop.

"We are here." Adil said no more as Rachel tumbled out the door, her legs still vibrating from the long, rocky journey up. And for a moment, what she saw before her literally took her breath away. She picked her way cautiously across a flat rock surface that seemed to lead to nowhere, until she stood a mere foot away from the rim and looked down sheer cliffs plunging straight into the valley below. It was the top of the world.

Rachel grabbed for her camera.

"We call it the Omani Grand Canyon." Adil continued to talk as Rachel's shutter began to click. "And the mountain, it is called Jebel Shams. The highest mountain in our country. 'The Mountain of the Sun', as it is the first to greet it in the morning and the last to say goodnight."

Rachel's shutter clicked again and again, over and over. She stood at the very edge of the abyss with her camera to her face, capturing the spectacle from every angle, the light gifting her with endless variations on a glorious theme as the shadows from the clouds drifted gracefully across the peaks. It was as if her eye had been taken over by another, very different type of photographer, she thought as she zoomed in on the goats in the distance grazing blissfully among the tiny terraced villages dotting the mountainsides. She'd never been into taking shots like this before. "Picture postcards" was how she'd always written off landscape photography. But this place practically throbbed with a vibe that she just couldn't seem to resist.

Perhaps, it occurred to her as she stood in the embrace of the soft breeze drifting up from the gorge below, she'd been wrong. It was possible, she thought, hurrying to get in the last shots before the mountain would bid goodnight to the sun, that she'd spent so much time focusing on the ugly that she had never allowed the beautiful to find its way through her lens.

14

Miza folded the large orange cloth diagonally until the message printed along its blue border became tucked inside like a secret. She then bent over as far as her belly would allow to lay the folded strip over the back of her head, winding the fabric tightly around and around until the two ends met on her forehead to be knotted together, the pointy tips hidden between the folds. The turban was made from her half of the *kanga* that her mother had used to carry her as a baby, and later that she, herself, had used to cradle the infant Sabra.

While a T-shirt or a greeting card might be used to share a thought or give praise in another country, where Miza was from it was the *kanga* that was used for this purpose. You could see them everywhere: tied around the waist as a sarong, spread across a table, hanging like a curtain at a window. *Kangas* were passed down in families from mother to daughter until they were only good as rags to clean the house. But the *kanga* was more than a piece of cloth; it was a symbol of the rhythm of Swahili life. Some offered messages of love or comfort or gratitude with a proverb or a riddle. Others were more critical, or came with a warning. *Nilikudhani dhahabu kumbe adhabu* was one Miza had seen. I thought of you as gold, but you are such a pain. *Halahala mti na macho* was another—beware, a stick and your eyes, meaning "danger ahead". Those were not the types of *kanga* one gave as a gift. Instead they indicated that the wearer was not on good terms with another, or had some strong political opinions.

The saying on Miza's *kanga* was one she had heard often as a child. Translated from Swahili it said "Every bird flies with its own wings". Some people took it to mean that everyone had limits, and should not go beyond their own possibilities. But it wasn't until she grew older that she understood the sense of power and independence her mother had read into the proverb and had wanted her to know, wrapping her little body tight in those words each morning until the day she was able to walk on her own two feet.

Now, as she stood before the hotel mirror and adjusted the wrap on her head, she struggled to see her mother's hopeful eyes looking back at her. How she missed her mother's touch, her smile, the sound of her songs that made every day feel like a holiday in their house.

At first, the demands of a new baby had kept Miza and her father too occupied to properly mourn. Their move to the village where her father was born came swiftly, as support from his family seemed the only answer for a man struggling to bring up two girls on his own. So when he turned listless and silent, Miza assumed it was the sadness finally catching up with him. She knew that sadness, as it was something she carried inside every single day, allowing the tears to flow only when the baby was sleeping and nobody was looking. But what was happening to her father was something different, as she found out the day he was silenced by illness forever.

With her father gone, things changed. Miza began to see her uncle for what he was—a bitter and crooked tyrant, whose powerful hands and cruel tongue could be provoked by anything or nothing. And in her uncle's household it was not only kindness that was scarce. Having two more mouths to feed added resentment to the man's long list of grievances, leaving Miza as the target of his outrage.

That was when Bi-Zena stepped in. Well aware of the way Miza's uncle bullied and berated the people of his village, and also well aware of the villagers' custom of turning a blind eye at the things that happened behind closed doors, she had worried for the girl. Miza would never forget the day the woman fearlessly strode up to her uncle's house, demanding that Miza come to work for her in the seaweed farm. Of course her greedy uncle could not say no to the promise of more money in his hands, so it was thanks to the old woman that the daylight hours gave her some escape.

But the sea could not save her from what happened at night. The first time Miza awoke to the touch of her uncle's dry hand on her breast, she let out a quick scream. Sabra stirred beside her in the bed and rolled over to face the wall. Miza clenched her jaws shut as she pushed the man away with all her strength, catching him with a surprise that was enough to send him out the door. But her uncle did not give up, and soon his visits became a recurring nightmare to be silently endured by Miza as the cost for keeping her sister from the same fate.

Not even when Tariq appeared, like an angel from above,

did her uncle stop his abuse. And when Miza told him that she and Tariq were to wed, and that her husband-to-be had rented a flat for her and her sister in Stone Town, he flew into a rage that lasted for days. "What," he had snorted, "you think that man actually cares for you? He already has a wife! You will be nothing to him, just a Zanzibar whore kept simply for his pleasure. And when he is done with you? You will be tossed away like yesterday's garbage."

Miza did not understand. Her uncle should have been happy at the prospect of his nieces leaving his household, freeing him of the responsibility and expense they had brought along with them, and to be receiving a handsome dowry as well. It wasn't until Tariq came and spoke with him, in a conversation Miza was not to hear, with an offer of an amount she was never to know, that he agreed to release both of his nieces into the hands of another.

Despite her uncle's stinging words, there was one thing Miza knew for sure. Her love for Tariq was real, and she was determined to do everything in her power to keep him from leaving this earth. She dug in her bag to make sure she had packed the little vial of water from the well. She was grateful her husband was getting proper medical care for the swelling in his brain, but if there was more that could be done, Miza was going to be sure to do it.

Though she had little experience with either the white arts or the dark arts herself, she'd witnessed plenty as a child. Zanzibar was filled with magic, as well as with famous witch doctors who drew others from places as far away as Haiti and the Congo to seek their advice. In her own family she had seen her mother's cousin turn to witchcraft when, half-crazy over her husband's wandering eye, she handed the man's underwear to a witch doctor for a spell of impotence, so that he'd be of no use to another woman ever again.

And in her uncle's village there was once a time when the entire town had been complaining of no sleep. Miza would never forget the children's excitement when the witch doctor arrived. They followed him up and down the winding streets like a pack of playful puppies as he chanted and prayed, until he stopped at the door of a shy old widower and pointed to him as the cause of everyone's problem. Not one person dared question the witch doctor's claim, as to anger the witch doctor might cause him to seek revenge the next time he was called. The poor widower was shunned, as was anyone in the village who was rumored to have the power to make others uncomfortable or ill by a simple look of the eye.

Miza also remembered when, as a young girl, she first heard the stories of Popobawa, the evil spirit named for the batwing shape of the dark shadow it cast over its sleeping victims. Every few years the panic would return, with horrifying accounts of the terrible odor, the sounds of giant wings and claws scraping across a tin roof, the overwhelming feelings of cold and weakness, and the terrifying acts of rape and sodomy. The tales spread like wildfire, as it was said the creature would instruct its victims to tell others about the attacks, lest it return for more. The hysteria that overtook the island was everywhere, with people trying everything they could to keep Popobawa at bay. They placed charms at the base of fig trees, smeared themselves with pig's grease, sacrificed goats, held exorcisms. Many tried to guard against the attacks by staying awake all night, or by sleeping in groups beside a fire outside their homes.

Miza arrived to find the hospital as quiet as a morgue. On the fifth floor she passed by the open door of her husband's room with caution, slowing just enough to check for a visitor's presence. Relieved to find it empty, she reversed her course and entered. Tariq looked the same as the day before except for the bandage, which now looked a little smaller. Perhaps a good sign, she thought. She bent over clumsily to kiss his dry cheek, the feel of his skin against her lips bringing an ache to her chest and a familiar, unspoken whisper to her ears. What was said in their touch was a truth that could not be denied: that as strong as her love was for him, his was equally deep for her. Their marriage was not some matter of impulse or convenience as her uncle had suggested; it was a blessing.

Miza stroked the back of her husband's cool hand with her fingers. Tariq was a beautiful gift brought to her from God. Why had he appeared on the beach that day if their union was a thing that was not meant to be? Although she wasn't the most devout Muslim, perhaps not as observant as Tariq had expected, she still held a strong and undying faith. She remembered the look on his face the first time she had left the apartment in Muscat without wearing a headscarf, and made a silent promise to herself. Should he recover—no, *when* he recovers—she would make every effort to follow his wishes and the traditions of a good Muslim wife.

She glanced over her shoulder before pulling the vial from her bag. The nurses and aides all seemed friendly enough, especially Neema, the one who had recognized her as a sister Zanzibari. But what Miza was doing was sure to be questionable—if not against the law—here in Oman. The Omanis' own tradition of magic was something they seemed to prefer to forget. This time she splashed a few drops onto Tariq's lips, which were held permanently open by the tube in his mouth.

As she was wiping his chin with the bottom of her sleeve, she remembered the copper coin. She put down the vial and removed the chain from beneath her scarf. Lifting Tariq's heavy head with one hand, she maneuvered the necklace into place as best she could, spreading it carefully over the top of his hospital gown. It wasn't until she was outside in the parking lot, where her taxi was waiting, that she noticed how nervous she had been. She paused to catch a breath, and reached into her bag for a tissue to wipe the dampness from her face. It was then that she realized her mistake. The vial of water was still upstairs, sitting in plain sight right on top of the bedside table. And the necklace! How could she have been so stupid as to not hide it beneath his gown?

She scurried awkwardly back to the elevator, her stomach churning in waves around the little one inside. The ward was quiet, except for one wheezing patient who'd been abandoned in his wheelchair. Miza rushed past the empty nurses' station and continued toward the end of the hall. But just as her foot neared the threshold of Tariq's room, she heard a dreadful screech erupt from inside.

"*Who was in my husband's room? Which one of you is doing magic on my husband?*" The shrieking was enough to rouse the dead.

Miza turned to run, but not before hearing a frightened nurse's response. "It was his wife," she said. "The other one. The Zanzibar wife."

15

The golden sunrise was just barely visible through the sheer curtains as Rachel grabbed her backpack and tiptoed around the debris-strewn floor. The hurricane that was Ariana had left the room in even more of a mess than the day before: piles of scarves, crumpled blouses, bags teeming with makeup, vitamins, and supplements, and a pair of white bras that stood tall and firm like a range of snow-covered mountains, among other signs of her unbridled presence. Now Ariana remained blissfully in dreamland in the bed closest to the window. Rachel envied her capacity for sleep, having had yet another crappy night herself, despite the Ambien she'd washed down with a glass of red wine hours before she was actually able to close her eyes.

She had heard Ariana return late to the room the night before, after Rachel had left her by the pool deep in conversation with Hani. The growing attraction between those two was so obvious it was ridiculous. They literally couldn't take their eyes off each other, and every little thing that was said by one was so very interesting or so funny or so poignant to the other that Rachel had felt it best that she, the lousy third wheel, simply roll away quietly into the night.

Rachel actually remembered having feelings like that herself, though not recently. Despite the best efforts of Maggie and her other friends, she hadn't been able to even remotely connect to any of the guys she'd been introduced to since she'd returned home to New York for good. And even before that, on the conflict trail, it had been mostly casual hook-ups or friends-with-benefits types of situations. She knew the deal. You never even dreamed of getting serious out there. The stakes were way too high, in more ways than one.

It had to have been with Jonathan, the last time she had felt consumed by the sort of blind fascination with another person that was keeping Ariana and Hani spellbound. She could still imagine the touch of his hand on the small of her back, a habit of his whenever they stepped off a curb and into the street. And she could still conjure up his smell, when she tried. A blend of sweet perspiration and clove cigarettes, with just a hint of laundry detergent. She wondered if he was still living in New York. He probably had another girlfriend by now. Hell, he probably even had a wife.

The glass doors leading into the hotel's breakfast room were locked, the tables inside set neatly and efficiently in anticipation of the morning rush. Rachel rattled the brass handle a little, hoping to draw the attention of someone who might take pity on her and allow her a shot or two from the espresso machine. But unfortunately there was not a soul in sight. The concierge had advised her to get to the Nizwa Souk early. The heat would soon turn oppressive, she'd been warned, so best to be there by six, when the gates were opened. Rachel pulled a piece of gum from her vest, popped it into her mouth and headed out front.

A lone, dented sedan idled outside the lobby doors, the driver busy on his cellphone behind the wheel. "*Salaam alaikum. Sabaah al khair*," Rachel said through the open window. Hello and good morning.

"*Wa alaikum a'salaam*," the driver answered her greeting, gesturing toward the back seat.

As the car took off with a screech, Rachel dug for her seatbelt, only to find the buckle cleanly sheared off, leaving the safety part of the safety belt pretty much nonexistent. They sped through the early-morning streets, Rachel bracing for disaster. The Omani newspapers were littered with stories of car accidents, which seemed to be just about the only bad news they saw fit to print. Just my luck, she thought as the driver slammed on the brakes, surviving all the dangers that came with the past thirteen years on the job only to be killed during this stupid assignment.

She turned away from the menacing traffic ahead and instead concentrated on the scenery flying by the window. The city, with its low, sand-colored buildings, sprawled seamlessly toward the brown mountains in the distance. For the number of cars already on the road, everything remained surprisingly still.

At the main gate she hastily paid the driver and said her goodbyes. From the street the souk looked massive, its walls towering fortress-like against the morning sky. Below was a sea of pale yellow and bright white *dishdashas*, the men and boys already congregating around the entryway, some lounging on a low stone wall that ran parallel to the high wall behind it. Not a woman in sight. Rachel wasn't bothered at all by that. In fact, it sort of felt like home to her, being used to finding herself the odd woman out in the company of men. Her presence here did elicit some stares, nothing more. But it was almost enough to make her wish she'd thrown on a burqa, as she had done a number of times while working on stories in Afghanistan and Iraq. The first time she'd covered, to gain access to some military bigwig, it had felt weird, but also surprisingly kind of cool. It reminded her of Halloween—her favorite holiday—when, from behind the safety of a costume and a mask, you could dare to be anyone you wanted to be.

Beyond the high walls, the sunlit corridors led past a string of markets: vegetables, guns, fruit, jewelry, meat, fish, spices. The bird market was somewhere nearby, as evidenced by a small boy swinging a fluttering mesh sack by his side. And there was plenty of pottery, most of it earthenware vases and urns lined up like orange soldiers in the early-morning sun. Perhaps a little too plentiful, and a little too similar, Rachel thought, to come from true artisans. And as she waded through the rows of terra-cotta toward the shops tucked behind, she saw she was right. The tourist tchotchkes here were even worse than what she'd come across in Muscat. There were the requisite "I ♥ Oman" key chains and mugs and refrigerator magnets, but it was the display on the far shelf that really made her cringe—bobble-heads and nesting dolls and salt and pepper shakers, all molded and painted into tiny figurines of women and men dressed in burqas and robes.

When she finally spied the sign—Omani Handicraft Market—Rachel breathed a huge sigh of relief. Tackling the stairs two at a time, the lens of her Leica cupped in her palm, she began to feel the familiar rush that came with the anticipation of getting the perfect shot. "*Salaam alaikum,*" came a voice from above.

"*Wa alaikum a'salaam*," Rachel answered as she reached the last stair.

"Omani coffee?" A short, trim man gestured to a silver urn resting on the table beside him.

Rachel nodded eagerly, the odor of cardamom and cloves enough to make her practically weep. She downed the first cup in one swallow and allowed him to pour another. "So," she asked excitedly, "these are crafts from Oman?"

"Yes," the man answered as he swept his arm across the doorways that surrounded them.

Rachel felt like hugging him, but instead simply followed as he led her into the first room, where the shelves were teeming with handbags made from tooled leather, looking suspiciously like one Maggie had brought back from Marrakesh. "Oman?" she asked.

The man shook his head. "Morocco."

The next few rooms offered no more promise. Pillows from Tunisia, dishes from Turkey, masks from Kenya. Finally the man stopped and pointed to a room lined with models of wooden boats, intricately carved dhows with elegant curves, complete with towering masts and working riggings. Beautiful, Rachel thought as she raised one eyebrow toward the man.

"Oman," he said, and smiled as he left her to explore on her own. She wandered from room to room, increasingly impressed with what she saw. A gorgeous chest covered with tightly woven red fabric and framed with dark wood, topped by touches of shiny brass as smooth as ice. The detail was astounding. Fringed blankets in colors so warm they made you want to curl up underneath right then and there. Even the bamboo walking sticks were tempting. Great gifts, she thought as she stroked the curved handles with her fingertips.

"Beautiful," she said when she met up again with the man and his urn at the top of the staircase. "So where can I find the people who make these things?"

"Oman," he answered, nodding with pride.

"Oman? *Ayna?* Where?"

"Yes, Oman." He lifted a cup. "Please, for you more coffee?"

"Well, *that* was a big help," Rachel muttered as she tromped wearily back down the stairs into the blinding sunlight, suddenly finding herself caught up in a stream of people heading toward the far end of the souk. As the gate neared, she thought she heard the sound of babies crying echoing off the walls. Then she smelled the smell. "The goat market," she remembered the concierge saying. "It is really something to see." She instinctively grabbed the Leica as she passed through the entry, and began to capture the chaos around her. Hurrying men dragged reluctant animals behind, impatiently scooping up the wriggly little things under one arm to rush toward the center of the square. Some of the goats seemed oblivious to their fate while others appeared to be fighting for their lives, twisting and pulling back on their leads.

Rachel was eagerly devouring it all from behind the lens. But as she moved deeper into the fray, her pace slowed. The bleating had become louder and more frantic, and through a wall of men she watched as the tethered animals were paraded in a circle around a crowd of buyers noisily shouting out their bids. A stir erupted beside her as a goat no bigger than a cocker spaniel broke loose and scrambled to escape, its eyes meeting Rachel's with a look that threatened to bring back all the feelings she'd been trying so hard to keep buried.

Behind her she could hear a mournful moan echoing from the edge of the square. In a dusty pen an emaciated cow was endlessly circling a metal pole, hopelessly determined to free itself from the short rope tied around its neck.

Rachel let the camera drop down against her stomach and pushed her way out of the crowd toward the exit, her head spinning. What the fuck?, she wondered as she tried to slow her breath. She'd seen so much worse than this before, so why this lame reaction now? But just as she was reaching the gate, something caught her eye that made her stop. It was a goat with a pink tail, and on the other end of the rope was the strange old woman she'd literally bumped into in Muscat, the one who knew her nickname. "Lil' Cherry Bomb," she'd sworn she'd heard her say that day.

True, there may be more than one goat in Oman sporting a pink tail, but still. She brought the camera back up to her eye with a shaky hand, pretending to focus on a group of men ten feet away. No matter how odd this woman might be, she was still a woman, and Rachel knew better than to take a picture of an Arab woman without first asking permission. Strictly speaking, taking a photo of anyone in the region without their knowledge was considered a criminal act under sharia, punishable both in this life and in the hereafter, or so they claimed.

But the gentleness of this country had made Rachel a little less prudent than usual, so when she pressed the shutter release and the aperture opened up to reveal the woman looking straight back through the lens with her one clear eye, Rachel was a little surprised. Yet instead of turning her head or shooing Rachel away, the woman was walking directly at her, her breasts swinging freely beneath her *abaya*, and was suddenly right in front of her face, pushing the Leica aside and poking her finger into Rachel's own chest. Rachel took a deep breath and steeled herself for a well-deserved scolding.

The old woman's words came out softly and silvery, like the vibrations from a harp. "My child, it is only by opening the eyes that one can open the heart. Know that there are times it will hurt, yet there can be no healing where there is no pain."

Rachel stood stunned for a moment as the woman retreated with her four-legged sidekick, its pink tail wagging happily behind them. "Wait, do you know me?" she finally managed to cry out, her voice battling the sounds of the frenzied market. But the old woman continued ahead, her back turned to Rachel, who stood transfixed in the middle of the bedlam surrounding her.

16

"Can we slow down a bit, if you don't mind?" Ariana's nervous laugh blended with the rush of water flowing through the ancient irrigation ditch below. Hani shortened his steps atop the narrow stone path that abutted the stream, the only route that led through the lush grove thick with date trees. The abandoned flip-flops and sandals littering the ground were a sign of just how difficult the walk might be for Ariana. He should have said something when he saw her shoes earlier that day, when they had met in the lobby of the hotel after his morning meetings for their excursion. But those straps that crossed three times around her slender ankles looked so nice that he lost his train of thought, and then they were in the car and it was too late.

The hours they had spent together the night before seemed to have flown by as quickly as a jet across the wide desert sky. He tried to remember what they had even spoken about. They had cautiously tiptoed around anything too personal, both of them still a little wary from the bumpiness of their initial encounter, and though he still couldn't quite figure Ariana out, he could see there was more beneath that makeup than a person would ever think. And Hani, he liked what he was seeing.

"It is not much further," he called back to her. "And trust me, it will be worth it." When he had come across Ariana this morning in the hotel lobby, she'd looked as though she had lost her best friend. Rachel, she'd told him, had gone off to the souk without her. "It's my job!" she'd said. "I feel like such a failure." Hani couldn't stand seeing her that way, and offered the outing as a distraction. He couldn't wait to share the *wadi* with Ariana. It was by far his favorite spot in Oman, one in which he'd spent countless days, first with his family and later with friends. Personally, he could have closed his eyes and still found his way safely along the little trail as thin as a beam, he was so familiar with the place. But now he shifted the bag he carried over his arm, and stopped at the bottom of a set of steep steps to wait for Ariana to catch up.

"I'm good!" she insisted with a confidence that rang false. Suddenly he felt her weight against his shoulder. "Oops." She righted herself before he even had time to fully turn. "Sorry," she said, the color rising quickly in her smooth cheeks. "Lost my balance."

Hani simply smiled. They continued to walk silently beneath the cool shade of the green palms until the walkway widened into a rocky path. "Now close your eyes," he instructed. "And hold on to my arm." Ariana did as told, pinching the cloth of his *dishdasha* between two fingers. Hani led her gently forward, up to the point where the landscape burst open to reveal a sparkling blue mirror sandwiched between the cliffs. "Okay. You can open them now."

"Oh, my." Ariana stood at the edge of the outcropping of rock, her eyelashes fluttering like black butterflies in the breeze.

"It is beautiful, is it not?" Hani beamed with pride.

"I'll say. Although spectacular is more like it, don't you think?"

Hani laughed and led her farther in, to a smooth, flat boulder hanging right over the water's edge, the view downward seeming to go as deep as that into the sky above. He took a light blanket from the bag and shook it, allowing it to sail back down gracefully over the rock's surface, and gestured to Ariana. Together they sat facing the shimmering epicenter of the oasis surrounding them.

"So you come here a lot?" Ariana asked, her eyes now hidden behind a pair of dark lenses as big as pomegranates, with purple frames that were the exact same shade as the color on her toes.

"I did. But I have not been coming much lately. My father used to bring us here, when I was a boy. I learned to swim in this water." Hani pointed to the young kids splashing around below.

"That must have been nice. Your family came all together?"

Hani nodded. "Yes, my father and mother, and all my sisters. My mother would bring a picnic, like I have today." He reached his arm into the bag and placed three packets, all neatly wrapped in foil, onto the center of the blanket. "She would sit on a rock, like that *jeda* over there," he said, pointing to a covered grandma shaded by a tree, "and shout at us to stop playing around, to be careful."

Ariana nodded as she watched a tall boy take a long dive from the cliff across from them, disappearing into the deep with barely a ripple.

"But my father," Hani continued as he removed more food from the bag, "he was just the opposite. He would only encourage our wildness, even the girls, when they were small. He would always dare us to jump off that bridge." Ariana's eyes turned toward the thin metal bridge that spanned the far end of the pool, where the water narrowed into a river that snaked through the mountains. "Now he is the same way with my little nieces." Hani pulled the lid from a Styrofoam container. "My father, you would like him. And he, I think, would also like you very much."

Ariana shifted a little uncomfortably on the rock. "So do you spend lots of time with your family?"

"Yes. I mean, as much as is possible. Though it is never enough for my mother. She is always pushing. But I'm with them whenever I can. I love to be with my sisters and their families. And I still have much to learn from my father. Would you like some *khubz*?"

Ariana took the piece of flatbread from his hand and dipped it into the hummus. "So your father is also a businessman?"

"Yes. And a doctor as well. Kebabs? They are chicken."

Ariana raised her eyebrows. "Wow. That's certainly impressive."

Hani lowered his eyes. "Not so impressive. It was all I could get from the hotel restaurant."

Ariana laughed. "No, I meant your father."

"Oh, I see. Yes, my father is quite an impressive man, known by many people. He has even been called on many times to travel to places like Jordan and often Dubai for his work."

"Well then you must take after him, with your running around from meeting to meeting. It seems like you have quite a lot of irons in the fire."

"And your mother, is she like you?" Hani helped himself to some chicken.

Ariana tilted her head up to the sky, as if it held the answer to his question. "Yes, and no, I suppose. I hope I am as kind as her, and as giving. But in ways she is far more traditional than I am. In that sense I am more like my father."

"And you and your father, you are close?"

"We are." Ariana chuckled. "My sister is constantly accusing me of being his favorite."

"I can understand that," Hani said with a smile that quickly erased itself. "I mean," he sputtered, "please not to offend your sister."

Again Ariana laughed. "No worries. You should hear it when the two of us go at it with each other. 'Ariana the prima donna,' she calls me."

Ariana. He loved the way her name sounded when it came from her own lips. Like a trill of soft notes from a worn wooden flute. "Your family, they sound very nice. Are you able to see them often?"

"Not often enough. A few times a year, when I go home or they come visit me in Dubai."

"So you must like Dubai very much, am I right?"

Ariana shrugged. "I don't know. It's complicated." She paused for a bite of flatbread.

"It is a very exciting city," Hani said.

"It is," she agreed. "I do like the crazy mix of people, and the outrageous scale of it all, and the feeling it gives that anything and everything is possible."

"And what is it that you don't like?"

"Besides being so far away from my family?" Once again Ariana turned her gaze to the sky. "Well, let me see if I can explain. You see, it's like sometimes I feel as though Dubai is one giant transient hotel. People are always coming and going, and don't really take the time to get to know each other very well at all. So that leaves everyone seeming pretty fake and superficial. It just doesn't feel like the real world. Does that make any sense?" Her eyes returned to Hani.

"Yes, it does," he said, nodding.

"And lately? I can't seem to stop thinking about how unfair it all is."

"Unfair?"

"You know, the great divide between the haves and the have-nots. Everywhere I look, I see all those poor laborers literally slaving away for the comfort and well-being of others. It seems like more and more of them are coming every day, but to most people they are invisible."

"I see," he said softly.

"I can't help but think that it could have been me, Hani. If my parents hadn't had the means to leave Pakistan, to bring me up and educate me in England, who knows what I'd be doing today? It's an awful situation. I just wish I could do something to help."

"So why do you stay there? Is it this job, this fixing job, that ties you?"

Ariana sighed. "Oh, Hani, I'm not really a fixer. I just took this job because a friend of mine couldn't, and because, frankly, I needed the money. But please," she quickly added, "don't tell Rachel."

Now it was Hani's turn to laugh. "I think that maybe, how is it said, the kitten has escaped its box?"

"Really? You think she knows? Wow, I'm gutted." Ariana dropped her face into her hands. "This is just so embarrassing." She raised her eyes to Hani. "Honestly? It was all so last minute, and I truly thought it would be easier, but I had no idea that everything was such a big secret in this country."

"Secret? What do you mean, secret?"

"Oh, you know. Like how when you Google all you get is the tourist stuff and the things the government wants you to see. Don't get me wrong, it's all very beautiful, but what Rachel needs is to go behind the scenes, and I feel like nobody wants us to get off the beaten path, or off any path at all for that matter."

"I see."

"Seriously, Hani. This is tough for me. I'm usually much better at what I do."

"And what is it that you usually do?"

"Well, I came to Dubai for a job in finance."

"I see," Hani said, surprised once again by this woman.

"But to be truthful with you, I don't really have a full-time job at the moment. I'm sort of at a crossroads, trying to figure out what's next."

"I see."

Ariana helped herself to a kebab and pulled a juicy morsel of chicken off the stick with her teeth. "I do often think about moving back to England," she continued after swallowing, "but that would almost feel as though I were giving up." She pulled a tissue from her pocket and dabbed at her lips. "Why am I telling you all this?"

"No, please. I like to hear it." Hani unscrewed the thermos and poured some juice into two little paper cups. "And what are the dreams, the ones that you are giving up?"

Ariana smoothed the front of her blouse. "Well, if you were to ask my mother, she'd tell you they were foolish dreams, dreams that either won't happen or, if they do, won't make me happy in the end."

"And why is that?"

"Basically because I want it all—husband, job, kids, travel— the complete package."

"And so what is wrong with that?"

"Nothing, I guess, in theory. But it's not that easy to find someone who wants to put up with all my crap, or at least one who doesn't feel threatened by it." Though her head was turned toward her lap, Hani could feel Ariana watching him from the corner of her eyes. "And believe me," she continued, "I've looked. I even did the whole online dating thing. My sister made me. Horrible. I'm done with that, full stop."

"Oh? With the way your phone dings and rings all the time, I would think you would be very popular."

"Popularity is *not* the issue. There's simply nobody good out there. And even if there were, I'm simply terrified of making the wrong choice again."

"Again?"

"I did tell you I'd been married, didn't I? Disaster. He was one of those guys who acts like a perfect Muslim man when they're with their family, but turns into a skirt-chasing perv the minute he gets away. I seem to keep coming across that type. Or worse, the ones who like to play around but then look for the nice little brown girl to take home to appease their parents. I can't go through that again. I just need a guy who is comfortable with who he is. Is that too much to ask?"

"I understand." Hani nodded gravely, masking his surprise at the news that she was divorced instead of widowed, as he had assumed. "And yes, making the right choice, it is very important."

The shadows from the cliffs had lengthened into long, dark fingers reaching out across the *wadi*. Hani wrapped up the leftover food, placed it back into the bag and stood. "Come," he said, pointing to the rocks below. "Let us go and relax next to the water."

Ariana unstrapped her sandals and placed them side by side on top of the blanket before attempting to follow Hani on the short climb down the cliff. He patted the ground beside him and she sat, pulling the wide hem of her skirt up to just below her knees.

"You know," he said as he dangled his two feet over the pool's glassy surface, "I am sure you would like to get a special Omani pedicure, am I right?" He pointed to her purple toenails. Ariana nodded, puzzled. "Well," he continued, "put in your feet." She hesitated as he plunged his own bare feet into the crystal clear water. "It is quite warm," he assured her. "You must trust me."

Ariana gingerly dipped in one foot and squealed, pulling it back in a jerk. "Holy crap! What the hell is that?"

Hani was laughing so hard he could barely speak. "They won't hurt you. Look." He pointed into the water, where an entire school of tiny black fish had attached themselves to every part of his feet. "They are the Garra rufa, but some call them the doctor fish. They just eat the skin that is dead. Come, try it again."

Ariana gamely slid her other foot under the surface, but only for a few seconds. "I just can't!" she said with a laugh. "It's *way* too creepy! Especially the ones that go between your toes. Yuck!"

"You will get used to it." Hani watched as Ariana continued to try, forcing her feet, one at a time, to remain underwater longer and longer with each attempt. He wiped his brow with his sleeve and plunged his own legs a bit deeper. Though the sun was low in the sky, he could still feel its burn through his *dishdasha*. The memories from childhood were still strong in this place—above all, the soothing caress of the water as it welcomed one's body from top to bottom. Suddenly he stood and whipped the *kuma* from his head, pulled the billowing white fabric of his *dishdasha* off over his shoulders, and sprung from the rock in his T-shirt and shorts, sailing through the warm air until his fingertips touched the glassy surface and the water gobbled him up in one giant swallow.

He came up shaking the water from his ears. Ariana was watching from the rocks, her smile a sweet delight that only made him feel even more like the child he used to be. "Help me up," he asked as he approached the shore, his arm extending from the water and up toward her. As she clasped her hand firmly around his wrist, Hani smiled slyly and jerked his arm back, bringing Ariana flying down next to him in a splash. Her head rose from under the water's surface as she sputtered and blinked, her arms flailing. "You can swim, can't you?" Hani said in a sudden panic, grabbing her under the armpits.

"Of course I can swim, you idiot." Ariana swatted at him as she whipped her head around, her eyes scanning the shore around them.

"It's okay, it's okay," Hani assured her. "There is nobody left to see us. We are alone."

"*Eeewwww!*" she suddenly screamed. "The fish!" Before he knew it, Hani found Ariana cradled in his arms, her own wrapped around his neck. He began to twirl in circles, the water churning in his wake, the absence of weight from her body making it all feel like the most splendid dream. "I will keep them away, like a knight defending his princess from the dragons."

Ariana laughed. "I'd rather they *were* dragons." He could feel her muscles soften beneath her skin, the thump of her heart against his chest begin to slow. How could something this wonderful be forbidden, this innocent touch between a woman and a man? Perhaps, he thought, this might be considered an essential circumstance under Islamic law, such as when a person faints or has a seizure, and it is allowed to touch to provide help.

But before he could reach a conclusion to his quandary, Ariana had loosened herself from his hold and was starting to wage a ruthless splashing battle against him. He retaliated with full force, the two of them yelling and laughing just as he and his sisters had done under his father's watch so many years ago.

"I give!" she cried out.

"Give what?" Hani continued to ply her with waves.

"I give up, you jerk!" Ariana paddled backwards to escape his assault.

"Give up?"

"It means I surrender! Stop! Enough!" She laughed.

But then it was Hani's turn to laugh, for when the splashing subsided it left Ariana looking like a melted clown, the makeup ringing her eyes and streaking her cheeks with colors that had no right to be where they were.

"My eyelashes!" She grabbed at the hairy fringes sliding down her face like drowned spiders. "Shit! Don't look at me!" She began to paddle toward shore. Hani stopped her with a gentle hand on the shoulder.

The kiss seemed to surprise them both, though it was clear neither one of them had truly wanted it to end. When it was over, they made their way to shore, an awkward silence between them. Hani didn't know whether he wanted to apologize or do it again. Instead he simply let the soft mountain air and the splendid orange sunset speak his words, and his thoughts, for him.

17

The needle pierced up through the cloth and back down again in a rhythm almost as rapid and precise as a machine. The tiny *kuma* Miza was embroidering for the baby was identical to the one favored by Tariq, in fact the very one he had been wearing on his head the day he appeared on the beach in the village.

The hospital ward was as quiet as usual. Neema had greeted her warmly as she stepped from the elevator, assuring her that she would warn her should Tariq's other wife appear. "You must be careful, my sister. That one's a wicked *ng'ombe*, an old cow," she had said. "Never have we had to deal with a healthy person who was so much more trouble than the sick. It took a good half-hour of our time to calm her down yesterday, after what she found in your husband's room." Miza sucked in a gulp of air, bracing herself for a scolding for the magic she'd attempted. But instead Neema offered a knowing smile. "You'd best keep your distance from that one. I cannot help but think of that old tale about the one named Miza, like you, who was turned to stone by a jealous other wife. You do know it, don't you?"

Miza knew it well. In fact, the story came from her mother's village, and told of the local chief's older first wife summoning evil spirits as she gathered well water from a cave with the younger second wife. The water Miza carried in her vial came from that very cave. She would try to steer clear of Maryam, no matter what. Even if the woman simply spied her in the hallways, she might recognize Miza's as a face from the past, and would likely put things together in the blink of an eye.

Neema's kindness had soothed Miza's nerves, to the point where she even found herself smiling a little as she sat with her bare feet curled under her, watching the drugged slumber that had erased the lines from her husband's face, leaving it as smooth as it had been when he was a boy. They had both been so carefree back then, as only children can be, when happiness seems as endless as a long day spent under the sub-Saharan sun. There were rare times, while she was living in her uncle's home, when tiny slivers of that kind of happiness had managed to seep back into her life. It was only Sabra who had made that happen, with her ready giggle and mischievous mind. And it was only on those special days when her sister would be allowed to accompany her down to the beach, to sit by the shore and explore the shells as Miza hung the seaweed to dry.

Miza knew Bi-Zena didn't mind her working slowly on those days, taking the time to play and chase around with little sister until they'd both fall laughing into the sand. But Miza was also well aware of the looks that would come from the other women out deep in the tide. That's when she'd quiet Sabra with the promise of one or two of her favorite stories, the old Zanzibari tales Miza's mother used to tell her as she drifted off to sleep at night. Even though Miza knew all those stories by heart, they always seemed endless, winding around in circles before they finally got to their point. And always the same themes: someone outsmarting or outwitting somebody else, one getting another to do something for them or taking advantage—even though the characters were often friends. And those characters, always the same. Fee'see, the hyena. Ko'bay, the tortoise. Kee'ma, the monkey. She used to wonder, as she listened to her mother's voice, which one was she? Was she like Soongoo'ra, the hare, the wiliest of all the beasts? Or was she more like Sim'ba, the lion, who usually played the fool?

What terrible tales, it now occurred to her. What terrible tales they *all* were, those little animal stories passed down through the generations by her ancestors, full of cunning and deceit, betrayal and killing. And really, what was the point they all seemed to be making? That good did not necessarily win over evil.

Miza put down her embroidery and got up to stretch her legs. Perhaps Sabra would be home from classes by now, she thought as she sent yet another message, hoping the sound of the phone would get her sister's attention. She'd received no response for two days now, and was praying her sister hadn't lost her phone yet again. As smart as she was, that girl seemed to lose track of everything, the way she flitted around, jumping from one thing to another with enough energy to light up an entire village.

This time a response came immediately. *Yes*, her sister replied to her message asking if everything was okay. Miza breathed a sigh of relief and waited for more. Sabra no doubt had a lot to share about the last couple of days. Usually it was regarding which teacher had been particularly mean, where she had stopped with her friends on the way home, who had said what to whom, which boy had looked at her. But today there was nothing.

And? Miza typed.

And everything is fine. I am fine, her sister replied.

You have no more to say? Miza waited.

How are you?

Something is wrong, Miza thought. Perhaps something happened at school, or perhaps it was because of a boy, or maybe Sabra had been alone long enough and simply wanted her to come home. But whatever it was, this just did not sound like her sister.

Suddenly Neema was standing over her, frantically waving her arms. "Quick!" the nurse whispered. "You must get out. She is here!"

Neema bent to help as Miza fumbled for her shoes. But it was too late. Maryam was there, at the foot of Tariq's bed, her pale cheeks flashing red upon seeing Miza's face.

"You!" the enraged woman hissed as the nurse flew from the room in search of help. "I remember you. I should have known that you were the one my husband took as his Zanzibar wife. Running after him like a filthy little dog ever since you were a child."

Maryam's voice held the same ugly sting as it had so many years before. Miza willed her eyes upward to meet the woman's own. She looked older, duller, heavier than she had been as a teenage girl, but Maryam's face remained as mean as Miza remembered it to be.

The woman took three steps toward Miza, her fists curled into tight balls and her chest heaving with anger. Then her cold eyes fixed on Miza's swollen belly. "And look," she said laughingly, "he has married a whore."

Miza pushed herself up from the chair, her arms instinctively wrapping around her middle.

"Tariq would not have had to marry you to get what you give away for free," Maryam scoffed. "What a fool he has been."

"Do not talk that way about my husband," Miza replied quietly yet firmly.

"*Your* husband. *Your* husband could not have done that to you." Maryam pointed with a jerk of the chin to the baby inside. "He is less of a man than the Queen of Sheba."

"This is his child," Miza said as she wrapped her arms tighter. "This is our son."

"Get out of here, and take your ridiculous lies with you!" Maryam screamed, flapping her hands at Miza, as if shooing away a fly.

"It is *you* who should get out," Miza snapped back. "You who treats such a kind man in such a wicked way."

Maryam lurched toward Miza and leaned into her face until the two women were practically nose to nose. "How dare you speak to me that way," she spat. "Just who do you think you are? You are *nothing*!" she screamed. "Just a stupid girl from a poor family in a forgotten land. You and yours were born only to be slaves of our people." Suddenly the woman seemed to have grown a foot taller. "You are nothing but a whore, just like all of them!"

Miza struggled to steel her trembling legs. "You *never* loved him. I could see it even as a child." She gulped, as if she could swallow the quiver in her voice. "You care nothing for him. Am I not right?" she now shouted, summoning the last ounce of bravery she could before it slipped away. All this anger, this could not be good for the baby. Though she was speaking the truth, Miza hated the sound of the ugliness coming from her own mouth. She wanted to stand her ground, to keep watch over Tariq, but right now it seemed more important to protect their child. She grabbed her bag, inched around Maryam and backed slowly toward the doorway as the woman continued with her tantrum.

"And you!" Maryam screamed, keeping pace with Miza's steps, the distance between the two no more than a hand's length. "You are not after all this?" She wiggled her fingers crudely in the air, the fluorescent hospital light bouncing off her rings. "Maybe it was you who made him this way in the first place, with your African magic, to steal from him and run back to your pimp in Zanzibar. Your voodoo will do nothing to help you and your bastard child!"

Miza closed her eyes and turned her head sharply as Maryam raised her arm. But instead of delivering the slap Miza anticipated, the woman yanked the scarf off of Miza's head and began to tug at her hair.

"Get away from me!" Miza yelled, pushing at Maryam's chest with all her strength.

Maryam suddenly spun on her heels and began to tear apart the hospital room, flinging towels and blankets, bandages and cloths in a rage. "What else have you done in my husband's room, you witch?" she screamed as she jerked the sheets off of Tariq, reaching under the mattress with one arm while frantically patting down his body with the other. When her hand reached his chest, she paused. Then, with two hands, she pulled down on the front of his gown, yanked the chain from his neck and flung it against the wall, where it hit with a clatter before sliding onto the ground.

18

The Scotch went down way too easily, but was doing its job just fine, easing Rachel back toward her rational self; the one who could come pretty close to blaming the morning's bizarre encounter at the market on the residue of sleep medication mixed with the ironic lack of sleep. But the alcohol was doing nothing for her anger. At first she had been a little relieved to find the hotel room empty when she returned from the souk, as she wasn't too anxious to share the story of the old woman and the goat with anyone, let alone a drama queen like Ariana. But when she found the note taped to the bathroom mirror with a band-aid, she was pissed. *You left without me! Off with Hani,* it read in perfect schoolgirl script. *Back soon. xoxoA*

Soon? What exactly was Ariana's definition of soon? And more importantly, at what time, exactly, was the note written? Not that she had any expectation that Ariana would have actually found anything worthwhile for her to shoot, but the woman was still technically under her employ. Maggie had not been receptive to the idea of her wandering the country on her own. So, with yet another afternoon lost, Rachel had spent the hours going through her images to see if she'd somehow miraculously captured even one magazine-worthy shot. And now it was getting late. The sun had already disappeared behind the mountains, and yet there was no sign of either Ariana or Hani. No voicemail, no texts, no nothing.

The poolside patio was nearly empty, much quieter than it had been a couple of evenings before, with only the flutter of birds bedding down for the night and the clicking of insects venturing out into the dusk disturbing the stillness. Rachel had just ordered a second drink and was settling in with one of the Oman guidebooks she'd spotted in Ariana's suitcase when she realized someone was speaking to her.

"You are American?"

She turned to see a large man, who sat with a laptop, an iPad, and a phone arranged neatly on the table before him. She nodded.

"I could tell by your accent. Texas?"

Rachel laughed. "No, New York."

"Ah," the man answered. "I have been to Texas. I have relatives living in Houston. But I would really like to go to New York."

Rachel nodded again.

"You are a tourist here?" he continued.

"No." She chuckled a little. "Not a tourist."

"So then what is it that brings you to Oman?" he asked, his eyes darting from her camera to her book before returning to her face.

Rachel sized the man up before answering. Wedding band, honest smile, clean white shirt, good haircut, well-trimmed beard, and firmly rooted less than an arm's length from his devices. A guy on a business trip, no doubt. "I'm a photographer. On assignment."

"Ah. I see. Well, there is no lack of beauty to be photographed here."

Rachel nodded again, and tilted her eyes back toward her book.

"Have you photographed Jebel Shams yet? Or the famous fort here in Nizwa?"

Rachel kept her eyes on the page as she answered. "It's not that kind of assignment. I'm supposed to be shooting crafts-people, and the handiwork specific to Oman."

"Oh. You mean like the *khanjar*, the daggers, and the silver jewelry?"

She lifted her head. "Exactly. But actually, I'm really not having much luck."

"And why not, if it is not too rude of a stranger to ask?"

Rachel closed the book and offered her hand. "Rachel. And not rude at all."

"I am Zayed." The man nodded his head politely, his hands remaining in his lap. "So tell me, what is your problem with the photographs?"

Rachel pushed back her chair a little and stretched out her legs. "Well, Zayed, I'll tell you. It just doesn't seem as though anything is really *made* here. And if it is, whoever is making it must be hiding out in a cave somewhere. Nobody around here seems to know anything."

Now it was Zayed's turn to laugh. "I understand. The Omanis are very good talkers, but only about the things they want to talk about. So let me ask you, have you seen Bahla?"

Rachel shook her head. "No. What's Bahla?"

"It's a town, not far from here, a walled city. It is where much of the pottery you see in Oman comes from."

"Bahla," she repeated slowly. "So they actually physically, literally, make the pots right there?"

"They do."

"You're sure?" She wrinkled her freckled nose and cocked her head.

"Yes, I am sure. They have been doing so for generations. Beautiful pottery. They're very famous for it. In fact, it is said that the potters of Bahla are born with magic in their fingers." He wiggled his own fingers in the air. "Of course, not many of my clients want to go there."

"Your clients?"

"Yes. I run a travel business in the Emirates. The Emiratis are not too big on magic, if you understand what I mean."

"Well, I'm all for it, if it will help me get the pictures I need." Rachel drained the watery mix at the bottom of her glass. "So what is it with these magical potters that freaks your clients out so much?"

"It's not the potters." Zayed smoothed back his hair. "It is that all of Bahla is supposedly filled with magic. They say it is the birthplace of the *jinn*."

"The who?"

"The *jinn*. In English I think you use the word 'genie'."

"Oh, right." Like what Adil and Ariana had been talking about that day at the restaurant, she remembered, when they told her about using her left foot to enter a restroom. Or was it her right?

"But the *jinn*," Zayed continued, "they're not at all like the genies they show in your Hollywood stories. They are said to be a whole species of intelligent beings—good and evil, ugly and beautiful—living here among us, but with powers that we humans do not possess."

"Is that so?" Rachel poked at the slivers of ice at the bottom of her glass. "Can they make people disappear?" She laughed to herself, having Ariana in mind.

Zayed leaned forward and clasped his hands together, his elbows resting on the table. "Well, actually, it is said that they can fly through the air, and transport humans from place to place."

"Hence the magic carpet," Rachel said.

"Exactly. They can even become invisible, only to reappear out of nowhere."

"Well that sounds pretty awesome."

"Yes," the man agreed. "I suppose it does."

Rachel was delighted to finally come across someone who spoke about more than the perfection of this place, as crazy a direction as this conversation seemed to be going in. "So what else can they do?" she asked.

"Many things. For one, they are said to change shapes, sometimes disguising themselves as snakes or dogs or cats. But what makes it very difficult," Zayed continued, "is that the *jinn* sometimes possess the bodies of actual humans, speaking and acting through them, or inflicting ill upon them."

Rachel nodded, her eyes focusing on a distant bird crossing the darkening sky. "Really. And why would they want to do that?"

Zayed sat back in his chair. "Well, from what I was told when I was a child, it would happen if the *jinn* feels he has been wronged in some way, and is seeking to punish the human responsible. My mother would warn me that the *jinn* hide in drains and wells, places that are dark and damp and deep. And if a human by accident urinates on a *jinn* or pours hot water on him, the *jinn* might feel it was deliberate and he will look for revenge."

"Seriously?" she said, shifting forward in her chair. "Let me get this straight. You're saying that if I were to meet one of these things, and maybe even make it mad, I wouldn't necessarily know?"

"No, probably not. Like I said, it can be hard to tell. And to make it even more confusing, it is said that the *jinn* are even capable of speaking the many languages of those they meet."

The old woman with the goat flashed into Rachel's mind, the thought leaving as quickly as it entered. She sat back and crossed her legs. "And so you believe in these things yourself?"

The man shrugged, but nevertheless answered. "If you ask anybody, not just people from here, but all around the world, you will hear the same. These are stories passed down from generation to generation. It is in the Koran. But also, I think, in other religions as well. Have you not been taught of something like this in your belief?"

Rachel was grateful for the sight of the waiter crossing the patio with a fresh glass of Scotch on a tray.

"Everyone has a story to tell about the *jinn*," Zayed continued. "But around here you will find that not many people will want to talk about such things. Watch," he whispered as the waiter approached. "Excuse me, my brother. My friend here was curious about Bahla. Have you been there?"

The young man nodded his head.

"And do you think it is a nice place to visit?"

"Sure. Why not?"

"You are not afraid?"

The waiter laughed. "Oh, you mean the *jinn*? That was a long time ago. Not now, *mashallah*."

Zayed looked at Rachel and shrugged his shoulders.

"Besides," the waiter said as he set down the drink, "it is said that if you are a good Muslim you can protect yourself. And if you need to, you can always go to a specialist."

"A specialist?" Rachel asked.

"You know, a doctor, a healer. There are said to be many in Bahla."

"So you wouldn't be afraid to go to Bahla?" Zayed asked.

The waiter shook his head. "Not me. It is the Emiratis who are most afraid. The whole Gulf is. Everyone says bad things about Bahla, but the Omanis are not scared anymore. Thanks to God and His Majesty we are more educated now." He picked up Rachel's empty glass and took a rag to the moisture on the table.

"So, wait, you're saying there's no such thing as *jinns*?" Rachel asked, confused.

The waiter stopped mid-wipe. "I did not say that."

Zayed laughed as the young man scurried off to wait on another table. "You see?"

"Wow," Rachel said. What the hell was up with everyone?, she thought. Were they all delusional? She'd heard ghost stories her whole life too—who hadn't? But that didn't mean she actually believed in them.

"Ah," Zayed said as the doors from the lobby swung open and a tall man in a light blue *dishdasha* approached. "Here is someone who will talk, no matter what the subject. I can guarantee it." He gestured toward the man. "Raheem, this is Rachel." He turned to Rachel. "Raheem talks so much that I sometimes have to ask him to stop before my ears fall off. It is a good thing he has found a way to make money from all his talking. Raheem is a tour guide." Zayed signaled for the waiter and pulled out a chair for Raheem to sit on.

"Pleased to meet you, Rachel." The tour guide smiled.

"Likewise."

"Rachel is very interested in the *jinn*," Zayed said.

Raheem raised his eyebrows.

"Do you have any stories for her?"

Raheem hesitated, his eyes darting around the patio as if checking to see if anyone else was listening. "Of course I have stories."

"Well?" Zayed asked with an impish grin on his face.

"Okay. Here is one. Let me tell you about my wife, Fatima. It is said she had a bad *jinni*. The story I was told came from when she was younger, before we were married. Someone sent the *jinn* to her to get revenge on her father, to hurt Fatima because she was her father's favorite. When it began, she would enter the house and fall down and faint. She would scream for no reason. One day her father and brother started asking her questions. The *jinn* started to answer. It wasn't Fatima's voice. It said it would make her life difficult. So they took Fatima to a healer. The first time did not work. And the second time did not work either. But the third time it did, or so they tell me. And when it was done, my poor wife had marks on her back from the healer beating the *jinn* out of her with his stick."

"*That's* how they do it?" Rachel coughed at a trickle of Scotch hitting her throat.

"Actually," the guide told her, "there are different ways they use."

"I heard of a healer who used a hot poker to brand someone's neck in order to heal a bad back," Zayed chimed in.

Rachel remained silent, baffled by these two men with their ridiculous tales.

"But you, you do not need to worry," Raheem added, pointing to the fading blue compass emblazoned on her bare forearm. "The *jinn* will not possess a person with a tattoo."

"Well, there you go," she said before taking a long sip of her drink. "So, I don't get it. Do you two believe in this stuff or not?"

The two men looked at each other, as if waiting for the other to answer. Finally Zayed was the one to speak. "It's complicated. To not believe is almost considered like not believing in Islam. But really?" He signed his bill and stood from the table. "You must go to Bahla for your pictures. It is no more 'haunted' than anywhere else. The *jinn*," he said as he waved his arm across the patio, "they are everywhere."

19

The morning sun was streaming through the Lexus's side windows, outlining Hani's perfect silhouette in an aura of gold that lit him up like a shining star. In the back seat, behind him, Miza lay curled up like a beach ball, a pillow stuffed under her belly and her head resting against the door. Rachel was scrunched up on the other side, busily rearranging the contents of her backpack. Ariana sighed contentedly. "Lovely day, isn't it?" she asked no one in particular before breaking into a whistle, a Katy Perry song from a few years back that she hadn't been able to get out of her head since yesterday.

"Ahem," Rachel objected loudly from behind her. "Do you mind?"

Rachel, apparently, was still mad. The woman had practically bit her head off when she and Hani returned from the *wadi* the night before. She'd tried her best to act normally when she spotted Rachel and Miza in the lobby, the two of them huddled together in a deep sofa like a pair of old aunties waiting up for a niece past curfew. She had worried that they might see something, as if she were wearing the afternoon's episode like a badge on her chest. But when she approached, she saw they had been too busy talking to notice her entering, and even appeared somewhat surprised by the interruption. But Rachel's anger was quick to surface. "Where the hell were you all afternoon?" she snapped, her eyes darting up and down Ariana's body.

"I didn't mean to upset you, Rachel. I left you a note!"

"But *all* afternoon? You didn't even call or text. You just left me here to wait."

"I am truly sorry." She squeezed herself onto the cushion next to Rachel and placed a hand on her knee. "But you were gone. I assumed you wanted to be on your own. And then there was my phone—it fell into the water. Honest. Hani is just now trying to get some rice, to help dry it out." She couldn't help but smile a little at the sound of his name on her lips.

"Whatever, Ariana. It just sucks that you're wasting my time with your fucking bullshit."

Ariana shot a look of embarrassed apology to Miza, but the woman seemed to be barely aware of the fuss around her. "I'll make it up to you, Rachel, I swear. I'm all yours." She held out her arms in an offering. "Whatever you need, I'm there."

"That's supposed to be your *job*, Ariana," Rachel snapped. "But don't trouble yourself. I've already made my own arrangements for tomorrow."

"But I want to make things right! I'm so sorry. Really I am."

"What is going on?" Hani asked as he plopped a plastic bag filled with uncooked rice on Ariana's lap. "Is everything all right?" He turned his gaze from Ariana to Rachel and back again. "Can I do anything to help?"

"I was just telling your friend here," Rachel said, jerking her head toward Ariana, "that I've made plans for tomorrow. I'm going to see the potters, the ones in Bahla."

Hani nodded slowly. "That is a good idea."

"I'll set up a driver." Ariana hopped up eagerly from the sofa.

"Don't bother," Rachel said. "I've already hired one. And no need for you to come," she added. "Miza has already asked. We'll go together."

Ariana was speechless. It was Hani who stepped in for her. "Why go with a strange driver? I will take you all. It would be my pleasure."

"Thanks, Hani, but that's okay. I can manage on my own." Rachel stood from the sofa and offered a hand to Miza.

"No, I insist. We will make a day of it," he said as his dark eyes shifted to meet Ariana's.

Rachel had finally given in to Hani's plan. And she hadn't seemed quite as angry in the morning as they gathered in the breakfast room for coffee before hitting the road. But Ariana had picked up a vibe from the two women that made her feel a little like the kid left without a seat in a game of musical chairs. Perhaps her happiness was too obvious. She'd have to try to ratchet that down a bit. Nobody likes a girl whose head is stuck on cloud nine. Even if she couldn't stop thinking about Hani, there was no need for the others to know that. "Everything all right back there?" she called toward the rear of the car.

"It's all good," Rachel responded flatly.

Ariana leaned back against the leather headrest, her mind returning to the *wadi*. She could feel the skin on her arms tingling at the mere thought of Hani's lips, soft and cool in the water's flow. How she wished those moments could have lasted forever, the two of them stuck in some fairy tale where time stood still. But she was lucky enough, she knew, to have yet another day to spend with him. She'd worry about tomorrow, well, tomorrow. Tomorrow! Ariana sat up with a start. Tomorrow was Friday, and that would mean nearly seven days had passed without talking to her parents. She dug for her phone, only to remember that it was still sitting, useless, inside a bag of rice. She turned around to Rachel. "Can I trouble you to borrow your mobile? I just need to check in at home. A quick hello. Won't be long."

Rachel tossed the phone into the front seat. "Be my guest."

The phone conversation started out just fine. Of course there was no way Ariana could even mention Hani to her parents, especially with him sitting right there next to her. She asked them about their day; they inquired about her job—the one she no longer had—happy that she claimed it was going well. It was when they asked exactly where she was at the moment that all hell broke loose.

"You're headed *where*?" her mother asked after a pause so long Ariana thought they had been disconnected.

"Bahla," Ariana repeated. "I'm on my way to Bahla."

"Oh, no you are not. You must turn around right away and go back to where you came from."

Ariana laughed. "What are you talking about, *Ami*? Are you all right?"

"It is not safe. Do not go near it. We have the experience."

"Please, *Ami*, put *Abu* on the phone."

Ariana heard the muffled sounds of her mother's voice as she handed the phone to her husband. "You must listen to your mother. I am serious."

"And hello to you too, Dad. Are you enjoying your day?"

"This is not a joke, Ariana. You must stay away from Bahla."

164

"Have you two gone mad? What on earth are you talking about?"

"You don't remember the accident?"

"Of course I do." Ariana would never forget that phone call telling her that her mother was in hospital, severely injured, after her parents' car had mysteriously spun off the road. "But that was in Saudi Arabia. You were on pilgrimage, to Medina, remember?"

"Of course I remember. And I also remember that the accident happened in the Valley of the Jinn."

"Oh." Ariana paused for a second. "I see. So you're saying that Bahla is the same?"

"I know this place," her father insisted. "It is full of *jinn*. If you go there, you are asking for trouble. It is like going to someone's house without an invitation."

"Please, *Abu*, I know what you're saying. I won't do anything stupid, I promise."

"What you will promise is that you will stay away from Bahla!" her father snapped with a sternness she hadn't heard since she was a child in trouble.

"I'll be fine. Don't worry. Love you!" she chirped a little too brightly before hanging up. She slumped back in her seat. If she were on her own, Ariana knew damn well she'd turn the car right around and head back. Why upset her parents? And really, why take the risk? But this was a job. And one she'd so far not been so great at. She couldn't very well run out on it. That would be totally unprofessional of her, and she knew how easily word got around in Dubai. And, she thought as she glanced to her left, that would also mean a day spent without Hani. Her parents were probably—hopefully—just overreacting.

"Is everything okay?" Hani asked, his eyes fixed on the road ahead.

"Yes. It's fine." Ariana smoothed her hair back, hooking it behind her ears. "It's just that my parents are a little bit worried about me."

"And why is that?"

"Well, actually, it's Bahla they're worried about. I had no idea it had the reputation it does."

"You mean the whole *jinn* thing?" came Rachel's voice from the back seat.

Ariana twisted around to face her. "You knew about that? Why am I the only person who doesn't seem to be aware of this?" She sat back in her seat and began to tap frantically on the phone. "*Bahla*," she read aloud from the screen. "*Also known in Oman as Madinat Al Sehr—City of Magic—due to its long association with* jinn *and sorcerers.* Even Wiki knows about it!" she squealed as she continued to search. "Oh my god. Listen to this. Here's a story about a guy who lives there, whose cement house burst into flames out of nowhere. *Then,*" she read, "*there's the matter of the awful cackling he heard echoing within the flames— and the pale woman in rags who stood atop his wispy sidr tree just before the blaze, who vanished as quickly as she had appeared* . . . blah blah blah . . . *outside—hidden among the endless sand and shrub— the evil demons that plague the desert town of Bahla, Oman, are almost certainly listening.*" Ariana gulped. "*Today, stories of* jinn *sightings in Bahla still range from*"—here Ariana slowed her pace and raised her volume—"*disquieting to downright bone-chilling.* Do you hear that? Disquieting to downright bone-chilling!"

Miza moaned and shifted in her sleep.

"There are *tons* of stories here," Ariana continued, her thumbs tapping frantically on the screen. "Mounds of rocks appearing out of nowhere, people hearing someone moaning but nobody's there. And listen to this—*a group of farmers talk of the* jinn *they have heard haunting the palm oases dotting the town, preying on them after dusk by calling their names across the valley until they are dangerously lost and bitterly cold.*"

"We get it, Ariana," Rachel said impatiently. "There are lots of *jinn* stories in Bahla."

"Seriously, you guys?" Ariana's voice rose an octave. "I think my parents might be right."

Hani laughed a little. "But surely you have known about the *jinn*."

"Of course I know about the *jinn*. In fact, I was there when one left my great-uncle and entered my aunt. It was a horrific sight. I'll never get it out of my head. And my parents, just a few years ago, had a horrible accident, driven off the road by the *jinn*. My mother was lucky to survive. Believe me, my whole family has been touched. And that is exactly why I'm beginning to think that going to Bahla is not such a great idea. Why invite trouble?" What she didn't mention to Hani was her nagging fear that the clairvoyant in Dubai had been right, that she, herself, had a *jinn*. What else could it be that was keeping her from finding love? She feared it was only a matter of time before the allegedly amorous spirit who had attached himself to her would cause whatever this was with Hani to also head south.

"Okay, okay," she sputtered when she clicked on the next link. "Now tell me I'm wrong. *National Geographic* has named Bahla the fifth most haunted city in the world. *National Geographic!*"

"Respect to Bahla!" Hani chortled with a fist in the air.

"It's not funny!" Ariana returned to her search.

"Give me that." Rachel reached from the back seat and grabbed the phone out of Ariana's hand. "Here," she said after a minute. "TripAdvisor: *Picturesque oasis town. Impressive and lovely fortress. Friendly people.*"

"It's probably a *jinn* who wrote that!" Ariana protested. "To lure unsuspecting people to their town."

"You will be fine," Hani assured her. "Bahla is a nice place. I know it well. And I will have you back in Nizwa by nightfall. It is my promise to you."

20

It was actually surprising to Rachel to see just how much about Bahla seemed to be *jinn* related. Scrolling down through the links, desperate to put a stop to the hysteria building in the front seat, she struggled to find any other tidbits of interest at all. It was all black magic, *jinn*, witchcraft. And a fort. Which, apparently, was also haunted. Were ghosts the only thing this place was about? It seemed so. And it also seemed all like a bunch of nonsense to her.

Miza stirred in her sleep, her legs bent up against her belly and her feet resting alongside Rachel's thigh. The woman's reaction when Rachel had mentioned Bahla the night before had been sort of pitiful, the way she had grabbed Rachel's arm with both her hands and begged to be taken along. The poor woman would have probably gotten down on her knees if she could manage it. "Sure, you're welcome to come. No problem," Rachel had assured her. "But I'm going to be spending pretty much all day getting shots of the guys making pottery there. Might be pretty boring for you."

"No," Miza insisted. "It will be fine. I think I might be able to ask around and find someone in Bahla who can help me."

Rachel had noticed her ashen skin and wobbly legs the minute Miza entered through the hotel's glass doors, and had invited the visibly shaken woman to join her in the lobby to share a pot of *chai*. "Help you how?" she had asked as she poured them each a fresh cup. "You mean like a doctor? You're not feeling well?" Miza had, in fact, appeared increasingly distraught by each day. Rachel had wanted to reach out to her, to offer some sort of comfort, but was made awkward by the woman's reserve.

Miza nodded. "Yes, a doctor," she said quietly.

"Wait," Rachel said, recalling the conversation on the patio earlier in the evening, "are we talking a *doctor*-doctor, or something else?"

"I need to find a person who has the power to help me. To help us," Miza added as she lightly rubbed her belly.

"Oh. I see." Rachel leaned back on the sofa. "So you're saying you think someone's done a number on you?"

"A number?"

"A spell. Bad *juju*."

"I know so. And I must hurry to put a stop to it, to protect my child."

Rachel blew the steam from the top of her cup. "Hani told me your husband had an accident. Is that what you're talking about?"

"Yes, it is true he had an accident. But that is only part of my trouble."

"So what's the other part?"

170

"It is his other wife," Miza said quietly, making certain there was nobody around to hear.

"His ex?" Rachel asked.

Miza shook her head. "Not an ex. The other one he is married to."

Rachel tried not to let the surprise show in her face. "So you and another woman are both married to the same guy?" She knew such arrangements weren't that uncommon in Muslim countries, but she had never spoken with anyone involved in one. Personally, Rachel couldn't imagine having to deal with a bunch of sister-wives.

Miza nodded shyly. "I married Tariq more than one year ago. He has been so kind to me, and to my sister. I love him, and he loves me as well."

Rachel couldn't help but raise her eyebrows.

"It is different," Miza rushed to explain, "than being a mistress." She looked down at the ground. "In some ways," she added.

"I'm sorry, Miza. I don't mean to come off as all judgy." Rachel paused for a sip of tea. "So you say the other wife is now causing some sort of trouble?"

"She saw me today." Miza pointed to her belly. "In the hospital."

"Oh." Rachel drew the word out long, her mind struggling to wrap itself around how that meeting might have gone down.

"Yes. Today she saw me, and saw that I was with child. And she knows that if Tariq does not live, and our child is born a boy, she could lose almost everything to us. So I know that to her, it is best my son not be born, no matter what."

"And?"

"And I am sure she is doing something to make sure it does not happen."

"To make sure Tariq doesn't die?"

"If only that were so. But I'm sure it is me, and the child, she is after. She took some pieces of my hair. That is all she needs for a *mganga*, a witch doctor, to inflict a spell. That is why I must seek help in Bahla."

"Okay." Rachel took a deep breath. "But really, Miza. Do you know what those guys, those so-called healers, do? Let me tell you—"

"Oh, I know all about it." Miza leaned back stiffly into the cushions. "In my country we have many ways of dealing with the *sheitani*."

"Okay, but seriously, do you really think you should be doing this to yourself? In your condition?"

"It is because of my condition that I *must* do this," she suddenly snapped. "Why do you think I dared to leave my husband's side? How could I have let myself do that if it wasn't my baby, *our* baby, that was in danger?"

Rachel rubbed her forehead. "I'm sorry, Miza. I'm trying to understand, I really am. But are you sure it's really what you think it is? Personally, all this hocus-pocus stuff just seems to be so—" Rachel paused mid-sentence, stopped by the blatant desperation on Miza's face. "Okay, okay. We'll go to Bahla tomorrow."

Now, with Miza still asleep beside her in the car, Rachel took the opportunity to probe a little deeper. "So maybe you can explain it to me, Hani." She leaned in and rested her forearms on the back of Ariana's seat. "What is it about the whole *jinn* thing that gets everyone around here so worked up? It just all seems so archaic to me."

Hani looked back at her through the rear-view mirror. "Well," he began, "it is true that it is an old belief."

"The way we were taught it," Ariana chimed in, "was that angels were originally created by Allah from light, and that the *jinn* were created from smokeless fire. Then there was Iblis, one of the *jinns*, but he was raised to the rank of the angels."

"Yes," Hani agreed, "and what you have to understand is that, unlike the angels, the *jinn* have free will. So what happened is that when Allah created man, Iblis was jealous, and refused to bow down before Adam, claiming he was superior because Adam was made from clay, and he, Iblis, was made from fire. So, for his disobedience, Iblis was driven from paradise and condemned to Hell."

"But," Ariana added, "he begged God to delay his punishment until the Day of Judgment, and that is why the *jinn* live all around us, making trouble from their parallel universe."

"You don't have this in your religion?" Hani's eyes once again turned to the rear-view mirror.

Rachel thought for a moment. "Well, I guess for Christians, Satan would be their Iblis. But I'm not sure where the *jinn* come in. And in my religion? I think it's looked at sort of differently, not that I know much. But then again, I'm not really a religious person."

Ariana whipped her head around and flashed Rachel a look.

"Really?" Hani paused before saying more, as if he were pondering a notion he'd never considered before. "So tell me, how does that work?"

Rachel laughed a little. "How does it work? It just does. I live my life, I try my best to be a good person, and if and when I'm not, it's totally on me."

"So you believe in nothing other than yourself?"

173

"Believing in myself, that's a whole other issue. But if you're asking if I think there's some all-seeing, all-knowing being up there running the whole show, then the answer is no." Rachel saw Ariana shrinking down in her seat.

"And can I ask," Hani said, "why do you feel this way?"

"I suppose it's the same reason you feel the way you do. It's the way I was brought up. And seriously, how could I believe in a god after seeing all the horrors I've seen in every corner of the world? Especially because so many of those horrors were committed in the name of religion."

"So you are saying that your religion is atheism?"

"Actually, atheism isn't a religion at all. That would be like saying that bald is a hair color, or that health is a disease."

Hani nodded slowly. "I see."

"I mean," Rachel continued, "I just believe in taking responsibility for myself, for my own actions. To you guys, it seems like everything is about fate."

"Yes, it is true that Muslims believe that their life is left up to the will of God. But as human beings we are given absolute freedom to do as we please, and believe that God loves his people and will always be forgiving," Hani said.

"Well, with all due respect, to me that kind of feels like a cop-out."

"Cop-out?" he asked.

"You know, an excuse, a way out of something."

"I don't understand."

"Okay," Rachel explained, "so like with this whole *jinn* thing. Someone has bad luck, someone makes a poor decision, maybe someone even does something bad. It was the *jinn*! It's like saying the devil made me do it, right?"

"It's not that black and white, Rachel," Ariana interrupted. "Can you honestly say that you've never experienced anything out of the ordinary in your life, anything that made you think, even a tiny bit, about the things we can't explain?"

"Oh, there are plenty of things I've seen that can't be explained." She snorted. "With what I do for a living? Trust me."

"That's not what I mean. I'm talking about the things we can't necessarily see, the sense of another power, or another dimension."

Once again the image of the old woman with the goat came into Rachel's mind, but she decided to keep that to herself.

"Yes," Hani said. "I am also curious about how you think. For us, the only purpose in life is to serve and obey God. And where do you find your purpose?"

Rachel had to laugh a little. "That's a good question, Hani. But the thing is, I have a real problem with the whole servility thing. I know that Islam means 'submission' in Arabic, submission to Allah's will, right?"

"And obedience to His law."

"Do you know what the philosopher Karl Marx called religion? 'The opium of the people.'" With no response from the front seat, Rachel worried that she had gone too far. "Look," she added, "you two are good people. You're not hurting anyone by being so devout."

"I should hope not!" Ariana gasped a little.

"All I'm saying is that I respect you both for your beliefs."

"And I respect you for yours," Hani said. "I am just trying to understand better what they are. You see, in Oman, it is very open. We live with other religions without any problem. We cannot say that other religions are not true. We believe that we are all brothers and sisters."

"Well that I can agree with."

"It is just difficult for me to understand that believing in *nothing* is believing in something."

"I think we're talking in circles, my friend. I say live and let live. To each his or her own." Rachel leaned back and inserted her earbuds, ready for a little Wu-Tang Clan to take her back into Rachel's World. But before she could even press play, the talk about her had started up in the front seat.

Didn't you tell me she was Jewish? I think that's what she said. A Jewish atheist. How can there be such a thing? I feel sorry for her. Anyone who willingly does the job she did must be crazy. I think she's lonely. I think she must spend her life trying to prove there is no God.

Before long their chatter turned into a droning lullaby in Rachel's ears, and she drifted off to sleep to the sound of her own psyche being pulled apart like a loaf of soft bread fresh from the oven.

21

The silence came as a welcome relief to Miza as she watched the others disappear behind the heavy iron gates of the pottery factory. She had pretended to sleep during the ride, had in fact wanted to sleep, but how could anyone sleep with that constant yammering going on? And all that talk about the *jinn*. If she hadn't been so weary from her lack of sleep the night before, and if her mind hadn't been so dizzy with worry, she could have told all of them a thing or two about the *jinn*, about the *juju*, the *sihr*, the *sheitani*, about the white arts, the dark arts, all of it. Where she was from, there was a long history of magic.

Miza took some brief comfort from the baby's movement inside her. But the panic remained close to the surface. How long would it be before Maryam would hand over whatever amount it took to buy the services of a *mganga*? Miza strained to remember the rules her mother had sworn by when she was pregnant with Sabra, measures her ancestors had taken for generations in order to keep the evil spirits at bay. *A woman with child does not sleep alone. A woman with child does not go outside during the night. A woman with child does not watch a movie that will make her scared. A woman with child does not go out alone to use the toilet.* And, of course, her mother had also hung the *azma* from their ceiling, just as everyone else did. All throughout the shops and homes in Stone Town one could see the brown scraps of paper fluttering on the end of a piece of cotton tied to the beams, carrying the words from the Koran that would ward off evil and bring in good.

How she wished she were home in Zanzibar, where she'd know just who to go to for help with warding off Maryam's evil magic. That's where the true experts were. All the Omanis who had family ties to Zanzibar preferred to go there for healing. If only she weren't about to give birth she'd hop on an airplane and go tomorrow. But the doctor had said it would not be safe this far along, so she could only hold on to the faith that one of the healers in Bahla would know what to do.

Miza thought about how Rachel had reacted the evening before, when she had told her of her interest in going to Bahla. The woman obviously didn't believe her story. Why should she? From what Miza had heard in the car, she didn't seem to believe in anything. A woman like that wouldn't understand the fears of someone like Miza. A woman like that would have no problems, would have no idea of what real problems were. A woman like that would be blind to the magic even if it bit her on the ass. And the other one! With her eyelashes and high-heeled shoes, poking into everyone else's business as if it were her own. Acting so high and mighty, and then practically crying like a baby when her daddy brought up the *jinn*. And why was she not there at home with her parents and the rest of her family instead of living alone like a spoiled diva in fancy Dubai? What Miza wouldn't give to have her mother and father still in her life. How could Hani stand it, tending to those two day after day?

Miza checked her phone for a message from Sabra. If only she had arranged for someone in Stone Town to check on the girl, to make sure she was okay. She should have gotten a phone number from her neighbor. She should have left someone other than that silly Hoda to care for Sabra. She should not have left the girl behind at all.

The baby continued to stir, roused by Miza's agitation. She dropped her head into her hands and paused. What was the matter with her? Perhaps it was Maryam who was causing her to think this way. It was not right of her to judge Rachel so harshly. She meant Miza no harm. In fact, she had acted almost warmly when Miza had returned, so upset from her clash with Maryam, getting her tea and soothing her nerves. And though Rachel may not have had the types of trouble Miza had experienced in her own life, it was clear that something had happened to her, to make her appear so hard and doubtful and shut off from the world.

And Ariana. Ariana had been nothing but kind to Miza, handing out compliments like candy, and giving up her room in the hotel so that Miza would be comfortable. It was clear that the woman's mind was now fixed on Hani. The way the color rose in her cheeks when he spoke to her. The way her eyes seemed to turn into two soft pools of warm chocolate when she looked at him. And last night, the way she appeared when the two of them arrived back together at the hotel after dark. Miza knew that look, the look of two people who had indulged in the touch of one another. But even so, Miza had a sense there were things troubling that woman, and to Miza it came through as loud and dissonant as the call to prayer blaring from all corners of Stone Town.

Miza plumped up her satchel and stuffed it between her head and the window, desperate for some real rest. If only she weren't so eaten up by her own troubles, she thought as her eyes slipped closed, she might try to help the others to see what was right in front of their eyes, to listen to what was in their hearts. She would not be so selfish, thinking her problems were so much bigger or more important than those of others. If only.

Kila ndege huruka kwa bawa lake, came the words in the voice of her mother as she drifted off to sleep. *Kila ndege huruka kwa bawa lake*. Every bird flies with its own wings.

22

"This place is owned by the government," Hani warned, pointing to the Omani flag flying high above the entrance of the pottery building Rachel had spied on the outskirts of town.

"I don't care who owns it," Rachel called back as she scurried ahead through the parking lot. "If there are real people making real pots in here, it's where I want to be."

After Hani offered an extended greeting and an explanation of the reason for their visit, they were told to wait. Before long a heavyset man in a *dishdasha* the color of mustard appeared. "Welcome," he said with a broad smile. "I am the one who will give you a tour today." He clasped his hands in front of his belly and turned on his heel. "My name is Sa'id. I am the head of finance for the factory," he explained over his shoulder.

"Factory?" Rachel's shoulders slumped at the word.

He paused and turned to her. "Actually, we are a school." They followed as he began a slow and deliberate path down a long hall. "Over here," he said as he pointed the way through a doorway to a mud-caked machine that was churning like a giant dentist's drill, "is where we mix our sand. And there is where it goes next." They turned to see a long blue machine with dozens of spigots jutting out from the bottom, the purpose of which was not explained. "And then it goes to here." He pointed to a large block of wet clay oozing out from a rectangular opening, reminding Rachel of the old Play-Doh Fun Factory she had as a kid.

"So where are all the potters?" she asked impatiently.

"We will get there," Sa'id answered, holding up one hand like a cop slowing traffic. She hated when people did that.

"And this," he said as they reached the next room, "this is our drying room." He smiled at the tables crowded with dozens of perfectly identical bowls, still glistening with dampness under the harsh industrial light. It was hard to believe these clone soldiers actually came from the hands of real people, they were so exact in every way. Next came the glazing room, its shelves lined with pinker, drier versions of the same bowls, arranged in squads divided by height and width. And still no potters in sight. It was as though all of it had been created by elves in the night. Or staged for the benefit of visitors like her, the more cynical side of her offered. "These will be glazed by our workers later," their guide said, as if reading her mind.

The next room held a hulking brick kiln that dominated the space. "Our oven burns wood, and has been used for many, many years." Sa'id stood back with pride and waited for them to admire the massive apparatus. "No pictures?" he asked Rachel, who shrugged her shoulders before obligingly clicking a few frames.

"And this," he said from the hallway outside the next doorway, "is where the detail is being done." Rachel readied the lens in her palm and stepped over the threshold. Inside, a dozen humorless faces turned toward her from beneath their black headscarves. Each woman held a thin, delicate brush, capable—under the guidance of a steady hand—of producing the most intricate of strokes. Rachel squinted to admire the painted bowls lining the shelves around her. With hope in her eyes she turned to Sa'id, who responded with a flat palm and a shake of the head. "No photos of the women."

After a stop in the packing room they finally came upon a handful of men who seemed to freeze in place as they approached, their mouths falling silent at the sight of visitors. It was clear they had been in conversation, standing in clusters along the far wall, next to a row of potter's wheels sitting idle.

"And this," Sa'id said, beaming, "is where the clay is turned into the pottery." The men, dressed alike in baggy pants and short-sleeved shirts that matched the brown of the clay, continued to stare as Sa'id spoke. "Like I said, we are a school, not for profit, with the purpose of keeping the artistry of our area going." One of the potters flashed a toothless smile at Rachel. All of them looked way too old to be in school. "It will take more than three years for these men to learn," Sa'id said with pride. And way more, Rachel thought, if they continue to spend this much time standing around doing nothing.

It was, for her, yet another morning lost. And she was pissed. "Is it true," she asked with a sidelong glance at Ariana, "that the potters of Bahla are born with magic in their fingers?"

"Pardon me?"

"Ouch!" she yelped as the edge of Ariana's wedge clipped her foot. "I said," Rachel repeated, louder this time, "is it true that the potters here are born with magic in their fingers?"

"No magic!" Sa'id snapped back, his face turning suddenly cold. "That was two hundred years ago. It is education! No magic," he repeated. "Magic is against the law."

Ariana rolled her eyes at Rachel and dragged her out the door by the arm as Hani said his goodbyes.

"Don't worry," he said when he caught up with the two of them in the parking lot, "I will introduce you to the real potters of Bahla. Their place is just past the old souk." He opened the car door for Ariana. "We will stop at the souk first. Perhaps there will also be some of the craftspeople there for you to photograph."

As they left the main thoroughfare and wound their way through the narrow roads toward the old center of Bahla, things became eerily quiet. To Rachel it almost felt like an old western town just before a high-noon duel, without a soul to be found on the sun-bleached, shadowless streets. In the main square, under the darkness of columned archways, the stores stood shuttered behind peeling paint, their garish signs the only hint of actual commerce. Barbershop, phone shop, jewelry shop, electronics shop, and at least five men's tailor shops—which seemed very odd to Rachel, seeing as how almost every man she'd seen in Oman wore a baggy *dishdasha*.

"It is almost lunch time," Hani offered in explanation of the closed stores. "Everyone is getting ready for prayers." He parked at the edge of the square and turned off the ignition, beckoning the three women to follow him through a dark passageway barely visible behind the shuttered shops. "Let us hope that there are still some people here," he called back. "Nothing will open again until five o'clock—after the meal and a rest."

The moment Rachel's feet touched the sunbaked ground of the market square, she felt something was not right. Her legs buckled slightly beneath her, her breath caught in her throat, her heart began to race, and her head felt as if it were floating above her like a balloon on a string. She stopped for a moment to lean against an ancient doorway as the others went ahead. Must be the heat, she thought as she shaded her eyes with one hand and gazed across the silent courtyard, allowing the blend of frankincense, cardamom and goat shit to do the work of smelling salts for her quavering senses.

There were very few stalls still open, and those that were seemed abandoned. The harsh sunlight had taken its toll, leaving everything cracked and faded. Wheelbarrows and shovels spoke of work underway, and in one corner she could see beautiful beamed eaves and intricately carved wooden doors that had recently been restored with care. Rachel pulled a filter from one of her vest pockets, screwed it onto her lens and began to shoot. Though she couldn't quite put her finger on it, there was something about this souk that made it different from any she'd seen before. And if it weren't for Ariana and Miza and Hani in her line of sight, or the scaffolding that climbed up the crumbling earthen facades at the far end of the market, she might have thought she'd been transported hundreds of years into the past.

"Everything okay over there?" Ariana shouted from the shade of a broad tree in the center of the dusty square, the last half of her words swallowed by a sudden cicada chorale that crescendoed as it bounced off the worn shop walls.

"I'm good!" Rachel yelled back as she put down her camera and dug a bottle of warm water from her backpack, then started across the square on shaky legs to join them.

"He says you should not be leaning there." Hani tilted his head toward an old man who had joined them, a man so small he looked lost under his white robes.

"I'm sorry," Rachel said. "I'll try to be more careful. Good thing they seem to be fixing things up around here. Looks like a nice stiff wind could just about blow this place down."

Hani shook his head. "No, it is not that. It is sturdy enough."

"So then what is it?" Ariana asked, her gaze remaining on the doorway in the distance.

The old man answered something in Arabic.

"Where she was standing," Miza translated, "is called the Pillar of Goats. It is said that goats, and people, who lean against that doorway can disappear."

"Well, I'm still here." Rachel patted her arms and legs as if confirming her own existence.

"For now," Ariana muttered, loud enough for Rachel to hear.

"This is Khalfan," Hani said. "He has been the night watchman at the souk for many years."

"Yes," Ariana added with a crack in her voice. "And I'm sure he's watched quite a lot."

The old man drifted into an animated monologue in Arabic, turning to Hani for translation after he finally paused to take a breath.

"What? What did he say?" Ariana asked without taking her eyes off the watchman.

"It is nothing. Just an old tale." Hani turned to lead them away.

"I want to know!" she insisted with a little too much force.

"Well." Hani paused, then responded patiently. "Khalfan was telling the story of the tree."

"This tree?" Ariana pointed at the leafy umbrella above. The tree's trunk was surrounded by a four-foot-high cement wall that was littered with faded red splotches.

"Yes. Well, actually, no. It was another tree. The one before this one."

"What's so interesting about a tree?" Rachel asked from behind her camera as she pivoted around, captivated by the strange aura of the souk.

"Well," Hani answered, "it was believed that the sap from the old tree, a frankincense tree, was used in religious ceremonies for thousands of years, back to the times of King Solomon and Cleopatra."

"And?" Ariana asked.

"And what?" Hani answered.

"I know he said more than that."

"Well, this is a new tree now."

"What happened to the old tree?" Ariana demanded.

"It became too large. It was old, and twisted. The roots were coming up from the ground. The men were cleaning and sweeping up leaves every day. So they cut it down."

"That's it?"

"That's it," Hani insisted, in a not very convincing attempt to hide the fact that he was obviously more familiar with the story than he was letting on.

The old watchman chimed in again.

"The branches burst into flame when they tried to cut it down," Miza eagerly translated, her eyes bright with expectation. "He says that people were putting little papers with magic spells inside and around the tree. It was the government who wanted it cut down."

Khalfan interrupted Miza to share more.

"They hired workers to do the job, he says. In the night. Their bulldozer caught on fire. Two men died. Others became ill. This is a new tree, but the old roots are still there."

Ariana clutched her purse close and began to back slowly away. The old watchman nodded his head, and said something else to Miza.

"The *jinn* are still there, in the tree, he says. But they won't come out unless you disturb them."

By now Ariana was halfway across the square.

"And what's with this wall?" Rachel asked as she maneuvered around for a better angle of the tree.

"The wall is where the goats are chained for auction in the mornings."

"So what's that red stuff all over it?"

Hani hesitated to make sure Ariana was out of earshot. "It is the blood of the birds. When someone says something bad about another person," he explained, "a bird is killed against this wall to get the spirit out."

23

Ariana stood over the jumble of rusted bowls and dented teapots, the cartons and tubs and buckets teeming with candlesticks and coins, key chains and spoons. Although it appeared to be overflowing with what looked like flea market junk, the last stall in the far corner of the souk had called to her, her addiction to shopping stifling the echoes of her parents' warning. What was she supposed to do anyway? Run away from the tree and the souk and lock herself up in Hani's car? She bent to pick a silver ring from the top of a pile in a woven basket. The watchman's stories hadn't made her feel any better about being in Bahla, but as he said, *the jinn won't come out unless you disturb them.* And she had no intention whatsoever of doing that. Besides, the last thing she wanted was to look like an idiot in front of Rachel. And Hani.

At first she didn't notice the man standing in the darkness of the tiny shop, amid the ropes and rifles and drums and canes hanging down from the ceiling and covering the walls. But how could she have missed him, she now thought as she took in the sight of the dark figure as big as a bear, in a crisp white *dish-dasha*, with eyes that seemed to look right into her soul. She smiled politely and twisted the ring off her finger.

"*Salaam alaikum,*" she heard Miza say beside her.

"*Wa alaikum a'salaam.*" The man's voice was rough like sand-paper, yet at the same time as soothing as honey. "Please," he said as he dug two small stools from under the rubble, "come in from the sun."

Ariana turned to find the others, but Hani was still deep in conversation with the old watchman, and Rachel was wandering the perimeter of the empty souk as if in a trance, her camera glued to her face. She reluctantly followed Miza up the two steps and into the crowded stall that was barely as big as a one-car garage.

"Sit." The big man gestured toward the low stools with his arms. Miza pointed to her stomach and shook her head. The man swept his arm across a small table, clearing the way for Miza as papers fluttered to the ground. Ariana lowered her rear slowly down toward the little plastic seat, taking care not to disturb the teetering heaps of merchandise as she folded herself into the shape of a paperclip, her knees poking uncomfortably into her chest. The surprisingly cool air was a welcome relief, but when the man reached across with a steaming cup of Arabian coffee she could feel the perspiration running down her neck. What she wouldn't give for a Starbucks iced latte, she thought as she politely sipped at the hot, dark brew. A plate of sticky dates was passed, buzzing with black flies. She watched as Miza simply shooed the pests away and helped herself.

"You have such lovely things here," Ariana said, fingering the random bits of hardware in the open box beside her.

"Thank you," said the man with a smile that revealed an impressive row of sparkling teeth. Following the path of Ariana's wide eyes, he turned to unhook a dagger from a spot high on the wall. "This one is a very old *khanjar*," he said as he pulled the heavy, curved sword from its silver sheath and handed it to her with pride.

"It would make a lovely gift for my father," she said, while imagining the look on her dad's face after he'd asked where she got it. She gingerly placed the blade down onto a pile of rags.

"Where is your father?" the man asked as he searched the overflowing walls for more treasures to share.

"St Albans. England. But I live in Dubai."

The man nodded. "Zanzibar?" he asked, pointing at Miza.

"Yes," she answered.

"Boy?" he asked, his dark eyes resting on her middle.

"Yes," she repeated softly.

Ariana chided herself for never asking. In fact, it was ridiculous how little she knew about this woman with whom she had spent much of the past four days. She must be losing her touch.

"It is the reason I am here," Miza added shyly.

At first the man seemed to not hear. It was Ariana who felt the need to respond. "To have your baby? Here? In Bahla?"

"Not to give birth. To get help."

Ariana noticed the man's thick eyebrows go up and down almost imperceptibly. "Help?" she asked, her voice cracking. "What kind of help?"

Miza shot her a cautious look and turned back to the man before posing her response, in Arabic.

The man seemed to hesitate, his eyes shifting back and forth between Miza and Ariana. After what felt like an eternity, he pushed back the sides of his curly salt-and-pepper hair with his thick fingers and said something that seemed to make Miza soften a little.

The conversation continued in Arabic, leaving Ariana alone with her dizzying thoughts. There was no question about it. She simply had to get out of this place, and sooner rather than later. There was obviously nothing here for Rachel, who, oddly, instead of huffing around impatiently like she usually did, appeared to be in her own little world, aiming her lens at who knows what. What was she seeing that Ariana wasn't? Ariana placed her empty cup on top of a tarnished tray and pushed herself up from the tiny stool.

"You need some handbags?" The man paused in his conversation with Miza to flash a creased smile in Ariana's direction, grabbing two straw purses from a hook. "Take them. A gift from me."

Ariana stood in the darkness of the shop as the words of her father rang in her ears. *If you go there, you are asking for trouble. It is like going to someone's house without an invitation.* And on top of them came the words of the watchman. *They won't come out unless you disturb them.* She backed out of the stall and into the sunlight. As charming as this shopkeeper might be, she had the distinct feeling he might possibly be someone to mess with the *jinn.*

"Careful!" Hani warned a little too late as she backed right into him, her stacked heel landing smack on top of his sandal-clad toes. He steadied her and then turned his attention to the big bear of a man, stepping up into the stall to greet him with three nose-to-nose touches, a custom she had noticed among the men of Oman. To Ariana, it seemed slightly unsanitary. Finally, after a little more of the usual back and forth, Hani uttered the words she longed to hear. "It is time to go."

Unfortunately, the four of them didn't get quite as far as Ariana had hoped. From the parking area in town Hani turned up a hill onto a street so narrow in places that the Lexus could barely squeeze through. Behind faded pink walls—scraped raw from unavoidable two-way encounters—only the tallest of homes and the tips of the palms were visible above the jasmine and bougainvillea. Even the intricate metal gates that led into the residences stood as barriers to the outside world, painted in thick coats of yellow and purple and green and blue. A quick look down an alleyway revealed a few signs of life—trashcans and hanging laundry, and a tree heavy with pomegranates pushing up valiantly between two stone facades—but all in all it was pretty quiet.

"So this is the scenic route back to the highway?" she asked.

"It is nice, yes? But no. It is the way to the potters."

"But—"

"They are very special, these potters," he insisted. "They are the ones who learned to do what they do from their fathers, who also learned it from *their* fathers. Rachel will get many photos. And I promise you, I will have you back in Nizwa by nightfall."

Ariana slumped down in her seat just as the car pulled into a dusty lot. Hani kept the engine running as he nodded at the crumbling buildings.

"You're not coming in with us?" she asked.

"They are expecting you. It will be fine. I will come back for you after I take Miza for an errand." Hani pointed at Rachel, who was already sailing through a massive iron gate that had been left halfway ajar. "And I know these men. They will allow photos of everything. This place will give her just what she needs. You will see."

Ariana slid out of the car and planted her two feet on the dry earth. Hani leaned across the seat and wound down the window. "I will be back in less than one hour!"

She shaded her eyes with one hand for a cautious look around. Pottery in every direction, resting on every available surface: crammed atop weather-beaten shelving, stacked to the ceiling in a little dark room behind an arched stone doorway, plopped onto each step of a steep stairway leading to a second landing. Some pieces were still orange, rough and unglazed; others had been painted. Some were wide and flat and others not, like the water holders drying bottoms-up under the sun, looking like an army of bald men seen from above. Across the lot she spied a pair of domed kilns made out of brick and mud, each with a tall smokestack teetering above. Indeed, the jumble of bricks and buckets and tarps and wooden planks was strong evidence of this being a genuine place of work.

She found Rachel standing quietly in a doorway, her camera pointed toward a dozen men crouched together on a woven mat, huddled over a tray of sliced pink watermelon, their sandals and shoes tossed off to the side. Their heads, some covered with *kumas*, others with turbans, bobbed up and down as they spat the slick seeds into their hands.

The first man to notice the two women standing there on the threshold smiled and rose from the floor. The rest of them followed, smoothing the fronts of their clothes as they stood. "Come," the tallest of the group said, ushering Rachel and Ariana into the darkness of a room illuminated only by the sunlight flowing through the open doorway behind them.

The first to get back to work was a bony man with a trim white beard and a short-sleeved button-down shirt, stiff with dried clay. He remained on his feet as a half-finished urn nearly as tall as he was began to spin beside him, its damp exterior wrapped in thick twine partway up its neck. Ariana and Rachel watched as he used a wet rag to smooth the outside with one hand while his other arm disappeared all the way up to the shoulder inside the urn. He shaped and reshaped until he seemed satisfied, then took one end of the twine between his fingers and let it unwind as the wheel continued to turn, unlashing the urn from its support. Ariana let out a breath she hadn't known she'd been holding in at the sight of the tall pot remaining firmly in place.

Next, a lanky younger man in an impossibly spotless white T-shirt and matching sarong gestured for the women to accompany him as he settled onto the seat behind a mud-splattered wheel. In less than four minutes he had turned a shapeless lump of clay into a delicate vase. Every part of his graceful hands had been used as a tool: the two thumbs that pressed firmly down into the wet mound at the center of the wheel, the steady fingers that gently coaxed the clay into a rising cylinder, the soft space between the fingers and thumb that smoothed the top, the edges of each fist to even the surface, the index finger that caressed the emerging neck until the other digits joined in with a gentle squeeze, the pinky that created a delicate lip with its steady tip. Ariana watched closely as his long brown fingers scissored around the top of the vase, leaving behind a fluted edge even more perfect than the ones she'd seen encircling the pies on that baking show back home.

The entire room was soon buzzing with activity. The men seemed to be moving in a dance they had practiced forever, their powerful hands and agile limbs working in sync as they paired up to stack fresh clay into piles of wet bricks, transfer partially finished pots onto empty shelves for drying, turn broken-down parts into more wheels that would turn endlessly into the evening. It *is* magic, she nearly said out loud, before the thought snapped her back to reality. She turned to hustle Rachel along.

But before she could speak, Rachel—at the urging of the younger potter—was removing the camera from around her neck and replacing it with a smock. She eased herself onto the round seat, pulled her hair back into a little ponytail and rolled up her sleeves as the man tossed a hunk of clay on the wheel before her. It began to spin between her knees. Rachel pressed first with her thumbs, just as she had seen him do, and when the pot-to-be rose a few inches she cupped her palms against the rotating surface as it wobbled from side to side.

"This is awesome," Rachel said in a voice Ariana had never heard before, with a smile she'd never seen. "I haven't done anything like this since art class in high school." The young man reached in to save her creation from collapse, then stood back to allow her to continue. Rachel seemed transfixed by the lump of wet earth before her, her eyes shining like two candles in the dimness of the room. "Really, Ariana. You should try it." She dipped her fingers into a bowl of dirty water as if it were a pot of gold. "It all just feels so incredibly amazing."

Ariana wrinkled her nose at the filthy brown mud splashed across Rachel's arms and the sludge embedded beneath her nails. She pointed to her own manicured hands and shook her head. But the truth was, it wasn't just the filth of the wet clay that made her keep her distance. There was no way she'd take the risk of touching *anything* in this place.

Rachel was too engrossed to notice Ariana slipping away to call Hani. It wasn't until she was outside that she remembered her disabled phone, still sitting useless in a bag of rice. The wind had kicked up, leaving the scattered tarps flapping and the palm trees swaying like hula dancers. Ariana checked her watch as she headed to the top of the driveway in search of the car.

It was then that she spied the roiling wall of sand in the distance. At first she thought it was smoke from a massive fire, but she'd seen this before from the windows of her high-rise in Dubai. Already the sky above her was becoming an orange haze. Suddenly the Lexus was right in front of her. "Get inside!" Hani yelled before jumping out and rushing through the gates to find Rachel. Through the back window Ariana watched the sandstorm approach like a slow-motion tidal wave, lifting the dirt up off the ground and whipping it into a frenzy.

"Wow!" Rachel slammed the car door and immediately turned her lens toward the barreling fury. "Where the hell did that come from?"

"We must hurry," Hani said as he started the car and turned up the hill. "First we must go get Miza," he explained before Ariana could question the route.

"We'll make it back to Nizwa before it gets too bad, right?"

"We will try."

Ariana's heart sank as she saw the doubt cross his face.

Hani turned on the high beams and emergency blinkers and stepped down harder on the gas, maneuvering the narrow roads as if he knew them by heart. Even the sudden gusts that seemed capable of pushing the car back the way it came didn't seem to sway his determination.

"Where is Miza, anyway?" Ariana asked as the dark horizon advanced like a distant herd of wild horses.

By now they had slowed, Hani squinting to make out the road ahead. Nobody spoke. The car echoed with the sound of sand against the glass as they continued to crawl up the hill that had all but disappeared from view. Hani spun the wheel sharply to the left and pulled to a stop just as day was turned instantly into night.

24

"Where are we? Whose place is this? Where's Miza?" Ariana's questions were snatched up by the howling wind before they could reach Hani's ears. She shielded her face with one arm and struggled against the violent force of the storm to follow him from the car toward a large, low house barely visible beneath the darkened sun. Rachel was close behind, the neck of her shirt hiked up to cover her mouth and nose. They managed to reach the front gate just as it, the house, and the three of them were swallowed up by an infinite cloud of red dust.

Holding tight to each other, they crossed a covered courtyard toward a heavy wooden door. Hani banged on it with his fist until it cracked open a sliver, the sand barging ahead like an unwelcome guest. A young woman, her black *abaya* billowing as if it were a parachute, hustled them inside and slammed the door against the ferocious wind.

Ariana stood and wiped the grit from her crusty, matted lashes as she took in the room around her. It was as long as a bowling lane and practically as narrow, the wood-paneled perimeter lined with brown velvet sofas, except for the one wall reserved for a huge television. She watched the muted screen in horror as a pack of spotted hyenas silently devoured a zebra, ripping it apart limb by limb.

"So what are we—" She turned to again question Hani before seeing he was involved in greeting two more women who had popped up in the room, indistinguishable from the others save for the hue of their headscarves. Like color-coded tokens in a board game, she thought. Rachel was busily brushing the thin layer of red from her jeans. Even despite the heavy front door shut tight and the room's only window buried behind heavy, thick drapery, the grainy dust was still managing to find its way into the room, gathering on every open surface like a new coat of paint.

A door to her left suddenly swung open as a little girl who wore a pleated yellow dress over long white leggings came barreling through. Hani bent and swept the child into the air, tossing her high above his head as she squealed with glee. The woman who had ushered them in from the storm appeared behind them, handing the girl a quick admonishment and a plastic tablecloth, which they both bent to spread smoothly across the overlapping rugs that covered the bulk of the tile floor. No sooner had they finished their task than the door flew open again as an even smaller child—a carbon copy of her older sister, right down to the jangling silver bangles on both dark ankles—joined the crowd, her hair still wet from a bath.

"Who *are* these people?" Ariana mouthed to Rachel, who simply shrugged her shoulders in response.

The woman in the purple headscarf, the one who had let them in, gestured toward the floor. Ariana raised her eyebrows at Hani.

"They are inviting you to sit and enjoy a meal," he explained.

"Oh no, I don't think so." Ariana shook her head as she adjusted the handbag on her shoulder. "We've got to get back." She wiped at the dust on the face of her watch. "Why, just look what time—"

Rachel took Ariana's wrist between her fingers, still flaked with clay, and gently pushed her arm back down to her side. She turned her eyes to Hani. "We'd be delighted."

The two of them lowered themselves to the floor as the rest of the group, including Hani, disappeared through the swinging door. "Bloody hell, Rachel!" Ariana whispered. "You know I can't be staying here any longer than I have to."

Rachel pointed to the front door and the dust that continued to infiltrate the room. "The storm? Remember?"

"I don't care about the damn storm!" she hissed. Already she'd felt too close for comfort to the mysteries of this town, as if she were on the verge of opening a gate that simply needed to stay shut. She felt herself shudder a little.

"Could you just stop already? Seriously, Ariana. Get a grip."

Ariana stood and climbed onto the sofa below the window and pulled back the heavy curtain, only to find the glass panes underneath not to be glass at all, but instead opaque, colored resin that suddenly made the room feel like a coffin.

"Is everything okay?" Hani had silently returned pushing a wooden teacart, its shelves heavy with plates of pears and oranges and bananas, dates, grapes and mangoes.

Ariana could feel her face warming as she reached one foot back toward the rug, knocking over a vase of faded plastic flowers in the process. "Just trying to check on the weather." She smiled weakly.

"Yes. It is supposed to be a very big storm. We will have to wait to see when we can go back to Nizwa." He left the cart behind and retreated through the door.

"I swear, I am done with this, full stop." Ariana thumped down to the floor next to Rachel. "And where is Miza, anyway?"

"Not sure," Rachel answered as she took out the camera she'd kept protected beneath her shirt.

"You know, I don't think it was just on a lark that she decided to follow you here."

"Uh-huh." Rachel twisted her torso and began to click, aiming her lens at anything and everything in the room.

"She had her reasons."

This time it was the green-topped woman who entered with food—a covered dish that she placed with care in the center of the plastic sheet.

"I said, she had her reasons," Ariana repeated in a loud whisper as soon as the woman was through the door.

"I heard you." Rachel turned her lens on the food before her. "So?"

"So what?"

"Don't you want to know what those reasons are?"

Rachel didn't respond.

"You know, the Zanzibaris, they're into all sorts of black magic."

"Uh-huh. I know."

"You know there are supposedly lots of healers here in Bahla, right?"

"I know."

"Well, I think Miza's here to find one."

"I know."

"And I think she might have found one at the souk. A witch doctor, like—Wait. What? Did you say *you know*?"

"Uh-huh."

"As in you knew she was coming to Bahla for that purpose?"

"That's what I said."

"How could you know and I didn't?"

"Because she talked. And I listened."

"And you didn't tell me this why?"

"Because it was her business. It *is* her business. Not mine, and not yours."

"What the hell, Rachel!"

Ariana sat fuming as Hani returned to join them on the floor. "We start with the sweets," he said as he dipped his fingers into a bowl of warm water before passing it to her to wash her hands. "You are not hungry?" He gestured to Rachel. "*Fadal.* Help yourself. Please."

Rachel dug in as if she hadn't eaten in a week. Ariana reluctantly picked an apple from the bowl.

"*Halwa?*" Hani held out a glass bowl filled with a thick, wobbly paste. Ariana scanned the floor for a spoon, or even a fork, but Hani shook his head, holding up his fingers.

Rachel reached across and scooped up a mouthful with her hand. "It's really good! Try it."

Hani waited with the bowl still resting in his hand. Ariana plunged two fingers deep into the mess and flung them into her mouth before the goo could ooze onto her lap. The sweet glop tasted of honey and roses, and might have been better if it weren't for the grit from the storm that remained in her mouth, and the unease that had settled in the pit of her stomach.

She licked her sticky fingers and checked her watch again, as if it held the key to her escape from this place. The door swung open and yet another platter was placed on the floor in front of her. Hani reached to remove the lid from a bowl of steaming rice and peeled back the foil from a platter holding saucy chunks of meat. The scent of cloves and cinnamon rose into the air. "There is fish also, I think," he said as he peeked under the covers of more dishes strewn across the plastic sheet. Again the door swung open.

"*More* food?" Ariana muttered as her eyes lifted upward. And there stood Miza, and behind her the big, dark man from the souk, his looming presence so intense that it made her feel as though she were melting.

Ariana remained motionless on the floor as Hani rose to greet him with a kiss on the hand, then one on the forehead.

"I think you have already met my father?" he said as he turned to Ariana with a smile.

25

Sabra clenched the damp pillow under her burning cheek as her tears continued to fall. Five days she had spent under her uncle's roof, five long days confined to the house under her aunt's watchful eye.

The woman had not been pleased at all when her husband arrived home from Stone Town dragging Sabra by the arm. She had been sitting outside in the empty doorframe as the children played in the shadows of the night, tossing pebbles against the rough cinderblocks, squealing at nothing Sabra could see.

"What were you thinking?" her aunt had screamed at her husband. "You can barely feed the mouths of your own children, let alone that of your dead brother's. Just what am I supposed to do with that useless creature underfoot all day? A girl who can barely keep her own shoes tied, let alone sweep a floor or cook a meal."

"I am only taking back what is rightfully mine," her uncle bellowed back, flinging Sabra inside through the doorway that had no door.

"So it is your pride that brings us this gift," she heard her aunt snort. "What, did her fancy sister finally tire of caring for her? Is she too busy with her rich Omani man to bother with this one?"

"It is clear that her sister cares nothing for her." Her uncle's words came out slowly and deliberately, as if he wanted to make sure Sabra heard. "But to me—to me she is of value."

"And what value is that?" her aunt snapped back.

"You will see. I am not a stupid man. I have a plan."

"You have a plan," his wife repeated, her words dulled by disbelief. "Well, your plan had better include a way to bring more food into this home, or we will all starve to death."

That night Sabra had lain awake in the creaky cot she had once shared with Miza. Though the moon was full, sending shadows to the ground as she and her uncle wound their way through the dusty roads after having been dropped off by the *daladala*, the bus that brought them from Stone Town, in the blackness of the familiar room she could not even make out the fingers of her own hand. Like the windows of most of the houses in the village, hers was blocked tight to keep out the sun. She remembered how she used to dream of prying the thin iron sheets open with a kitchen knife or the edge of the metal dustpan to let in the daylight during those long afternoons waiting for Miza to come home from the sea. Back then the room had felt like a secret cave. Now it felt like a prison.

Sabra could tell it was early morning only by the sounds of the roosters. She touched a match to the wick of the kerosene lamp and stretched, her long legs cramped from so much lying around. If only her aunt would allow her outside for some fresh air, she thought. And if she did, Sabra also thought, she would begin to run, and would not stop running until she was as far away from this room and this house and this village as her legs would take her. She wiped the dampness from her face and stooped to bring her eye to the one place where she knew the sunlight could sneak in—a tiny gap where the iron sheets did not quite meet.

"Sabra, is that you?"

She leaped back from the window, her heart pounding.

"It is me," the voice continued in a whisper. "It's Bi-Zena."

Sabra couldn't help but smile at the memory of the old woman who always seemed to save her toothless smile for Sabra, and even then only when no one else was looking. "Bi-Zena!" she whispered back excitedly, her lips held close to the open crack. "What are you doing here?"

"I'm here for you."

"Did Miza send you? How did you know I was here?" Sabra remembered how her sister used to tell her that Bi-Zena had eyes that could see it all, that she knew everything about everyone in the village. Miza had even used Bi-Zena's name as a warning to Sabra to make sure she behaved when no one was around to watch her.

"No, child, your sister did not send me. It was the other seaweed women who have been talking of your return to the village. They say your sister left you behind, that she went to go live in Oman with her husband."

"That is what my uncle says as well! But it's not true. Yes, she is in Oman, but only to have her baby. Then she is coming back home. Miza would never leave me."

"I was sure of that. They say she left you to live with your uncle. That I could never believe."

"It was my uncle who forced me to come here! He stole me from our home. Hoda, our maid, was watching me, but he threatened her and scared her away."

"Does your sister know you are here?"

"He took my phone from me. Usually we send messages every day, but without my phone . . ." Sabra struggled not to cry.

"Your uncle, he is treating you well?" Bi-Zena's voice hardened with the question. "He is not bothering you?"

"I have not seen him much."

"That is good."

"He must be very busy with his duties as the village elder."

Bi-Zena did not answer.

"And busy making his plan."

"Plan? What plan?"

"He told my auntie he has a plan for me. So she should not worry about the expense of having me here."

"And you know nothing more?"

Sabra shook her head, forgetting for a moment that Bi-Zena could not see her.

"Tell me the number for your sister. I will find someone who has a phone to let her know you are here."

"But I don't even know the number she is using." Sabra could feel the tears starting up again. "We just send our messages back and forth, that's all. Miza told me to memorize the number, but I didn't listen."

For a moment there was silence outside the window. Sabra had to wonder if her uncle had spied the old woman. But then Bi-Zena's response came through, with a sternness that made Sabra stiffen. "Listen to me, child, and listen closely. I have my own plan. Tomorrow morning I will come back.

I will be watching. And when your auntie leaves to go to the market, I will come and pay a visit to your uncle. When you see me, you must pretend you barely remember me, that you do not care. He must not know we have spoken. Do you understand?"

"Yes, Bi-Zena."

"Good. And in the meantime you must keep your eyes and ears open. If you should see or hear from anyone in the village, do not speak to them. We do not need our plans turning into their gossip. These people are afraid of your uncle, and will tell him anything if they think it will put them in good favor."

Sabra nodded. "I will be careful, *mama*."

"And listen carefully. Try to hear what your uncle is planning."

"Yes."

"I will be back in the morning. I promise."

"I know." Sabra put her hand flat against the cool iron sheet, as if it would bring her closer to the woman's soft touch. But instead what she felt was the tickle of something crinkly against her palm. Sabra lifted her hand and smiled as she watched the edge of a cellophane wrapper being pushed through the crack. A lollipop, the same as Bi-Zena used to sneak to her while she sat digging bottomless holes in the white sand, waiting for her sister to finish with her work. "Thank you," she whispered as the candy dropped into her hand. And then the old woman was gone.

As Sabra tucked the treat away, to be saved for later, her hand brushed against the *kanga* she'd so hastily stuffed in the satchel the day her uncle had come for her. Now she spread the piece of orange cotton over the cot, the missing half a painful reminder of her sister and the ocean that lay between them.

Sabra smoothed the blue border of the cloth gently with her hand as she took in the fading words she'd never before paid attention to, hearing their meaning for the very first time in her life. *Kila ndege huruka kwa bawa lake.* Every bird flies with its own wings.

26

Hani's father swatted the pile of tasseled pillows off the brown velvet sofa, sending them tumbling to the ground. When he bent to help Ariana up from her seat on the floor, Rachel noticed her flinch, and noticed as well her attempt to hide the reaction by pretending it was simply a sudden chill. Rachel understood why he had thought Ariana to be in trouble. When Hani introduced his father, Ariana looked as though she'd been kicked in the stomach. And though the color had suddenly drained from her face and beads of sweat seemed to be multiplying on her forehead, she was now waving away the man's concern with a delicate flick of her hand and a weak smile.

"I'm fine. No worries." Ariana's voice trembled. "If you don't mind, I think I just need to go spend a penny."

The others in the room turned to each other, confused.

"I'm sorry. I mean visit the loo."

"Visit who?" Hani's eyebrows practically rose to his hairline.

"Use the ladies' room?"

Hani's father pointed toward the courtyard.

"I will show you the facilities for our guests," Hani offered.

Rachel made a move to help her shaky friend up, only to find her own legs numb from the lack of blood. She remained on the floor as Hani cracked open the front door and motioned for Ariana to follow. "It is fine," he assured her. "The wind has quieted for now."

Hani's father lifted two half-empty platters off the mat and pushed his way through the swinging door with a heavy shoulder. Rachel flattened her palms onto the sofa behind her and hoisted herself onto the cushion, her two useless legs buzzing with pins and needles. She was bent over, massaging her calves when he returned through the door, tapping away at a phone as he lowered himself onto the sofa beside her.

"You have eaten enough?" Hani's father asked.

Rachel nodded. "Yes. Thank you."

"Good."

Rachel sat and listened to the sound of his pecking as it filled the silence of the room. "So where *is* Miza?" she finally asked.

"Resting." He cocked his head toward the swinging door. "She is with my wife and daughters. They are taking care of her." He went back to his phone.

Rachel shifted in her seat, a little unnerved by the presence of this giant of a man. "So she's okay?"

Hani's father grunted.

"Are you going to do something to, I mean, for her?"

He shrugged his broad shoulders without looking up from the screen.

She struggled for something else to say. What was it about this guy that was making her so uneasy? And who could he be so busy texting with anyway? He was as bad as Ariana with that thing.

As if reading her thoughts, the man put down the phone and ran his fingers through his curly hair. "And you, you are okay?"

"Me?" Rachel suddenly felt as though his dark eyes were looking right through her.

"Yes, you."

"I'm good."

"Your sleep problem, it does not bother you?"

She stiffened at the question. "What do you mean?"

"There is a remedy. To give more energy. But only if you are interested."

"How did you know I had a sleep problem?"

Again he shrugged his shoulders, and went back to his pinging phone. No way, Rachel thought. The guy's just trying to impress me with a little beginner's luck. Really, who doesn't have sleep problems?

"And your stomach? How is it doing?"

"Just like any other poor schmuck who's spent way too much time on the road." Rachel stopped her hand from traveling to the spot just left of her belly button, the one that had been prone to spasms for as long as she could remember. "But might you have something for my chronic thyroid issue?" she countered, remembering a drug ad she'd seen on television.

"Your thyroid is fine," he answered with a chuckle that said he knew she'd been testing him. "But that scar on your arm, that I could make fade to nothing."

Rachel's eyes flew to the spot of her tattoo, which remained completely covered by the cloth of her sleeve. The man stood and strutted away through the swinging door with the confidence of a rock star exiting the stage, leaving Rachel literally open-mouthed. It was the sound of raised voices coming from the courtyard that snapped her out of her bewilderment.

"That's not the point!" Ariana was shouting.

"Then you must explain," Hani pleaded.

"How could you not tell me?"

"Tell you what? That my father is a doctor? That he is a man who helps those who need him? I already told you that, when we were at the *wadi*."

"You call *that* a doctor?"

"*That?* And what is the difference what my father does with his time?"

"Oh, come on, Hani. You know how I feel about this. The next thing you'll tell me is that you're mixed up in all this crap too!"

"Well, in fact, I am mixed up in all this 'crap', and happen to be learning it from my father. I am his apprentice." Rachel could hear the pride in his response.

"Ha! That's just fucking perfect. Now please, just go get your keys and take us back to Nizwa."

"I cannot do that."

"Stop messing with me, Hani."

"I am serious. The storm is not yet over, and we are not sure what path it is taking. There is no way we can pass through on the road to Nizwa before tomorrow. The visibility is close to zero, and the sand will choke the engine of the car. We cannot leave until it is safe."

"You can't be telling me this!"

Rachel jumped at the desperation in Ariana's voice. "Is everything okay?" she asked as she poked her head out the door.

"No, everything is not okay *at all*!" Ariana snapped.

"It is fine," Hani assured her, his eyes still on Ariana. "It is just that Ariana seems to think she is too good for us, for my family, and all our 'crap'."

"That is not what I said!"

"Then what is it you said?" Hani spat out his words one by one. "Please explain it to me, so that I can understand."

"Maybe we should just go," Rachel suggested.

Hani turned to her, the anger in his face easing for a brief moment. "I'm sorry, Rachel. That will not be possible. The storm will prevent us from driving back to Nizwa for now. But you are both most welcome to stay here until it is safe."

"That is *not* happening," Ariana began. "No way I'm staying here. I can't even be in this house!"

"And what is wrong with this house?" he snapped back.

"That's very kind of you, Hani," Rachel interrupted, embarrassed by Ariana's over-the-top reaction. "But I think I saw a small hotel on our way up the hill, am I right?" She sighed at the thought of a long night ahead spent calming down her fixer.

"Well, yes, if that is what you want. I will walk with you there. But really—"

Before Hani could finish, Ariana was already gone from the courtyard and out the front gate. "Shit," Rachel said out loud, rushing back into the sitting room to grab her backpack and Ariana's purse. She stopped Hani at the door. "It's okay, Hani. I remember where the hotel is. Let me talk to her, and we'll check in with you tomorrow morning." Rachel ran to catch up with Ariana, fearing that in her frantic state of mind the woman would be hopelessly lost within five minutes.

Out on the deserted street the wind was still strong, sending garbage and debris flying through the darkness with each lusty exhale. Rachel had no idea of the time—the surrounding storm had made it impossible to tell when day had passed into night.

Ariana had not gotten far, and was uncharacteristically silent as they followed the labyrinth of roads leading from Hani's father's home. And though Rachel could practically hear her seething, she was too focused on the challenge of finding that damn hotel to offer any consolation. Despite the aid from a full moon that had appeared from behind the receding curtain of dust, nothing was looking remotely familiar, and with nobody to ask for directions it was beginning to look hopeless as they neared the bottom of the hill.

When she recognized the gates of the old souk, she grabbed Ariana's arm and hurried inside, seeking shelter from the erratic gusts and welcoming the chance to regroup.

Suddenly things fell quiet, the wind rebuffed by the thickness of the four ancient walls. They stood at the edge of a row of shuttered stalls, the shadows of the notorious tree reaching toward them like bony fingers from the center of the courtyard.

"What the hell are we doing in here?" Ariana's panic echoed through the souk.

"Jesus, Ariana, calm down. It's okay. I'm just trying to get my bearings, all right?" Rachel brushed the sand from her sleeves, the dizziness she'd felt in the souk earlier that day returning like a roaring tide to a battered shore.

"*Calm down?*"

"Ariana, nothing has happened." Rachel took a deep breath. "We're fine."

"Maybe you're fine, but I am far from it." Ariana sounded as if she were about to crack.

"What the hell is going on with you?" Rachel watched as Ariana began to pace in a little circle, shaking her head and muttering to herself as she went round and round, making Rachel even dizzier than she already was.

She finally stopped. "That man?" Ariana pointed toward the empty stall in the far corner. "Hani's father? He's the one Miza went to see, you know."

"So I gathered." Rachel shifted her backpack to the other shoulder.

"And his son! He is even worse, lying about it all."

"Well, technically, I don't think he lied. He may not have been specific about his family, but he didn't lie. Give the guy a break, would you?" Rachel closed her eyes, straining to remember the route they had taken from the souk earlier, in the car.

"Clearly he's not to be trusted! And if he lies about that, no doubt he lies about everything else. I'll bet he didn't mean one word of the things he said to me."

"Get a grip, Ariana. He seems like a perfectly nice guy to me."

"Ha! They're all like that. Always telling you you're different than other women, how smart you are, how beautiful you are inside and out. They see a woman who doesn't cover, and to them it means only one thing. A bunch of scam artists if you ask me. And apparently he's no different from the rest of them. I should have known better."

"Come on—"

By now Ariana was practically hyperventilating. "And being from a family like that, what kind of magic must *he* have used on me to make me fall for his lies? He probably put something in my food, or maybe in my drink yesterday at the *wadi*. What else could explain it?" Her head dropped down heavily into her hands. "Oh, why am I such an idiot?" She crumpled down onto the stoop of the stall behind them with a sob.

"Shit, Ariana. What exactly did you two do yesterday?"

"Nothing!"

"You did something. I know it."

"Stop, Rachel."

"Well, whatever. You're both adults." Rachel rubbed her temples. "Seriously? Hani seems to be kind of a great guy. And it's obvious that he does have feelings for you."

"No he doesn't." Ariana wiped at her face with her sleeve.

"Now you *are* being an idiot."

"Bugger off, Rachel!"

"Well, he does. And it's been pretty clear that you have the hots for him as well."

"I do not! And so what if I did? There's no way I could ever be in any sort of relationship with that kind of man, with that kind of family."

"Why not? They seem perfectly nice to me." All Rachel wanted was a bottle of water and a place to lie down.

"What don't you get about this? People like that are dangerous!"

"People *like that*? What the hell does that even mean?"

"It's *black magic*, Rachel. These people have powers that are not always used for good. Don't you think that if they can convince the *jinn* to leave a person alone they can also talk them into doing things for *them*? These people are not safe to be around, are not to be trusted. And believe me, they aren't the ones to turn to for help. It is God, and only God, who is the ultimate protector." Ariana's face dropped into her hands. "It's all my own fault," she cried. "Why didn't I listen to my parents?"

"Would you just stop already? Jesus, Ariana—wait, did you hear that?"

"What? Hear what?" Ariana's head jerked up, her eyes darting frantically from one end of the souk to the other.

"Nothing. I just thought—"

"Thought what? What did you hear?" She stumbled as she rose from the stoop.

"Someone. Something. *Shhh*, listen."

The whispers that had caught Rachel's ear were now multiplying, bubbling from the dark corners of the square like the buzzing of a curious mob.

"Who's there?" Rachel shouted. And then, in an instant, silence. "Shit. That was *really* weird." She heaved a sigh as she steadied herself against the archway's worn wooden pillar.

"Rachel! Don't!"

Ariana's screamed warning was the last thing Rachel remembered hearing before it all went dark.

27

Stupid. Stupid. Stupid. Stupid. Hani's thoughts echoed his heavy footsteps as he paced the length of the patio's four walls. *What was I thinking, letting things get so far with that ridiculous woman? I must have been out of my mind. A woman like that, with her fancy clothes and fancy ideas and her nose in the air, without an ounce of respect for who I am, who could never love or respect my family for who they are. How could I have been taken by her, knowing how wrong she was for me?* The argument with Ariana had left him bitter and bruised. But it wasn't until after he exchanged words with his mother that he realized just how selfishly he'd behaved with Ariana.

"Well, that will be that," his mother had said as she cleared away the rest of the meal.

"That will be what?" he asked.

"The way that girl looked at you, it is clear what she thought."

Hani could feel his face redden.

"Don't act like you do not know what I'm talking about. You are a man, not a boy."

"Don't worry, Mother. Ariana is not the woman for me."

"I know that. But do you think she knew that? At least now she does."

"So you were listening?"

"It was hard not to hear her squawking."

Hani tried hard to remember exactly what had been said.

"A woman of that age. I am sure she has been divorced. Am I right?"

Hani didn't answer.

"And does she not even know about the law that forbids an Omani from marrying a foreigner?"

"There are ways to get permission."

"Ah, so you *have* thought about this woman in this way!"

"No!" Hani protested. "It was just a response to your question."

"Well, it does not matter now."

"No, it does not."

"Good."

"Yes. Good."

Her words only served to reinforce what Hani had known all along. No matter what he had thought about Ariana, his mother would never have given her permission. And he would never have dishonored his mother by not heeding her wishes. But that did not mean he had to act like a snake. Imagine if someone had carried on with one of his sisters the way he had carried on with Ariana. He knew plenty of brothers who would do terrible things to avenge those who had dishonored their sisters the way he had dishonored her. The shame washed over him like blood from a slaughter. He had to go find her.

Though there was truly no forgiveness for what he had done, he nevertheless had to apologize. Hani headed to the front gate.

"Where are you going?" his mother called from the doorway of the house.

"I will go see that they got to the hotel without a problem."

His mother raised one eyebrow in a look he knew well.

"They are guests in our country," he said. "We cannot forget the way of our people, Mother. We must make sure they feel welcome and safe."

The hotel was dark, the lights coming on one by one as Hani pounded on the heavy wooden door. "We are closed!" a voice shouted from inside. "No more room!"

"Please," Hani pleaded. "I am looking for two women."

"We are not that kind of place!" the man yelled through the door.

"No, they are my friends. It is me, Hani. I need to know they are safe."

"There are no two women staying in this hotel. Say *salaam* to your father for me, and get home safely. Goodnight!"

Hani watched as the lights went off, then turned and peered into the darkness before him. "Ariana!" he roared into the night. "Rachel! Where are you?"

The streets were silent, save for the scraping of papers and leaves as they skittered across the ground under the spell of the winds. "Ariana!" Hani began the trek downward, his eyes peeled for any trace of the two women, pausing every few steps to listen for voices, footsteps, anything.

It wasn't until he was nearly at the bottom of the hill that he heard Ariana's shouts through the open entryway of the souk. "Rachel!" she cried. "Where are you?"

He found Ariana trembling on the other side of the gate, looking so frail and frightened that he was tempted to once again take her in his arms.

"She's gone!" Ariana sobbed.

Hani's eyes flashed around the shadows of the souk. The moonlight shimmered in a macabre dance across the silent square.

"I swear, one minute she was right next to me, talking to me, and then she just disappeared!"

"You were both here in the souk?"

Ariana nodded.

"Rachel!" Now it was Hani's deep voice that echoed across the courtyard.

"What happened to her, Hani?"

Hani quickly turned his focus from where it had become fixed on the infamous doorway, the mysterious Pillar of Goats, hoping Ariana hadn't noticed. "I'm sure she will be fine."

"How do you know?" she wailed. "This can't be happening. We have to find her!"

"We will find her. Don't worry." Hani peered into the far corners of the souk, searching for movement.

"How can I not worry? I know what goes on here. I'm not an idiot!"

"This is very strange."

"Strange? *That's* what you people call this?" she shrieked.

"No, I mean it is strange that the gates to the souk are open. They are usually left closed, locked for the night. Nobody comes here after dark." Hani struggled to mask the worry in his voice. Suddenly a shadow passed overhead that made them both raise their heads in alarm.

"What was that?" Ariana moved in closer next to him.

"A cloud."

"A cloud? That was no cloud! Stop lying to me, Hani. Enough. Just stop it."

Hani felt Ariana's words cut straight into his heart. "Come," he said as he hurried her out of the souk. "Let's go and search the streets. The storm has settled, the moon is bright. We will find Rachel."

They roamed the winding streets surrounding the market, with not a word between them as they scoured every inch of road with eyes wide open, both taking turns yelling out Rachel's name. Nearly an hour of searching turned up nothing but overturned garbage bins, stray cats, and parked cars nearly indistinguishable under inches of red-orange dust. Hani was about to suggest they return home and resume their search in the daylight when Ariana suddenly came to a halt at an intersection in the road.

"Quick, give me your phone," she cried. In the phone's bright light Hani saw what she had seen—the deep imprint of a small but heavy boot stamped squarely into the dust to their left. "It's her! I know it." Ariana exhaled with both a sob and a laugh. "Her and her stupid Timberlands."

"They continue that way." Hani pointed to where the road narrowed into a dim alleyway. "But where did they come from?" To their right, the road leading up to that first footprint was completely untouched, the thick layer of sand as smooth as a freshly vacuumed carpet.

"Come on!" Ariana started down the dark corridor, Hani following the beacon of light from the phone as it washed from side to side across the alley in front of them. "Up there!" His eyes followed the direction of Ariana's trembling finger to where, in the distance, he saw the silhouette of a hunched figure rocking back and forth like a pendulum, smack in the middle of the narrow road.

They rushed together to where Rachel stood, her matted hair and glazed eyes speaking of an experience far beyond that of a person who had simply lost her way.

Ariana threw her arms around Rachel and squeezed tight, only to be met by a stiffness that Hani could almost feel himself. "You're here! Are you all right? I was so worried about you!" She stood back a little and looked Rachel over from top to bottom and back again, as though reassuring herself that the woman was still in one piece. "What happened? Who did this to you?"

Rachel remained silent, her eyes clouded with confusion.

"We must get her home," Hani insisted as he slid the backpack from Rachel's shoulders. Ariana took the lead, holding fast to her friend's arm. "You are coming to my home as well?" Hani called from behind.

Ariana stopped and turned. "Of course I'm coming. I can't leave her alone in this state. What kind of a person do you take me for?"

"I'm sorry, Ariana. It's just that after what you said before—"

"Stop, Hani." She waited for Hani to pass, and then followed him back up the hill in silence with Rachel safely in her grasp.

The sitting room was quiet when they entered, the television off, the dishes and mat gone from view, the dust swept away, the pillows neatly arranged across the long sofas. Hani placed Rachel's backpack gently on the floor as Ariana guided her down to a seat, removing her vest and lifting her legs onto the cushion as Hani handed her a thick blanket to spread across Rachel's shivering body.

"I feel like the morning after an all-nighter. What happened to me?" Rachel's voice was indeed slightly slurred, her eyes glassy and dull.

"You're asking me?" Ariana scooched in beside her and took Rachel's limp hand in her own.

"Well, I sure don't know. Did I pass out or something?"

Ariana shook her head. "Not that I know of."

"I must have. I feel so weak."

"But I don't think you did."

"My camera!" Rachel bolted upright.

"*Shhh*, it's right here. Calm down."

She slumped back onto the pillows. "So how did I get there, where you found me?"

Ariana turned to Hani for an answer.

"Please," he said with a finger to his lips, "do not wake my family." He poured water from a pitcher on the teacart and handed the glass to Rachel.

"So how *did* I get there?" she asked again, this time in a whisper.

"I'm not sure," Ariana answered, her eyes still on Hani.

"What do you mean you're not sure? The last thing I remember we were together, in the souk. Right?"

"We were."

"And?"

"And then you were gone."

"That's crazy! Maybe we *both* passed out or something," suggested Rachel.

"That's not what happened," Ariana responded.

"Must have."

Ariana again turned to Hani. He shrugged his shoulders.

"Wait." Rachel raised herself up onto her elbows. "That old woman, the one with the goat. She was there! She grabbed my arm, and I left with her."

Hani saw Ariana's eyes suddenly widen, and then just as quickly return to normal. "There was no woman with a goat, Rachel. There was nobody there but us."

"She wanted to show me something. I think I might have taken pictures." Rachel lunged for her backpack, only to fall back dizzily onto the sofa.

"You must try to relax. For your health." Hani held his arms stiffly at his sides. "Please, have some more water."

"But you *must* have seen her, Ariana. She was right there!"

"I swear, Rachel, nobody was there. Nobody that I could see, at least."

"But she was! Maybe you were just too upset about everything else to notice."

Hani felt Rachel's eyes upon him as he turned his back to the two women. "I will get some tea."

By the time he returned with the tray, a restless Rachel had stepped out to the patio to wash the dust from her face and arms. He sat on the sofa across from Ariana. "I am sorry you are stuck here for the night," he said as he poured from the pot.

"Sometimes you do what you have to do." Ariana's gaze was pointed toward her feet. "What happened to her, Hani?"

"Don't worry. She will be all right."

"How can you be sure of that?" Her head shot up. "She vanished right in front of my eyes! I might have been upset, but I'm not blind."

Now it was Hani who looked awkwardly away. "I will take you both back to Nizwa first thing in the morning, after breakfast," he said.

"No need. I'll use Rachel's phone to arrange for a real driver. We'll be gone before you and your family are up."

"If that is what you want."

"Yes, it's what I want."

"Look, Ariana—"

"Please, don't."

Hani stood to hand her a cup, the steam curling over his outstretched hand like a thick morning fog. "I'm so sorry, Ariana," he blurted out. "*Inshallah* you will find all you want and all your dreams of happiness will come true."

"And you as well." Ariana bowed her head and blew gently into her tea.

"Well, goodnight then." He stood over her, mesmerized by the radiance of the dark curls tumbling over her shoulders. "I mean, goodbye."

"Goodbye then," she repeated, her voice nearly swallowed by the silence in the room.

28

The syrupy smell of smoldering incense crept up through her nostrils before Ariana coughed herself awake. She bolted upright to find the sitting room filled with smoke.

"Your friend, she could not sleep."

Ariana blinked twice at the sight of the huge man resting on his knees in the middle of the room. Beside him, atop a small prayer rug, sat Rachel with her back to Ariana, her head and torso shrouded in a sheer purple shawl embroidered in gold.

"What time is it? What's going on? What are you doing?"

"*Shhh*. Relax and go back to sleep. It is still night," Hani's father answered, his voice smooth and calm. "And no worries. She will be fine."

Ariana eyed the long, thin cane resting by his side. "Rachel? Is that really you under there? Are you okay?" She stood and started drowsily toward the covered woman.

"Please." Hani's father stopped her with an outstretched palm.

"It's okay, Ariana," Rachel said without turning around. "I'm hoping Hani's father might be able to help me figure out what happened tonight."

"Oh, no. You really shouldn't be—"

"Quiet. No talking." The man began to rub his hands together, his long fingers glistening with oil.

"You have got to be kidding me." Ariana plopped back down on the sofa with a knot in the pit of her stomach, praying that this was all just a bad dream.

"If you would like to wait elsewhere, that can be arranged."

Ariana's eyes followed the chain of tiny stitched flowers climbing the back of the gauzy purple shawl. Then she noticed the charred holes that had erupted between the sequined petals, telling tales of close calls with catastrophe in this very room. "If you think I'm going to leave her here alone, you're crazy." She hugged a pillow close and folded herself into a corner of the sofa, wishing for it all to be over.

"Now close your eyes," Hani's father instructed Rachel. "Do not open them. And please, no talking." Ariana's heart flew into double time as she watched him slide a smoking brass urn under the purple tent, where it nearly rested against Rachel's back. As the cloying odor of frankincense continued to fill the room, Hani's father leaned in close to Rachel's ear.

"It's hot," Rachel answered to a question Ariana couldn't hear. And then he began to chant. The Arabic words were spoken softly, in a continuous stream that reminded Ariana of the buzz from a swarm of insects. She wondered how the man could breathe, as he never seemed to pause for air. Finally, after a good ten minutes, the chanting stopped.

"How are you? How is your head?" He sat back on his heels.

"Okay. It hurts a little." Rachel sounded subdued, almost drugged.

The man began to drone again, his words becoming softer and softer, as if someone were turning down the volume bit by bit. Even Ariana was finding it calming to the point of being nearly hypnotic. Rachel remained quiet, her stillness broken only by an occasional bob of the head, as if she were fighting the urge to nod off.

"How is your head?" he asked again.

"Good." Now Rachel sounded as if she were in a trance.

"And your chest?"

"Good."

Ariana choked a little at the sight of the smoke thickening under the shawl. But Rachel's breathing seemed to remain remarkably untroubled.

Then Hani's father scooted around behind Rachel, slid the brass burner aside and gently guided her limp body down until she lay prone on the floor, her head resting on a pillow. He rearranged the purple cloth to cover her from head to ankle, leaving her bare feet sticking out like two flags in the wind. Ariana leaned forward to confirm the sight of Rachel's chest slowly rising and falling as if she were checking on a sleeping infant.

Hani's father picked up the cane and placed it at an angle across Rachel's stomach. Taking the crown of her head into one large palm, his thumb resting on the middle of her forehead, he resumed his recitations. He paused only to adjust the cane, straightening it across Rachel's upper thighs. Leaning in toward her ear, his voice became a whisper. Rachel's legs jerked slightly. The man nodded with satisfaction in Ariana's direction, and lowered the cane slightly to a spot right above Rachel's knees, never once breaking his mumbled lullaby. As he continued to chant, the movement in her legs increased. It was as if they were awakening to a life of their own, the movement following the path of the stick as Hani's father gradually placed it lower and lower until it was resting on Rachel's ankles. Then he stopped.

"Come and sit." He stood over Rachel and waited as she pushed herself halfway up with her hands and scooted backwards until her spine was resting against the bottom of the sofa, across the narrow room from a wide-eyed Ariana. Hani's father removed the purple covering from her head and spread it across her legs. Though pale and dazed, she seemed more relaxed than Ariana had ever seen her before.

"Wait, what is that?" Ariana asked as the man handed a tall glass of orange liquid to Rachel.

"No worries. It is a blend of herbs. Twenty-four herbs. It is made special for her by me."

"Which herbs?" Ariana continued. "Exactly what is in there?" She grabbed the glass away before Rachel could finish.

Now Hani's father turned his attention to Rachel's feet, which seemed to be twitching even more than before.

"They're so cold," Rachel complained quietly.

The man simply nodded. Then he took her right ankle into his hand and turned her foot inwards. "Now we wait."

"Wait for what?" Ariana asked nervously.

"Watch," he answered. "You will see."

The shawl across Rachel's legs began to vibrate. Faster and faster it shook from the force of the spasms raging through her. Then, just as Ariana jumped to her feet to somehow come to her rescue, Rachel let out a wail that shook the house, as if something deep inside had burst wide open.

Hani's father waved Ariana off with a hand, and helped Rachel up to a seat on the sofa. "Now you must lie back and sleep," he said to her.

29

The sun seemed to pause directly behind the thick colored windowpanes, making them glow, for an instant, as if they were the most magnificent stained glass in the Sultan's mosque. Ariana stretched her weary limbs and rose silently from the sofa, careful not to wake Rachel, who remained as still as a corpse under a blanket.

Slipping out the front door and into the covered courtyard, she stopped to savor the calm before performing her morning ablutions. The fury that had swept the earth to the skies the day before had completely passed, leaving a thin coating of dust that had piled high into little mountains in the corners as the only evidence of its visit. By the light of day things didn't seem quite so frightening, but that didn't mean she was any less anxious to leave.

The water from the marble sink felt like cool velvet as it splashed across her face, washing away the last remnants of the storm while giving her the strength to face a long day after a sleepless night. Ariana helped herself to a clean towel from a pile beneath the sink, shook open the folds and floated it down to cover a spot on the dusty ground. She then pulled the scarf from her handbag and draped it over her head and shoulders, and, using the sun as her guide, she kneeled facing Mecca for her morning prayers.

Rachel was up by the time she returned, perched on the edge of the sofa with her head in her hands.

"How are you today?" Ariana brushed Rachel's hair from her face.

Rachel lifted her eyes, looking surprisingly bright and alert. "I'm good, I guess. When I finally did sleep, I slept like a log."

"It's no wonder. Who knows what he slipped into that drink? Personally, I didn't sleep a wink."

"Sorry. I'm sure the whole thing must have freaked you out."

Ariana laughed a little. "That's putting it mildly. I am so ready to be gone from here it's not funny." She took a tube of gloss from her purse and dabbed it onto her lips with her pinky finger. "I have to say, from my perspective it was quite terrifying. Yet you seemed so calm! Weren't you scared?"

Rachel hesitated for a moment. "No, not scared. But when he put that cloth over me and told me to close my eyes, that was kind of creepy."

"It must have been terribly claustrophobic."

"And hot! Oh my god, his hands felt like they were burning each time he touched me. Did he warm them on the fire or something?"

"Not that I saw. And all that smoke! It's a wonder you weren't choking under there. Or sneezing at least." Ariana sat down next to Rachel.

"I know. Weird, right? But once he started doing his thing, I did feel pretty calm. Only hot. And after, when he sat me up, I was totally freezing. Especially my feet."

Ariana looked down at Rachel's feet, now still and warm beneath her thick white crew socks. "I hope you don't mind me asking, but what was it that made you scream and cry like that, right when he had you sit up? Now, *that* was horrifying."

Rachel closed her eyes. "I'm not sure," she sighed. "It was sort of like one minute I was feeling completely overwhelmed, like a balloon pumped up over the max. And then all of a sudden, *whoosh*! Like someone had popped a hole in the soles of my feet and everything went flying out all at once, like a purge." She leaned back against a cushion. "What the hell do you think that was about?"

Ariana stood and shook out Rachel's blanket, folding it hastily into a tidy square. What she thought it was about was something she'd rather not speak of. "So are you all set to go? Adil should be on his way. We'll be out of this place before you know it."

Rachel rubbed her forehead with her palms. "I really wish I could figure this all out. After the thing with Hani's father I had the strangest dreams. But they didn't really feel like dreams. Has that ever happened to you?"

Ariana didn't respond.

"I kind of think I was starting to remember a little bit of what happened to me last night." She stood and began to pace the room. "There was a place with palm trees, sort of like the ocean at that fancy hotel in Muscat, but not."

"There are palm trees all over Oman." Ariana checked her watch.

"And there was a lot of sand."

"That too, Rachel. Especially last night."

"No, I mean it was a real place. At least I think it was. Shit, I feel like Dorothy after Oz."

"Right. And there's no place like home. Which is just where I intend to go as soon as I can get us out of here." She plumped up the pile of pillows that had been resting under Rachel's head overnight and began to arrange them in a neat row across the sofa.

"I'm not kidding, Ariana. Maybe we shouldn't be in such a hurry to leave. I really would like a chance to talk to Hani's father again."

Ariana paused with a pillow in her hands. "No, Rachel. Absolutely not. We have to go. Haven't you had enough of all this?"

Rachel stopped and turned to Ariana. "Well you're the one who believes in it all. So what, all of a sudden you're singing a different tune? I'm just saying."

"And I'm just saying let's not get swept into anything more than we already have while we're here." Ariana tossed the pillow onto the sofa.

"I think it's a little late for that, don't you?"

"That's not what I'm talking about," she spat back.

"Jeez, lighten up, would you, Ariana?"

Ariana remained with her back to Rachel until the warmth left her cheeks.

"Look," she finally said. "You know and I know that I came here against my better judgment. But I did it. I spent the night in this house having absolutely no intention of doing so, but here I am. I've been scared out of my wits by things we should not be messing with and that may never be explained, and I can't deal with any more of that right now. I admit I've made the worst decision ever, and the sooner I can leave it all behind

237

the better." She plopped down heavily onto a sofa. "I'm glad I got the chance to meet you, Rachel. I really am. But honestly?" Ariana's voice had risen with each anxious word. "I should never, ever have agreed to take this job."

"Pipe down!" Rachel whispered. "Do you want to wake the entire household?"

With that they both turned to the sound of someone stirring in the courtyard.

"If you ask me, it's more than just the *jinn* that's driving you out of Bahla," Rachel whispered.

"Oh, please," Ariana whispered back.

"Don't pretend you don't know what I mean. There's a lot I do remember quite clearly about last night, you know."

For a moment the room was silent. Ariana looked down at the carpet as she began to speak. "You may think you understand, but you really don't."

"How do you know I don't?"

"You don't understand because you are not me, Rachel," Ariana hissed, her eyes meeting Rachel's. "That's how I know. There is no way you could truly understand my culture. And there is no way you could understand how betrayed I feel. For me, finding out that Hani had been hiding the fact that he was involved in magic was as if I had found out he was an escaped convict. That shocking, and that disturbing. What kind of guy does that? If he truly cared about me, he would never have lied."

"But he didn't lie!"

"Please. The man has made it quite clear that he thinks I'm not worthy of his respect, and I have only acted to prove him right."

"Stop blaming yourself for what happened at the *wadi*. My god, Ariana. It's only sex. It's natural."

"I never said anything about sex!" Ariana snapped. "And I'm no prude, if that's what you're thinking. I was married once, remember? But just so you know, that is not the way things are done around here. You have to understand, we are not like you, sleeping with whomever you find yourself with at the end of the night. Trying men out as if they were competing for a spot on the team, tallying them up like points on a scorecard. It's not decent. And it is not allowed."

Rachel was saved from having to defend herself by the sudden sound of voices coming from behind the swinging door.

"So they are gone?" a woman asked.

"Yes, Mother. They were being picked up before dawn. I offered to take them but Ariana refused."

"Of course," Hani's mother answered. "Well, good. I have better ways for you to spend your day here with me."

"Whatever you need, Mother."

"*Inshallah*, I am a lucky woman, with a son like you to depend on."

"And I am a lucky son as well," Hani answered in a singsong voice that made it sound as if these were lines they had delivered back and forth to each other many times before.

"Imagine life with a woman like that," his mother continued. "A woman who has no respect for tradition, no respect for the normal order of things in a household."

If Hani had an answer, Ariana didn't hear it.

"That type brings nothing but trouble. Nothing but arguments and defiance."

"Why are you telling me this, Mother?"

"A woman like that can get her hooks into a man and not let go. I have seen it happen."

"Don't worry. You can see there are no hooks in me. She is gone."

"And I am sure she does not even cook."

"All right, Mother."

"And she is too old to bear children."

"Okay, Mother."

"A woman like that would be a curse on a man. I thank God you are not marrying her."

"Please, Mother."

"No, you will settle down with a good wife. In fact, I have the perfect girl already picked out for you."

"I'm sure you do, Mother."

"A woman who is young and pure, who has not been married before."

"That is enough, Mother."

"She is ten times better than a woman like that."

There was a pause in the conversation that, to Ariana, seemed to last a thousand years. She held her breath as the first words of Hani's response came roaring from behind the door.

"A woman like that? How can you speak of a woman like that? You do not even know one thing about a woman like Ariana. She is kind and sweet and gentle. And she is smart, and curious, and can make a person feel as though they are the only other one in the room. She would do anything for anyone. A woman like that worships her family, and loves her faith just as deeply. She does not need to be covered from head to toe to prove her devotion. She does not need to hide her hair of silk or her slender waist to hold her beliefs. And do you know what? Even though I do like what is on the outside, it is what is inside Ariana that I find the most attractive. There are not many women I have met who are as true to themselves as Ariana.

In fact, there are no other women like Ariana. A woman like that? I would be lucky to marry a woman like that."

A soft cough coming from the direction of the courtyard drew Rachel and Ariana's attention away from the argument behind the door. Hani's father poked his head in and turned his dark eyes from one woman to the other and back again before crossing the room in a purposeful stride and pushing his way through the swinging door that led to the rest of the house. His sharp words penetrated loud and clear in a serious-sounding Arabic scolding that neither of them could understand. The discussion between Hani and his mother came to an abrupt halt and then, silence.

Hani's father returned to the sitting room and handed Ariana a box of tissues to wipe away the tears she realized had appeared on her cheeks. "And you," he said as he sat himself down next to Rachel, peeling an orange while he spoke. "How are you feeling today?"

"I'm okay. But can I ask you—"

"You know, it usually takes many sessions for the healing to properly work."

Rachel laughed a little. "Right. Like a chiropractor."

"But what I did should help."

Ariana sat quietly, straining to hear the sound of Adil's tires on the driveway.

"It is a start," Hani's father continued.

"Do you have any idea what happened to me down in the souk?" Rachel asked.

Hani's father popped a section of the juicy citrus into his mouth and swallowed. "Of course I do. But that is not where your problems come from."

"My problems? All I want to know is how I lost all that time last night."

"Ah," he said as he stretched out his long legs in front of him, "but you see, everything is connected."

"How?"

"You are one who has wounds that run deep, deeper than the one that gave you that scar on your arm. These are the wounds that cannot be seen by the human eye, the kind of trouble from spirits that have been living within you for years."

"Well, I suppose if by spirits you mean memories—"

"I mean what I say. Can you tell me that you didn't feel something last night, here on this floor?"

"No," Rachel answered in a whisper.

"Exactly. And if I have done my job well, it means I have cleared the way for the one still inside to get what she wants from you."

"She? Who? Get what from me?"

"We need to go, Rachel," Ariana said quietly. "Let's go wait out in front for Adil."

"Just a sec, Ariana. I just need to get some answers before we head back."

"You are going back to Nizwa?" Miza stood in the sitting room doorway, her arms cradling her belly and her eyes clouded with worry. "Please, will you take me? I must go to Tariq. The hospital called to say they have lessened his medications. They are hoping he will awaken soon."

"Of course we'll take you. Let me help you gather your things." Ariana stood and took Miza's arm.

"*I* will take you," Hani's father offered. "Your time is quite near." He nodded toward her middle.

"Really," Ariana insisted. "We can do it. It's no problem." There was no way she was going to leave the poor woman alone, open to the influences of Hani and his family, in her vulnerable state.

"That scarf!" Rachel raised herself slowly from the sofa with her eyes fixed on the orange and blue cloth wrapped around Miza's head.

"Rachel, this is hardly the time . . ." Ariana turned to Hani's father for backup.

"No, really," Rachel persisted, reaching her hand out to touch the worn fabric. "I've seen this scarf before. I saw it last night."

"You mean in your dreams?" Ariana asked as she watched Hani's father finishing his fruit with a satisfied smile on his face.

"It was the exact same pattern," Rachel continued. "Only I think it was wrapped like a skirt. On a child. A girl."

"Maybe you were just remembering seeing it on Miza, before. I'll get your things, Miza." Ariana plumped a pillow and urged the pregnant woman to sit.

Rachel shook her head. "I swear I haven't. And the scarf, that girl, they were as real to me as the hand in front of my face." She jumped up and grabbed her backpack from the floor. "I'll show you guys! I took pictures. The old woman wanted me to. I remember now!" Rachel gripped the Leica in her shaking hands as she pressed with her thumb to scroll through the images.

"It's okay, Rachel. Seriously, this isn't the time." Ariana narrowed her eyes and shook her head.

"But I think I might have photos of the girl! I swear!"

"I do not need to see pictures." Miza's voice came out low and hushed. "I know who it was. It was my sister you saw wearing the *kanga* last night. My sister Sabra."

30

"*Harakaka!* Hurry, hurry! I do not have all day to wait for you to finish your bread." Sabra watched as her little cousin rolled the dough between his fingers, his round eyes seeming to dare his angry mother into taking action. The woman instead turned her attention to Sabra. "You are to finish your chores and go to your room and stay there until I return. Do you understand me?"

Sabra nodded her assent as she stood by the bucket, washing the plates and cups.

"I did not hear you! What did you say?"

"Yes, Auntie," she muttered to the rough rag in her hand. On the other side of the house her uncle's broad back was silhouetted in the open doorway as he squatted in the early sun, smoking his cigarettes and watching over the morning comings and goings of the people of his village, the vibrant greens and yellows and reds and blues of the women's clothing in sharp contrast to the dullness of the cinderblock homes and dusty road. They looked like a sisterhood of peacocks as they descended to the market, their parade scattered with a handful of men heading down to the fruit stand to gather for a morning of idle chatter. Some would pause to say a quick hello to the straggling train of weary fishermen—the unlucky ones who had returned empty-handed from a night bobbing around on the water in their little wooden canoes, and the luckier ones who had already made their bargains at the market—all of them heading toward home. No matter who they were or which way they were going, all would be sure to stop and offer polite greetings to Sabra's uncle and give pats to the heads of her cousins, already busy at play in the sandy soil.

"And don't forget to put the laundry to dry on the line!" her aunt snarled.

Sabra lifted the last plate from the mat on the floor and slowly wiped it clean, anxious for her aunt to scoop up the children and head out to the market herself. She inched around her uncle's unyielding frame and out the door with the heavy basket held firmly atop her head, dropping it down beneath the rope strung taught between two palm trees. As she bent and stretched to fill the line with damp clothes that flapped like bright flags in the ocean breeze, Sabra's eyes remained wide and alert, scanning the distance for any sign of Bi-Zena. It wasn't until after her aunt and cousins had rounded the path and were finally out of sight that she saw the woman approaching, her steps heavy and deliberate against the dusty road.

"*Ninakusihi salamu.* I bid you greetings," she heard Bi-Zena call out in a voice thick with sweetness. Her uncle grumbled a greeting in return as he ground the remains of a cigarette into the soil.

"And how are you feeling this fine morning? I trust all is good?"

"All is good, Bi-Zena," her uncle answered without looking up.

"I have heard she was back," the woman said as she cast her eyes dismissively toward Sabra. "It is a shame that her sister does not choose to care for her."

Her uncle swatted at a fly with his hand. "Yes, isn't it? But it is no surprise."

Bi-Zena nodded. "No. No surprise. And it is even more of a shame for you, and your poor wife, having yet another mouth to feed."

The laundry basket empty, Sabra lowered her eyes and hurried past the two of them and back inside. She could almost hear her own heart pounding as she took a broom to the ashes from the fire that still smoldered beneath the kettle. She had been emboldened by Bi-Zena's visit the morning before, feeling hope at last that she might find a way out of this horrible prison. But by the time darkness fell, her courage seemed to have disappeared with the sun, down below the horizon into the depths of the sea. Then, long after the other children were fast asleep, she heard her name spoken, her uncle's sharp voice bouncing off the walls of the patio and through the flimsy curtain covering the bedroom doorway.

"But it will be all taken care of. I promise you."

"And when? When exactly is this astonishing windfall supposed to arrive?" her aunt hissed.

"Soon. It will be soon. Sunday I will be going to Stone Town to meet with the brokers to make the deal."

"I don't believe you."

"Call them yourself. I will give you their number."

"I have heard your crazy plans before. If you are so smart, then why are we not yet rich? You are a fool."

"Do not doubt me, my dear wife. I am no fool. This time it is for sure. Do you know how many there are in the Middle East looking for 'household help'?"

Her aunt spat out a laugh. "As if that girl could be a help in any house."

Sabra knew that housekeeping was not the real future for the girls who were sold to those in other countries. She had heard the terrible stories of girls who became slaves to rich Arab women or, worse, playthings for their husbands. She had been warned not to get involved in talking with strangers, to never wander the streets alone. The thought of being sold like a cow or a chicken made her meager breakfast rise to her throat.

Sabra peered from the doorway to see her uncle still holding court from the threshold. Bi-Zena remained before him, her heavy arms crossed at her belly. "Of course, it won't be easy, getting a spoiled girl like that to put in a hard day's work."

Her uncle laughed. "You sound like my wife."

Bi-Zena clucked and shook her head back and forth. "That poor woman, with her hands already full with your beautiful children," she sighed. "But this, it is something I can do, a small way for me to thank you for all you have done for our village."

Sabra now understood Bi-Zena's plan. Just to be free of this prison for a few hours a day, to be out in the salty air and clear blue sea within the comforting reach of the watchful woman, that would be enough to make each day bearable. But what Bi-Zena didn't know was that those days might be few, and that Sabra was facing a future even more devastating than the one inside her uncle's house. She held her breath and waited for her uncle's reply.

"But the girl will be paid for her labor, am I right?"

"*Hakuna matata*, chief. Of course. I assure you that I will bring her wages directly to your door, every day."

"And she can start today?"

Sabra could almost see her uncle's greedy brain at work as he tallied the money she'd reap from a few days in the ocean.

"Of course. I will take her with me now."

"Sabra!" her uncle shouted. But Sabra was already at the door, her sleeves pushed up past her elbows, her worn orange and blue kanga draped loosely over her head.

31

The shadows were growing long in the afternoon sun as the Lexus wove through lanes thick with trucks and cars that had been sidelined by the storm the day before. Everything seemed to have happened so fast. One minute Rachel was waking from the best sleep she'd had in her life, and the next she was in an adrenalin-fueled race to the airport, just like the old days.

At first Miza had shown little surprise at the images in Rachel's camera. "That is the road in the village, the village in Zanzibar where I was living before I married Tariq," she explained, her eyes narrowing, as if trying to make more detail appear in the frame.

"Are you sure? Look again," Rachel insisted.

"It is my village," Miza replied.

"But that makes absolutely no sense!" Rachel swiped to the next image.

"And that is the fruit market, near to where I brought seaweed in from the ocean. I am sure of it. Do you see the orange wall

249

behind the tables? And the man sitting there, behind the scales? I would go there every morning before I went to work. I would buy a mango or a citrus fruit. We would say hello. I know it is him."

Rachel took the camera back for another look. "What the fuck? I've never even been to Zanzibar!" Out of the corner of her eye she could see Hani's father smiling a little. "So this," she persisted, shoving the Leica back toward Miza, "what's this picture?"

At the sight of the following image Miza seemed to stiffen. "That is the house," she said, pointing to the screen. "The house of my uncle." She raised her head up toward Rachel. "But where is my sister? You said you have photographs."

Rachel pulled the camera toward her and frantically searched for more. But the screen displayed only those three images of the village. The remaining shots were of the factory and the old potters and the souk and the sandstorm and the room they now sat in—the only photos she remembered taking since they first arrived in Bahla, which now seemed so very long ago.

"Let me see that one again." Miza held out her hand for the Leica. "The one of my uncle's house."

Rachel returned the image to the little screen.

"Can you make it bigger?" Miza watched as Rachel zoomed in on a tighter frame of the little cinderblock building. "Lower." Miza poked at a button with her finger. "On the ground. To the side of the doorway. That is what I want to see."

Rachel made an adjustment, this time focusing on the bottom part of the frame, and again handed the camera to Miza.

Miza gasped, her hand flying to her mouth.

"What?" Rachel grabbed the camera and looked again. "I don't see anything."

"There. The lion, drawn in the sand. My sister and I used to leave that as a sign for each other, right there beneath the window, when something was wrong inside the house."

"A lion?"

"From the old tales. The lion was always the boss, the bully. He would demand that the other animals bow down to him. He would terrorize their villages, just like our uncle. So if our uncle was in a mood to take out his anger on us, we would give the other a warning."

Rachel looked at the image again. "But I don't even see a lion."

"Look," Miza insisted as she pointed to the screen. "There is one leg. And there is another. And the tail."

"I still don't quite—"

"Nobody knew about the lion but us. My sister is there, in that house. I know it. And something is very wrong." The tears began to escape from Miza's eyes. "I have not been able to reach Sabra for days. I know something terrible has happened."

Ariana pulled a handful of tissues from the box at her side. "I'm sure everything is fine, Miza. It must be difficult being so far away, am I right?"

Miza shook her head. "My uncle is a very bad person. He has done unspeakable things to me. And Sabra, she is only fourteen."

Ariana paled a little as she tucked her arm around the weeping woman's shoulders. "I'm sure there is some sort of an explanation for all this," she said with a rocky confidence that wouldn't fool even a child. "Honestly, you really do need to calm down a bit."

Rachel turned her eyes to Hani's father, who remained silent on the sofa, his attention riveted to the screen of his phone, either oblivious or indifferent to the drama around her. Rachel wasn't sure which.

"What if Miza's right?" she asked Ariana.

"Rachel!" Ariana glared at her from behind Miza's back.

"No, really. I can't totally explain it, but I have a feeling that what Miza says might be true. Her sister needs help."

"Please, Rachel." Ariana cocked her head toward Miza, who was clutching her belly as she slowly rocked back and forth.

"I'm serious, Ariana. And you can't tell me I'm wrong, or crazy. You said it yourself that there have to be things in life that can't be explained, that we can't necessarily see, didn't you?"

A soft moaning from Miza silenced both women. Rachel flipped quickly through the shots in the Leica once again and then shut her eyes, struggling to summon an image of the girl she had seen the night before. After a minute a spindly form appeared in sharp focus, as clearly as if it were a photo. Rachel zoomed in on the girl's ebon face, her skin smooth and creamy, her teeth straight and white. How young she looked. And then a close-up, her eyes filling the frame like two deep, dark pools that seemed to lead into a sea of despair.

Suddenly Rachel jerked back with a start, the eyes of a thousand children and women, men and boys, each soldier and refugee and prisoner, all the wounded and the hungry, every desperate person she'd ever seen through the lens of her camera looking right back at her through the eyes of this young girl.

"I need to go to her," she heard Miza say.

"No, love, you really can't." Ariana took Miza's hand in her own. "There's no way you should be flying in your condition."

Rachel turned again to Hani's father, her heart pounding. "Can't you do anything about this?"

Hani's father looked up from his phone. "Me?" He smoothed the front of his white robe with one large hand. "I am not the one who can be of help in this situation."

"What do you mean?"

Hani's father didn't answer.

"Tell me. What do you mean?" Rachel pleaded. "There's something I'm not getting here."

"What's to get?" he responded.

Rachel looked up at the ceiling, her head and her heart still reeling. But even as those images from her past began to slowly fade away, she was left with one that remained in crisp, sharp focus—the tall, dark girl wrapped in the orange and blue cloth. The words were out of her mouth before she had a chance to think.

"I'm going."

"You're going where?" Ariana asked. "I hardly think this is the time for us to be dealing with your issues, Rachel." She pointed her chin toward Miza.

Rachel felt Miza's hand clamp down on her wrist. She turned to face the woman and slowly nodded. For the first time in ages she could feel the fire that came with a sense of purpose. And for the first time *ever*, it wasn't about the attention and admiration that came from appearing brave or noble, it wasn't about the accolades that came with landing a front page. It wasn't even about her at all.

"You must go to the village, to the ocean, and look for the seaweed women," Miza told her. "Ask for Bi-Zena. She will help you."

"What?" Ariana's head turned from Rachel to Miza and back again. "What's going on?"

"Ariana." Rachel stood and reached for her backpack, wrapped the strap around her camera and placed it carefully inside. "It looks like I'm going to Zanzibar."

*

The traffic slowed as they approached the outskirts of Muscat. "Hani, can you explain it?" Rachel asked.

"What is it that you would like me to explain for you?" He checked his watch and craned his neck to peer over the lanes ahead.

"How did those images get in my camera? How could I be in a place, let alone a place that's a five-hour flight away, without even knowing?"

Hani shifted his eyes from the road to Rachel for just a quick second, as if debating whether to answer.

"Seriously, how long was it between when we left your house and you guys found me? A half-hour? Maybe a little more?"

"It was two hours."

"Two hours? Where the hell *was* I, Hani? I mean, if I had gotten hit in the head or something, if I had been unconscious or dreaming, I could maybe understand imagining a place I'd never seen. But the images are right here!" She patted the backpack on the seat beside her. "Tell me how that happens."

The traffic had come to a standstill. "There are some things we cannot completely understand."

"Apparently." The hairs on Rachel's arms rose a little just thinking about her experience with the man's father the night before. "But I can't help but wonder."

"It is good to wonder." Hani took a deep breath. "It is like this, Rachel. One cannot live their life with everything in black and white, right or wrong, true or not true. A life like that, what is its purpose? If we think we know everything, then we know nothing. And we think there is nothing left to learn."

"I guess. But shouldn't we try to figure out the things we don't understand?"

"Who knows? Maybe not. Sometimes it is the things

we cannot explain that make life beautiful. Because you never know what might happen."

Rachel stared into the trail of red lights ahead.

"Think about it. You and I have met. Was that just an accident? How do we know? And now we are friends, are we not? That is a good thing, and perhaps one that was meant to be, for a reason. And was it an accident that you met Ariana? Or Miza?"

"I'm not sure, but—"

"And what is it," Hani continued, "that causes a person to connect with another, what makes them determined to do something they never dreamed of doing before, even if it makes no sense, even if it goes against everything they ever believed? What makes a heart say one thing when the head is saying another?"

Hani turned off toward the airport exit and again checked his watch. "You should be fine. The last flight for Zanzibar City leaves in one hour."

"You're going back to see Ariana, aren't you?"

Hani smiled.

"Ha! I knew it!"

Hani's smile grew wider.

"I'm rooting for you, Hani. I want you to know that."

"And I am rooting for you as well, Rachel," he said. "But somehow I think you will be fine without my roots."

32

Ariana barely had a chance to say goodbye as Hani rushed Rachel out the door and into the car. Everyone had assumed that she would be traveling with them back to Muscat airport and straight home to Dubai. But the sight of Miza had held her back, and she simply could not imagine leaving the woman behind.

And then the pains began.

Hani's father had taken control, asking Miza to show him exactly where it hurt.

"Here," she said, pointing to her lower abdomen.

He went to summon his wife. The woman brushed past Ariana as if she weren't even there before sitting herself down on the other side of Miza. Hani's father sat with his phone in his hand, noting out loud the time of Miza's every wince as his wife spoke quietly into the anxious woman's ear. As Miza calmed and the pain seemed to lessen, Hani's mother turned her attention to Ariana with a question lobbed at her husband in a contemptuous snarl. Though she spoke in Arabic, the meaning of the woman's words was clear on her face.

"I *am* still here. I've stayed to help Miza," Ariana answered for herself, emboldened by the astonishing turns the morning had taken.

Hani's father bit his lip and tried not to smile as the color rose in his wife's cheeks.

"Then make yourself useful, and go into the kitchen and ask my daughter to make some tea," she answered in English, unable to look Ariana in the eye. "And you," she said to Miza, "lie back and let us see if your pains go away."

By the time Ariana had returned with the tea, a decision had been made. "My wife does not think she is in true labor, does not think the baby is coming now. So we will go to Nizwa, to the hospital. Miza will see her husband, and we will ask the doctors there to look at her. Just to be safe."

Ariana had no other choice than to agree. Adil had still not shown up, and by now she doubted he ever would. And the sooner Miza got to the hospital, and to Tariq, the better.

With Miza stretched out on the back seat of a sparkling new Toyota, Ariana took her place in front by Hani's father's side. As he cautiously inched the car onto the crowded highway, she heard him sigh. "Too bad there is no magic for this, am I right?"

Ariana laughed nervously. Although she had to admit that she was impressed by the man's gentle way with Miza, and by the favorable effect he seemed to have had on Rachel, she was still not entirely comfortable in his presence.

"I am sorry about my wife," he said. "She is not a bad woman."

"It's okay. I understand."

"I do not blame her for the way she is. Hani is very special to her, as you can see. Her baby boy. Finally, after five daughters, a son."

"I get it."

"But to me? It is a struggle. I beg for her to let him go, to let him be the man he is, to make choices on his own."

Ariana nodded. They drove in silence for a while, comforted by the sound of Miza's rhythmic breathing as she dozed behind them.

Hani's father was the first to break the silence. "You know, there is nothing to be frightened of by me, by my son."

Ariana shifted uncomfortably in her seat. "Oh, I'm not—"

"It is okay. There are many like you, who misunderstand what we do."

"Well, you know what we've all been taught. That we should trust in God, and only God."

"And you do not think that I do? You do not think I am a pious man?"

Ariana didn't know how to answer.

"Me, I am just part of a power bigger than myself, here on earth to give people some comfort from what ails them and some direction. It is with God's power that I can do what I do. Did you not hear the Koran coming from my lips last night?"

"I did," Ariana said quietly.

"And to be clear, I do not ask for anything in return for those I help. I help because it is something I can do, something I must do."

Ariana watched as the man pushed back his long, dark curls with one hand, seeing something of Hani in the softness of his eyes. "You know, it's kind of funny," she said. "Everyone swears that the best way to avoid the magic, the *jinn*, is to stay away from it and everything related to it, to just trust in God to protect us. But why would so many of us who have done just that have stories to tell if that were the case?"

Hani's father laughed a little. "And you?" he asked. "What is your story?"

"Honestly? My entire family seems to have been touched in one way or another."

Hani's father nodded, his eyes turning to her for a quick moment, one eyebrow arched in question. "And you?" he repeated.

Ariana hesitated before answering. "Okay," she finally said, before taking a deep breath. "So, once? Once I was told that I have a *jinn*. One who is in love with me."

"Ah." Hani's father smiled a little. "And have you done anything about this?"

"Of course not!" Ariana cringed as she suddenly remembered who she was talking to. "I'm sorry. I didn't mean to offend you. It's just that it's so ingrained in us to stay away from those things. I should have never even put myself in the situation I did in the first place, when I was told about this *jinn*, about how it's supposedly keeping me from the love of others."

Hani's father drove in silence, his eyes firmly on the road ahead.

"So do you think it's true?" she asked shyly.

"Your *jinn*?" he asked.

"Yes."

Hani's father shook his head.

"You don't?" Ariana turned in her seat to face him.

"No, I do not."

"How do you know?"

259

"It is easy. You heard my son's words to his mother, just as I did. Those are the words of a man who has found his voice from the love of a woman. There was no *jinn* standing in his way."

Ariana felt a warmth rising from her heart to her head.

"I see the way he listens to you, as if every word from your lips is the start of a sweet song. Only a man in love would have ears like that."

"Oh," Ariana said, her voice a whisper.

"And I have seen the way my son looks at you. It is in those eyes that I can see the true magic, the magic that is the most real. And the magic that makes me the happiest."

Ariana melted back into the upholstery, her mind heavy with the weight of his words, her heart light with the hope they carried.

Now the two of them sat together, sipping tea in the hospital's cafeteria while waiting for visiting hours to begin. Miza had been wheeled off to an examination room but was desperate for a glimpse of her husband. Ariana had promised to check on Tariq for her, only to be turned back by a pair of officious nurses and told to return in an hour.

At 2 pm on the dot they both rose from their chairs and headed to the elevator, crowding in with the others anxious for a visit with family or friends. When the doors slid open on the fifth floor, Ariana felt herself nearly knocked over from behind. "Excuse me," she said pointedly to the woman in a hurry, who instead of responding simply bulldozed her way in front of them, using her handbag as a battering ram. They stood and watched from behind as she marched down the long hallway, her high heels pecking at the shiny floor like woodpeckers on a tree. "They did say Tariq was in room 506, didn't they? The second from the end?" Ariana asked Hani's father as they saw the woman turn and enter through the door.

"I will go check with the nurses." But as soon as the words left his mouth, the other elevator door opened and out came Miza, being pushed in a wheelchair with a blanket across her lap.

"Have you seen him? Have you seen Tariq?" she asked. "Please," she implored the aide behind her, "please go faster."

Ariana and Hani's father followed closely behind as Miza was wheeled into the room.

A shrieking voice came blasting through the doorway. "Her! Take her away! Get that woman out of here now!"

"Who the hell is that?" Ariana said out loud upon spying the pushy woman from the elevator hovering over the motionless figure in the bed, as if waiting to pounce over it toward Miza like a tiger.

"I am his wife!" the woman screeched, spit spraying from her lipsticked mouth. "And I demand that this whore be taken from his room immediately. You, go get security!" she demanded, pointing with a shaking finger at the bewildered aide. "Go get somebody!"

Ariana rushed around the bed to confront the woman face to face, the blood boiling in her veins. "How dare you talk about my friend that way! Who the hell do you think you are? *She* is his wife," Ariana insisted, pointing to Miza, who sat gripping the arms of the wheelchair. "And that is his child she is carrying. What is wrong with you? Are you crazy?"

"How dare you!" the woman seethed. "I was married to this man long before this witch from Zanzibar got her clutches on him. And I am *still* his wife."

Ariana was speechless.

"Yes." Hani's father was suddenly standing between the two women. "It is true that Miza and this woman are both his wives. But only one of them treats him with the love and respect a good husband deserves."

"And who are you?" The furious woman whipped her head around to confront Hani's father.

"I am a doctor."

Maryam's eyes traveled from his head to his toes, noting the absence of the white jacket and tie and stethoscope hanging around his neck. There was no identification badge hanging on a cord, as every person who worked in the hospital wore. Just a big dark man towering over her in his *dishdasha* and *kuma*.

"You are no more a doctor than I am Cleopatra."

Hani's father shrugged his shoulders. "I am enough of a doctor to see the sickness inside of you."

"I am perfectly fine! At least, I will be once *this* one is out of my sight." Maryam jerked her head toward Miza.

Ariana returned to Miza's side and took her trembling hand in her own.

"But you won't be fine," Hani's father continued calmly to the raging woman. "Even if she disappeared into thin air, that would still not be enough to soothe the demons that have taken over your soul."

"You have no idea what you are talking about," Maryam protested.

"Ah," he responded with a nod. "But I do. I see the greed that is gnawing at you like a pack of rats. It is not good for your mind." Hani's father tapped his head with two fingers.

"Oh, I see. So you are a psychiatrist," Maryam sneered.

"I am not that kind of a doctor," he answered.

"Well, if you can be of no help to my husband, then I insist you leave this room as well."

"But you are not the one who has concern for her husband. Clearly, if it were not for this," he said, pointing at Miza's round belly, "you would be just as happy if he never woke up."

"What has that witch told you?" she snapped. "She has been filling your head with lies."

Miza's hand tightened around Ariana's fingers like a vise.

"She has filled my head with nothing. It is through my own powers that I see all of this." He circled his palm in the air, as if conjuring a vision. "I see the treachery in your heart. This treachery is a poison that will harm only you. To wish ill upon an innocent unborn child, that is a crime that can never be forgiven. And no one, or nothing, can protect you from the horrors that will be unleashed upon you should anything happen to him. Do you understand what I'm saying?"

Maryam blanched as the meaning behind his words began to dawn on her. "Then you are a witch, just like her." Her voice began to crumble. "And I never—"

Hani's father held up a thick finger. "Do not try to tell me what you did or did not do. If you continue to wish harm on this mother and child, you will be punished in this life, up until its very end. Only Allah knows if you will be punished in the next. And there will come a day when you wish you *were* Cleopatra. Even her end was dull compared to what will happen to you if any harm comes of your evil actions."

He began to chant in Arabic, the singsong words evoking a dirge in an ominous minor key. Then he reached his fingers deep into the pocket of his *dishdasha* and suddenly flung something toward Maryam, a cloud of what, to Ariana, looked simply like a mix of sand and lint, straight into her startled face.

The woman let out a gasp and clutched her handbag close to her body, her chest heaving like that of a person who'd run a hundred miles. The looming man stood his ground, until she finally began to slowly back around him. As she disappeared through the door, Hani's father turned and winked at Ariana, the corners of his mouth curling up into a little smile.

33

The fishing boats appeared like a scattering of bobbing fireflies as the plane made its descent over the moonlit sea. The flight had seemed interminable. Rachel was accustomed to using her time in the air to brief herself on an upcoming assignment, research her subjects, make her plans. But here she was flying into a situation totally unprepared, her only leads being the three mysterious photos, the paper from Miza holding the directions to her uncle's village, and the matching half of the orange and blue *kanga* that Miza had urged her to take along. There would be no one on the ground to guide her, to pave the way for her mission. Even Ariana would have been a welcome sight, as lame of a fixer as she was. But somehow Rachel knew she'd figure this out. It felt as though some unseen hand was guiding her. Or, she thought, it was simply the unfamiliar feeling of her old confidence making a comeback.

With her backpack slung over her arm, Rachel followed the other passengers down the stairs from the plane and into a line trailing halfway back to the runway. Even long after midnight the tiny airport was in total chaos. Amid the murmurs of confusion a sharp voice shouted, "Yellow fever! Yellow fever!" She instinctively began to wave her arms at invisible mosquitos, and then remembered the vaccination certificate that had been required for her entry into South Africa back when she was covering a violent miners' strike a few years earlier. *Shit.* Was it still in her pouch, perhaps stuffed behind her passport? She doubted it. The line inched forward as people without the proper papers were told to step aside. Rachel continued to fumble through her backpack, acting as though she was certain it had to be in there somewhere. She grabbed the first piece of paper to touch her hand and waved it at the man. Her ruse worked, and she was pointed through the door and into the building.

The visa process was a true test of patience. So many questions, on top of a photo, fingerprints, and $100, thank you very much. Finally she pushed her way through the glass exit doors, the smell of the country hitting her like a pie in the face. It was salty, fishy, spicy, all at the same time. The warm, soft breeze seemed to envelop her in its sweetness.

"*Jambo! Jambo!*" The dark sidewalk leading to the taxi stand was lined with men young and old shoving past each other to get to the tourists exiting the building.

"*Karibu.* Welcome to Zanzibar." A man, or really a child, reached out his hand to remove the strap from her shoulder.

Rachel backed away. "I've got it," she insisted, hoisting the backpack up closer to her neck. "I'm good!" she repeated louder, hastening her steps as the kid closed in on her. "Seriously?" she demanded, stopping dead in her tracks and spinning around to look him in the eye.

"*Kuacha!*" came a sharp voice from behind her. The kid backed off as Rachel turned to find herself face to face with a gorgeous young man, looking just as if he'd walked out of a magazine, his muscled shoulders bursting from his sleeveless T-shirt, the smile in his eyes as bright as the one on his lips. "Do you need a taxi?" he asked, his voice now smooth as silk.

"I do," she answered, looking around for his car.

"Are you staying at the beach?"

Rachel didn't answer.

"*Hakuna matata.* No worries. I know a hotel that is close. It is fine."

"And *I'm* fine. Thanks for your help, but no thanks."

He continued to walk with her toward the waiting taxis. "Okay," he said as he opened the back door of the first car in line for her. "Get in." Then he rattled off something to the driver before settling into the seat next to her. "My name is Kanu," he said, his teeth sparkling in the darkness of the night. "In Swahili, it means wildcat," he said with a wink.

Ariana couldn't help but laugh. "Okay, Kanu, but really, I can take it from here."

"It is okay. I live near the hotel. I will make sure you get there safe. It is late, not safe for a woman like you, alone."

Rachel rolled her eyes in the cover of darkness. She had heard from colleagues who had traveled here for a little R & R about the *papasi*, the beach boys of Zanzibar, hustlers who hang around the tourist hotels offering help with luggage and drivers and sightseeing, encouraging visits to souvenir shops owned by their "cousins". Often they were rented by female tourists to act as escorts during their stay, the young men's services extending far beyond that of a mere tour guide.

On the outskirts of the city center the car came to a stop. "We must walk from here. No cars allowed." Rachel paid the driver and watched from under a streetlamp as he drove away into the darkness. The streets around her were silent, snaking off in opposite directions like the tentacles of an octopus.

"Come on," Kanu urged. "It is this way."

She hesitated a moment before hitching the pack higher onto her shoulder, then began to follow as Kanu led her through a maze of abandoned alleyways, the sounds of their footsteps echoing off the ancient buildings that were barely visible in the darkness.

"This is the old part of the city," he explained. "Very nice, but not very exciting at this time of night, right?"

Rachel wondered if she wasn't being stupid. Alone in a strange city, lost, in the middle of the night, with a complete stranger? *A recipe for disaster*, her mother would have said. But then again, she reminded herself, she'd done much, much stupider in her life. And she was pretty certain this guy was just a gigolo, and not an axe murderer.

"So do you work here in Stone Town?" she asked a little nervously.

"I have a little shop," he said. "Right in the center. But I can have someone work for me tomorrow, if you would like to see the sights."

"Uh-huh," Rachel murmured, now sure of her instincts.

"It is too bad it's so late. It would be nice to get a drink, don't you think?" he asked.

Rachel ignored the question. "So where are you from?" she asked him as they turned onto a narrow street that looked exactly the same as the one they had just been on.

"The mainland. Tanzania. I left with my brother, to get money to send to our family. My brother works now with the tourists in Kilimanjaro."

"And where did you learn English?" Indeed, his English was impressive.

Kanu shrugged his shoulders. "The tourists. It was easy. No problem."

They continued down the deserted streets. "How do you like it here in Zanzibar?" she asked, warming a little to this savvy young man, who to her seemed way too smart for the path he was on.

Kanu shrugged his shoulders. "It is nice here. I can make money. But it is also difficult, in a way."

"How so?"

"I mean with the girls. I cannot date the Zanzibar girls. Their parents would never allow it."

"Because?" Because you're a gigolo? she thought.

"Because I am not Muslim."

"So you're a Christian?"

Kanu shook his head. "I am not much of anything. My father is a Muslim, my mother is a Christian. But me? I have seen too much in this world to put my faith in anything beyond what I can use to put food on the table tomorrow."

"I hear you. But then again," she said with a chuckle, "you never know." Rachel stopped under the halo of a dim streetlamp, squinting to get a better look at him.

"What?" he asked.

"Listen, I have to ask you something."

He flashed a practiced smile and placed his hands on his hips in a pose that must have paid off in hundreds of tables of food in his life. "Anything you want. I am here for you."

"Kanu, *really*?" She shook her head.

"You know I am very good at making a vacation more than just a spice tour or a snorkeling excursion. I know how to make special memories."

"Please, just cut the crap. I am not on vacation, and I think I may need your help."

He dropped his arms and stood up straight. "Okay. So what is it?"

Rachel pulled Miza's map from the pocket of her khakis. "There is a girl," she explained. "In this town. She needs my help."

Kanu took the map from her hands and held it up to the light. "Somebody needs help? No problem. I am like a superhero."

Rachel had to chuckle. "I'm sure you are. And a superhero just might be what I need. Do you think you can get me to this village?"

"I will take you, of course!"

"Good. And one more thing. I'm not sure what I'm looking for when I get there, but whatever it is, it might not be easy."

"Easy? Who said things had to be easy?"

"Nobody ever," she agreed. Gigolo or not, Rachel was impressed by the young man's confidence. They continued down the twisting alleyways. She had no idea what direction they were going in, or how far they had gone. Every street seemed the same, each one lined with ancient buildings behind massive wooden doors, every one shuttered tight for the night.

She arrived at the hotel worn and disoriented, grateful for Kanu's presence. She stood back as he pounded on the heavy front door with his meaty fist, and listened as the locks were undone one by one. As the right half of the domed entryway swung open, she stuck out her hand. "By the way, my name is Rachel." They shook. "Please, come in so I can pay you," she said as she crossed the threshold. Then she noticed the disdainful eye of the hotel worker standing on the other side of the door.

"No," Kanu said from outside. "There are some things I offer that money cannot buy. I will see you in the morning." And he was gone.

34

Ariana woke to the sound of footsteps, the squeak of sticky rubber soles coming up against newly polished floors. Her eyes remained closed, her body achy from the night spent in a hard chair. Miza had been given a room, as well as something to help her relax and sleep, though she had only agreed to it after both Ariana and Hani's father convinced the head nurse to allow them to spend the night by Tariq's side. The nurses seemed to be hopeful about his recovery. His vital signs were strong, and it might be only a matter of time before he came to, they said. Miza did not want him waking to an empty room.

She stretched her arms high above her head and straightened in the chair. At first she thought she was mistaken, but as her eyes adjusted to the light it was clear she was not. In the chair across from her, where Hani's father had dozed off under an avalanche of snores the night before, sat Hani himself, his chest pulsing up and down in the rhythm of contented sleep.

Ariana smoothed her messy hair and ran a finger under both eyes, not daring to attempt more lest he wake. How beautiful he looked, dappled by the tiny rays of sunlight peeking through the hospital blinds. So innocent. So pure. So good. She sat frozen in place, watching him as he wallowed in the last of his morning dreams. But at his first stirrings she jumped from her chair and tiptoed toward the door. She wasn't ready to let him see her like this. And she certainly wasn't ready to have a conversation like the one that was bound to follow.

"Where are you going?" she heard him ask just as she reached the threshold, his voice scratchy with sleep.

"Hello," she answered without turning around.

"Hello back. Are you okay?"

"I'm good." She looked back toward him, one hand remaining on the door handle.

"Your friend Rachel got off fine." Hani yawned and checked his phone. "She should be in Zanzibar by now."

"That's good."

"Yes, it is."

"And your father?"

"He had to go back to Bahla. There were things he needed to take care of."

Ariana nodded. "Your father is an interesting man."

Hani nodded as he rubbed his eyes.

"He was very impressive last night. Did he tell you about Tariq's other wife?"

Hani laughed as he shook out his legs. "Yes. He can be quite a force, even without his magic."

"I can see that."

They remained for a moment in an awkward silence that filled the distance between them, both grateful for the arrival of a nurse coming to check on Tariq. She looked at his monitors and plumped his pillows, scribbled something down on a chart.

"So I guess you will be going back to Dubai soon," Hani said once the nurse left, closing the door behind her.

Ariana nodded slowly, her eyes focused on the window behind Hani's head.

Hani cleared his throat. "Look, Ariana—"

"I really should go check on Miza," she claimed as she once again reached for the door handle. But no sooner had she pulled the door halfway open than she felt it being pushed closed again. Hani stood behind her, his breath warm on her neck.

"Please, Ariana. Let me talk." He rubbed his face with the palms of his hand. "I am very sorry for the way I have treated you. I don't know what happened to me. It's like my head got turned around backwards."

"There's no need to apologize. Trust me. I was the one who said things I should never have. Everything's just been so crazy during the last few days."

Hani shook his head. "There are no excuses for the way I behaved."

"Seriously, Hani. I mean what I say."

"As do I."

She again reached for the door handle.

"Please, Ariana, don't go." He placed his hand on top of hers and together they retreated, hand in hand, into the silence of the room, their eyes focused on Tariq, his presence a welcome excuse to not have to look at each other.

It was Hani who spoke first. "So what are we going to do? Spend the rest of the time we have together apologizing to each other?"

Ariana laughed a little. "That would be a waste, wouldn't it?"

"It would be. So maybe there are more important things to talk about."

"Like what?" Ariana's heart seemed to jump a little at his words.

"Like this?" His eyes turned down to the two hands still clasped together between them. Ariana pulled hers back with a little jerk.

But Hani wouldn't let go. Instead he took hold of her other hand as well and planted a kiss on each of them before placing them against his chest.

Ariana stood open-mouthed, for once at a loss for words.

Hani led her by the hand to the chair he had slept in, still warm from the weight of his body, and pulled the other up beside it. "You are so quiet. Are you okay?" he asked.

"I'm fine," she assured him with a little smile. "Just thinking."

Hani nodded. "I have been thinking as well."

Ariana nodded and began to twist a strand of her long hair around one finger.

"Tell me what you've been thinking," Hani pleaded.

"You go first," she insisted.

"Okay." Hani took a deep breath. "So, you know I have many businesses I am involved with. Enough to keep me busy all of the time."

"Yes, that seems to be the case."

"So, here is what I am thinking. If I only worked on these businesses, and stayed away from the magic, then would you then be willing to give me, give us, a chance?"

"Oh, Hani," she gushed. "I know now that I could never ask that of you. It's a part of who you are. That would be like asking a tiger to give up its stripes."

"But neither could I ask you to put yourself in the middle of something you and your family are so opposed to."

"Well maybe it's high time that my family and I step out a bit from our comfort zone, and open our minds to something different."

Hani laughed. "Can you imagine? A holiday meal with our two families, together? Just think about how that might go."

Ariana laughed as well. "My mum would probably not set foot within a six-yard radius of your dad. And my father would no doubt spend an entire week praying in the mosque afterwards."

"And *my* father would not be able to keep himself from sharing stories that would surely scare the life out of both of them."

Their conversation came to a halt as a janitor entered to empty the wastebasket.

"Okay. So maybe not," Ariana continued once the man was gone. "I'm just so confused, Hani. But I keep coming back to something Rachel said, about making choices and controlling our own destiny, about taking responsibility for our own lives."

"That's funny. I just had a talk with her about the complete opposite. About how we must leave ourselves open to the things we cannot understand."

"Huh," Ariana said, trying hard to imagine Rachel's side of that conversation. "But think about it for a minute," she said. "Maybe life isn't about being one way or the other. Perhaps the answers we are looking for come from everywhere—our faith, our brains, *and* our hearts. Listening to just one of those may not be enough in every situation. Do I make any sense?"

Hani sat back with a satisfied smile. "Of course you make sense."

Ariana smiled back. "This isn't just some crazy notion?"

"There is nothing crazy about it."

"You don't think I'm being foolish?"

"You are the least foolish person I have met. In fact, since the first time I saw you, I thought—"

"Okay, enough, Hani." Ariana laughed. "Now you've gone completely too far."

She suddenly stopped, as from the corner of her eye she saw a stirring from under the sheets of the hospital bed. And there was Tariq, eyes wide open, with an odd little smile of his own that made it seem as though he'd been following their conversation all along.

35

"We're going on *that*?" The tiny motorbike purring under Kanu's legs looked no bigger than the old Huffy Rachel used to cruise around on as a kid.

"Sure. Why not?" He revved the engine, as if to prove the bike's worthiness.

"What if we run into trouble? What if we need to get out of there fast?"

"My bike is as fast as a cheetah."

"And what will we do if we need to take the girl with us? There's no room for three on that thing."

"I know people. I have friends everywhere. One word from Kanu"—he snapped his fingers in the air—"and they will come running."

"But what if—"

"Relax. *Hakuna matata*."

"No *hakuna matata*. I'm serious."

"It's okay, Rachel. I have this handled. Trust me. And here, put this on. It is the law." She took one look at the black helmet he'd unhooked from the handlebars and burst out laughing. *Bad Girl*, it declared in sparkly silver gothic lettering splashed across a pink love heart.

And they were off, Rachel on the seat behind Kanu with her arms wrapped around his rock-hard six-pack in true biker-chick fashion as if it were something she did every day. She wore Miza's *kanga* tied around her neck, flapping behind them like a flag carried into battle. As bumpy as the ride was, a bike was clearly the way to go, especially given Kanu's agility at dodging the dogs and cats and goats and donkeys—not to mention the pedestrians—who all seemed to think the road belonged solely to them.

It was nearly midday before they reached the village, the shadows from the wiry palms short and stubby, reminding Rachel of half-burned candles on a birthday cake. Kanu pulled over at the village square, the bike skidding to a stop on loose gravel. He rested it against a tree and stretched his sinewy arms and legs while Rachel retrieved her camera from the backpack. Nothing in the place seemed at all familiar to her, but then again, she thought, why should it? The road they stopped on did resemble the one in the picture a bit, but honestly it could have been any road leading into any little village—sandy, bumpy, empty. To her right a tall plume of white smoke curled toward the sky.

"That is the village kitchen," Kanu explained. "For people who don't have a place to cook in their homes."

To Rachel's left sat two cars that looked as if they'd been parked there for years, their sunbaked roofs curling with peeled paint. Beyond that was a low white building with a green tin roof.

"And that is the mosque. Does it not look familiar to you?"

Rachel shook her head. "No. But he does."

Kanu followed her gaze to the man sitting behind the tables heavy with fruit, the orange wall behind him gleaming in the light.

"*Jambo!*" Rachel yelled as she trotted toward the stand. The fruit vendor responded with a sweep of his arm across the tables, a gesture of offering of all he had for sale. "Do you remember me? From the other night?" The man raised one eyebrow in puzzlement. Rachel waited as he and Kanu had a quick exchange in Swahili.

"What did he say?" she asked anxiously.

"I asked him if he knows you, but he does not."

"With the camera," she insisted, holding the Leica up to her eye, hoping to jog his memory. The man shook his head. "Ask him if he knows anything about a girl showing up here recently," she urged Kanu.

As Kanu finished his question, the fruit seller pointed a dark finger toward a cluster of houses near the shore.

They continued on foot down the rubbish-strewn road toward the heart of the village, past simple homes made of unpainted bricks, their windows covered with newspapers and faded cloth, past a few shops shuttered for the noonday break, past more cows than people. Rachel suddenly yanked Kanu's arm.

"What is it?" he asked.

"That's it! The house. The one in my photo!"

She quickened her pace, Kanu hustling to keep up.

From the outside the house was quiet, the only movement coming from the laundry stirring gently on the line. Rachel was almost at the open front doorway when Kanu grabbed her shoulder. "Stop," he advised, his eyes darting from side to side.

"Let me check it out. You go wait by the trees. If there is somebody here, they will be less suspicious of me than of a *mzungu*."

"A what?"

"A white person."

Rachel watched as Kanu called hello through the doorway. A woman in a purple turban appeared with a small child on one hip and an annoyed look on her face that melted into a smile the minute Kanu opened his mouth. They exchanged a few words Rachel could not hear, but when Kanu returned to her side he seemed sure there was nothing amiss in that house.

"Just a woman and her children," he assured Rachel. "Her husband was not home."

"But what did you say to her? What did you ask?"

"Oh, this and that. Just enough for me to look around at what was behind her back. You know."

"No, I don't know."

"Just a little conversation. It is what I am good at, talking with the ladies."

"Apparently so." Rachel paused to give the house one last look. "Come on, let's keep going toward the water." But they had barely taken two steps when Rachel turned back.

"Now what is it?" Kanu asked.

Rachel pointed toward the front of the house.

"What? What is it?" His forehead was wrinkled with confusion.

"Under the window. Can't you see?"

Kanu moved in closer. "What is it I'm looking for?" he yelled back over his shoulder.

"*Shhh!* Here," she whispered as she reached his side, pointing down toward the ground. "The lion."

Kanu cocked his head and squinted into the dirt. "Ah. So there is a drawing of a lion. So what does that mean?"

Rachel looked down at the fresh outline etched deep in the sand. "It means that Sabra is here. And in trouble."

Kanu raised his eyebrows. "A lion means trouble?"

"It does. Just trust me." Rachel had to laugh, listening to herself. Here she was, tossing all logic into the air and instead taking her cues from a crazy dream and a bizarre set of photos that seemed to come out of nowhere. What was the matter with her?

"Okay," Kanu said. "So now what?"

"Now we go down to the water."

The turquoise sea was dotted with women squatting in a low afternoon tide that seemed to stretch out for miles, the rainbow of colors of their clothing making them appear like flowers rising from the shimmering ocean. Rachel stood at the shoreline with one hand shading her eyes, squinting to make out their faces. But the women remained hunched over the rows and rows of little sticks supporting their harvest, their images reflected in the water as if they existed in two worlds at the same time. "I'm going out there," Rachel said to Kanu as she handed him her backpack and bent down to untie the laces of her boots.

"I will come with you," he insisted as he kicked off his sandals.

"I'm good, Kanu. Believe me, I've done way more dangerous things than this in my life, all by myself."

Kanu stood looking at her for a moment, as if trying to figure her out. "Well, okay. But be careful of the rocks. And the shells. And the fish," he warned as he parked himself under a shady palm. "I will be here if you need me."

Rachel rolled up her pants and waded in, the memory of another sea, another time, another Rachel propelling her toward the horizon and the women busy at their work.

Nobody seemed to notice her splashing through the shallow water past the pair of fishing boats marooned by the tide, listing to one side like a couple of beached whales. It wasn't until she was about halfway out to the seaweed women that one of them, set a distance apart from the others, finally stood, her hands held against her broad back as she slowly rose.

Rachel picked up her pace and called out from behind the woman. "*Jambo!* Hello! I am looking for someone named Bi-Zena. Do you know where she is?"

The woman continued to stretch as she faced out to sea, her thick body draped with long, clumpy strands of slimy seaweed fresh from the muck.

"Excuse me!" Rachel shouted. "Bi-Zena. Do you know her?"

The woman began to turn, water dripping from the hems of her skirts. "I am Bi-Zena," the woman said, her hands coming to rest on two hips as wide as the ocean itself.

"My name is Rachel," she said, her eyes cast cautiously downward as she picked her way through the sharp shells that seemed to be multiplying underfoot. "Miza sent me." She held out the *kanga* as if it were a calling card.

"I know who you are," the woman said in a voice that Rachel could swear she'd heard before. And when she looked up, she found herself face to face with the old woman with the goat. Except with no goat. And with about three times as much heft on her body, and with skin as black as the nighttime sky. On second look it seemed as though the only thing the two old women really shared was that one cloudy eye.

"But—"

Bi-Zena held up a finger. "There is no time for questions. You have a job to do."

Rachel wiped the sweat from her brow. "Sabra. Where is she?"

The seaweed woman pointed to an orange speck in the distance. "She is working. She is safe here, in the ocean."

"Thank goodness," Rachel sighed.

"But that does not mean she is not living in danger. You must take her with you, back to her sister. Take her to Oman. It is the only way. Her uncle is planning to sell her, just like a goat at auction."

At those words Rachel's eyes flew to meet the woman's own, expecting some sort of sign of recognition at last. But there was none, just one milky eye that looked nowhere and a clear eye that had turned its focus back to the girl in the distance. Rachel turned to Kanu, who was just where she had left him, resting under the palms. "Okay," she answered Bi-Zena slowly. "We will come back. Tomorrow. I can take her with me then."

"No!" the woman barked. "It must be today! There is no time to waste. Her uncle is a fast-moving evil, one that waits for nothing. You must take her today."

"Today?" Rachel took a deep breath. "Today. Okay. Let me go try to arrange for a car. I'll be back. I swear."

"Wait!" the woman commanded. "It is not so easy. The people of our village," she said, pointing to the other women still hard at work, "they are all wanting to get into the uncle's good favor. They are gossips, with tongues as quick as wildfire. I can see them already wondering why I am speaking with you. They cannot know, they cannot witness, what will happen. You must find a way to make the girl disappear."

"Disappear?" Rachel was tempted to laugh, but under the woman's stern watch didn't dare.

"I mean you must get her away in secret. Without the others knowing. And quickly, please."

The sun had dropped halfway toward the horizon by the time Rachel arrived back at the beach with her plan fully in place. The women were finishing up their workday, hauling the seaweed toward the shore, dragging their bundles behind them like the train of a wedding dress. Bi-Zena was leading the way, her large breasts swinging under her seaweed boa.

Rachel stood in the white sand among the empty coconut shells, between the crude wooden drying racks made from sticks and twine. For now the structures were serving as a playground for the village children freed from a day spent in school, who jumped and ran and skipped along the shore before heading home for the day. She tugged at the camera around her neck and headed into the shallow surf.

"*Jambo!*" she called out as she neared the women. "Photos?" Bi-Zena shook her head theatrically and wagged a finger in Rachel's face. The other women all scowled and shook their heads as well, some covering their faces behind their damp arms.

Rachel waited for Bi-Zena to pass before reaching out with a fistful of bills toward the other women. One peered into Rachel's hand and raised her eyebrows. The next did the same, looking to her friends for support. But then came a bony young woman who gladly pocketed the cash, holding up her heavy bundle toward Rachel's lens like a trophy.

Others soon followed, suddenly cured of their camera shyness by Rachel's bottomless pockets. She clicked away as the crowd grew around her. Through the throng of women clamoring for her attention, Rachel struggled to catch sight of Bi-Zena abandoning her harvest on the shore and heading back out to sea for the girl in orange.

By now the seaweed women were competing with poses straight out of *Vogue*. After taking what seemed like a thousand photos, Rachel doled out the last of her bills and held her empty hands up in a sign of surrender.

As the women went back to their bundles of seaweed, she turned toward the white smoke billowing from the village square. But before leaving the beach, Rachel let out a piercing whistle in the direction of the playing children, holding a bag of candy above her head as a lure. They came running. "Yes!" she said to herself as she tossed a handful of sweets over her shoulder.

The parade behind her grew as she made her way up the gravelly road, the shouts and squeals of delighted children bringing others from their homes to take part in the tourist bounty. Even some old men, and mothers cradling babies in their arms, turned to watch the joyful free-for-all, a scene that had become exactly the distraction that Rachel had hoped it would be, enough to keep prying eyes off the large woman and the tall, skinny girl also scurrying toward the village square.

The candy rained down in a steady stream onto the children's heads as they scrambled to keep up. As they neared the tiny mosque, Rachel turned from the crush to see a taxi parked behind a cluster of palm trees, with Kanu behind the wheel. With the screaming and scrambling keeping the chaos alive, she slipped away to help shuffle Sabra into the back seat and under the half of the *kanga* Rachel had been wearing around her neck.

Once the girl was safely tucked away, Rachel turned to Bi-Zena, standing tall and proud with her arms folded on her chest. "Thank you," Rachel said as the woman's mouth broke into a wide, toothless grin.

"No, it is you who is to be thanked, Lil' Cherry Bomb," she answered.

And with that the woman turned and headed back toward the sea.

36

The warmth of her sister's hand pressed against her own was as comforting as a blanket to a baby. Sabra shifted her weight from a cross-legged position on the floor and leaned her shoulder against the arm of Miza's chair. The atmosphere in Tariq's hospital room was giddy, almost as if there were a party going on. Sabra lowered her head to cover a yawn. Though exhausted from everything that had happened the day before, she did not want to miss a word.

Tariq looked good to her, though perhaps thinner and paler than the last time she had seen him in Zanzibar. He seemed so hungry to hear about everything that had gone on while he was in his long sleep. How strange it must have been, to be there but not, to be on the earth as it turned yet know nothing beyond your own mind—a thought that made her wonder. "Did you have dreams while you were asleep?" she asked.

Tariq hesitated for a moment. "I suppose they were dreams. I can remember hearing some voices. Maybe it was nurses, maybe not. Sometimes I felt as though I was watching myself in this bed, as if I were somebody else, but I would see the whole thing from under the water, like being in the ocean, but in the sky." He laughed a little. "I know it makes no sense. I'm sorry."

Sabra closed her eyes for a second, just to see what it would feel like to be in a state like that. But all that she felt was her sleepiness trying to lure her into its soft clutches. She jarred herself awake and tried to catch up with the conversation swirling around her.

Tariq's friend Hani was very handsome. She admired the way he remained so calm, so attentive to everyone else's needs, like how he seemed to appear with tea or water or something to eat before you even said you were thirsty or hungry. It was almost as if he could read your mind. And his friend! At first Sabra had assumed the dark-haired woman was his wife, the way they were always looking at each other, making little comments that nobody else could hear. But when Sabra had said something to Ariana about her husband, the woman blushed and quickly corrected Sabra's mistake with a giggle that nevertheless made it clear that having Hani as a husband was something she'd delight in.

She loved Ariana's look, so glamorous yet so real at the same time. As the others talked, she made a quick study of the woman's style—makeup but not too much makeup, eyebrows strong and neat, lipstick that was not too shiny, small earrings that glimmered through the strands of her thick dark hair. She reminded Sabra of those girls in the music videos that Miza didn't like her to watch. And those eyelashes! She could capture a fly in those things. But more than her beauty, what Sabra liked most about Ariana was her kindness, and her generosity. When she had noticed Sabra looking at her bracelet, made of heavy blue and gold beads, she immediately took it off of her own wrist and placed it on Sabra's. And when she heard that they had left Zanzibar in too much of a rush to pack a proper bag for Sabra, Ariana had darted out of the hospital and returned with a bag full of everything she might need: a toothbrush and hairbrush, some clean undergarments, and even a small tube of pink lip gloss, which had made Miza frown.

And then there was Rachel. Unable to sleep from the excitement of being on an airplane for the first time, and anxious to practice her English, Sabra had peppered Rachel with questions all the way from Zanzibar City to Muscat. *How many cities have you been to? How many languages do you speak? Have you seen the pyramids? Were you ever in an avalanche?* This woman had done everything. She had lived history, instead of just reading about it in boring schoolbooks. And the people she must have met, so many different faces and customs and beliefs.

Sabra could not wait to finish her studies and become a famous photographer, just like Rachel. But *she* would make sure to dress better for the job, she now thought as she eyed the woman in her rumpled pants and thick, heavy boots. Rachel could be so pretty if only she tried to be a little more like her friend Ariana.

Now she heard Rachel talking about what happened when they got to Stone Town. They had already shared with everybody the details of how they made their escape from the beach, Rachel describing how the seaweed women had closed in around her like a swirling cyclone, and Sabra telling how she had dashed from the ocean straight to the taxi with its motor going. She had even made them laugh with her description of Bi-Zena running alongside her, her breasts flopping up and down like two fat fish out of water, and her massive shadow providing as much cover as a canopy.

It all seemed so very long ago now. They had rushed back to Zanzibar City, determined to catch the last flight of the day to Muscat, to put as much distance between Sabra and her uncle as possible before anything more could happen.

But a stop at the apartment in Stone Town was necessary, as Sabra would not be allowed out of the country without the proper paperwork. Fortunately Miza had secured a passport and visa for her months before, when she had been unsure about leaving her sister behind. And luckily, Sabra knew exactly where her sister would have put them, in the bedroom closet on the highest shelf with all the other important papers.

"So there we were," Rachel was saying. "The main front door to the building was open a little, so I ran up while Kanu waited in the taxi with Sabra, still hidden under the *kanga*, just in case. Just before I got to the second landing, I heard steps coming down toward me. These two shady looking guys shoved their way past me, as if I weren't there."

"The men who were to pay my uncle for me," Sabra added with a scowl.

Rachel continued with her story. "The key to the flat was just where Sabra knew it would be, under the doormat."

"We must find a better hiding place, Mi-mi," Tariq said, frowning.

"Anyway," Rachel continued, "just as I stood to insert the key in the lock, the door swung open, and there I was, face to face with the meanest looking son of a bitch I've ever laid eyes on. And I've seen a lot of mean sons of bitches in my life, trust me."

"My uncle," Miza murmured.

"I figured. So I just slid the key into my palm and pretended to be lost, confused about which apartment I was looking for. Then I wandered up the hallway until I was sure he was down the stairs and out the front door, and scrambled in to get the papers."

"And I had just come up for some air when I heard the big wood door slam," said Sabra. "I screamed, and Kanu took one look at my uncle and stepped on the gas! I am lucky he was in a hurry and did not see me."

"Yeah," Rachel added. "And imagine me coming out to find nobody there. Thank god Kanu had only driven around the block and back." She gulped at a bottle of water. "So what went on around here while I was gone?"

Sabra saw a look pass between Ariana and Hani. "Not much," they answered in unison. Ariana began to slide a pendant back and forth along the chain around her neck, a pendant that Sabra recognized as the lucky coin her sister had worn for as long as she could remember.

Rachel cast a worried glance at Miza. "And what about Maryam?" she asked, her whole face scrunching up as if she did not really want to hear the answer.

"Oh, Hani's father took care of her, and good!"

Sabra saw Rachel's eyes widen at Ariana's words.

"What do you mean 'took care of her'?" the American asked.

"Oh, please, Rachel. It wasn't like that at all. He simply told her off." Ariana laughed. "And then kind of scared the shit out of her a little."

Rachel's head shook quickly back and forth, as if she were trying to rid her mind of something. She took another gulp from the water bottle. "So she's out of the picture, or okay about all this, or what?"

"We shall see," Tariq said with a shrug. "I am thinking it will be all right. Whatever happens, I am going to live in Zanzibar now, all of the time." Sabra felt her sister give her hand a tight squeeze. "And I am hoping that when I assure Maryam that she will have the money she wants, that will be enough for her to be content. It is a small price for me to pay, as I have all of my riches right here."

"You must all come visit!" Miza said with a smile.

"Oh." Rachel grabbed the straps of her backpack and slid it toward her. "I almost forgot." She pulled the wrinkled half of the *kanga* from inside.

Miza shook her head. "No. You must keep it."

"But—"

"I insist. Do you know what the words mean?" Miza asked, pointing to the faded letters barely visible across the blue border of the cloth.

Rachel shook her head.

"It is something our mother wanted us to remember, to make us strong as girls growing into women. It says, *every bird flies with its own wings*."

"That's beautiful, Miza. But I couldn't—"

"Do you know what, though?" Miza continued. "I do not think it is right. Because I have seen how some birds fly together in lines, taking turns being the one in the front, falling back when they get tired, every bird flying a little above the one ahead to help shelter it from the wind, each one making it easier for the next so that they can all go farther." Miza gestured toward the *kanga*. "And so you understand why you must keep it. It is yours now." Miza's one hand remained clasped with Sabra's as she reached out for Rachel's with the other. "You are our sister now."

37

"Are you sure you've got everything in there?" Ariana eyed Rachel's backpack with wonder. "Need water, or tissues, or something to read on the plane?"

"I'm good." They stood together near the curb as others sped past them pushing carts heaped with luggage and cartons and bags, looking as though they were moving entire households across the globe. It was well past midnight, and the Muscat airport was as busy as if it were midday.

"How long is your flight?" Ariana asked.

"I don't know. I think about seventeen hours or so. I'll be back home tomorrow, with the transfer in Doha and the time difference and all."

"Ugh. Sounds awful. But I guess you're used to it."

"Yeah. No biggie." Rachel shifted her backpack to the other shoulder. "It's okay, you know. I'm fine here. Hani's waiting for you." She pointed to the car parked across the road.

"I know. I'm just not very fond of goodbyes."

Rachel looked down at the ground. "Yeah. Me neither."

Ariana yawned and checked her watch.

"So when are you headed back to Dubai?" Rachel asked.

"I'm not sure. I'm at least going to stick around until Miza has the baby, and until Tariq is back on his feet. Maybe I'll even try to make friends with Hani's mother," she said with a laugh. "Who knows?"

"I'm betting on you in that match."

"Thanks. And you?"

"I've got to get back to work. Actually, I guess I *want* to get back to work."

"That's good. Very good. I'm sort of anxious to get back to work as well, though I'm thinking of doing something quite different this time around. I've got my mind set on something a bit more meaningful." She shifted her weight from one foot to the other. "Will I be seeing you again?"

"You never know. Maybe I'll need a fixer!"

The two women laughed, their arms flying around each other for a warm embrace.

"I'll miss you, Rachel."

Rachel wiped her eye with the back of her sleeve. "Yeah. Likewise."

"Have a safe journey."

"And you as well, my friend. Wherever it takes you."

Rachel settled into the window seat with her phone as she waited for the plane to begin taxiing. Already there was a selfie from Ariana, sent from Hani's phone, the two of them grinning into the lens from the front seat of his car. Rachel reversed the direction of her own phone's camera and stuck her tongue out in response. Then she turned her attention to her work.

Maggie—she texted to her friend in New York. *Leaving Oman. Assignment was an epic fail. Sorry.*

Rachel accepted a glass of wine from the flight attendant and took a hearty sip. On the other side of the little window the sky was splattered with stars, each one glimmering like a tiny pinhole leading to the promise of another, brighter universe.

But, she added in a second message, *I do have a whole other story, a very different one, that you just might be interested in instead. xoxoR*

Acknowledgments

I still have to pinch myself when I say it: *The Zanzibar Wife* is my fifth book. Seriously, I can't believe it! Each step along the way, from researching to finding the characters, has been both fascinating and challenging. So many remarkable people worked with me or supported me through the process that allowed this book to exist.

First and foremost, I want to thank Ellen Kaye, whose wisdom, sense of story and writing gifts never cease to amaze me. I am so ecstatic we are a team. I often think about the crazy research we did with *The House on Carnaval Street* (aka *Margarita Wednesdays*) and *Return to the Little Coffee Shop of Kabul*. You were right beside me all the way, Ellen, from the sacrifice you made to be with me in Oman (I thank your family for that too), and then through many revisions. You are always my rock. I hope we have many more travel adventures and books in our future.

A huge shout out must go to Beverley Cousins and her team at Penguin Random House Australia. What can I say? Without you, there is no book. Beverley, working with you and your team is a joy. You took this book to places I didn't know it could go. And hats off to the designer who did the cover. It's my favorite so far.

Maddie West at Little, Brown UK and Sphere Fiction, you always have faith in me and my stories, even when they are just budding in my head. Knowing you believe in me gives me the courage to think outside the box and keep looking for those stories.

My rock star and always faithful agent and friend, Marly Rusoff. I love our conversations on the phone when you are trying to help me sort through a storyline or when you flat out tell me it sucks, and then come up with something better. You are the one who pushes me to find that story deep down in my soul, and it's you who has always believed in me. I am so grateful for you and Mihai (Michael) Radulescu. Can you believe it's been fourteen years since you both decided to take a chance on me? Everything changed the moment you walked into my life. I don't know if you realize the positive trickle-down effect you have had on so many lives, and the direct impact that you have had on my family. I have huge love for the both of you. Thank you so very much.

I aspire to be like you, Eliza Ilyas. You are smart, funny, beautiful, and have an unwavering faith. Thank you for opening your home, and your life, to me. I loved the research that we did together, the adventures we shared, and the many selfies we took. You are such an inspiration and loyal friend. I can't wait for more crazy selfie-filled travels.

Karen Kinne, you are my best friend. Or, really, you are my sister. We have very seldom lived in the same country at the same time, but I know you are only a phone call or flight away. I love that you will help me sort out difficult plots in a book, even if it takes hours. I love our friendship.

Jayne Lowe, our meeting was designed by a force greater than ourselves. You took a leap of faith when you hopped on a plane to Mexico because you thought we should meet. I adore you and your sweetness. Thank you for taking time out of your busy life to help me do the research in Zanzibar. You are a gentle soul with a huge heart. Our friendship may be new, but it will last a lifetime.

Denis Asahara, my one and only. You are uncomplicated, easy, and allow me to just be me, even if it drives you a bit batty. You often have more confidence in me than I have in myself. You seem convinced that I am a strong woman, even when I feel weak and scared. I remember commenting on how worried you must have been when Ellen and I were lost in the mountains of Mexico. You calmly said, "Really, Deb, you drove over the Khyber Pass from Afghanistan to Pakistan, and you didn't seem to be worried about the Taliban. Now I'm supposed to be worried about you driving in Mexico?" Okay, Denis, you made your point. But you also make me freakin' crazy and happy all at the same time. I can't imagine life without you.

Andy Besch, you are such a cool dude. You and Ellen open your home to me and welcome me like family. Thank you for sharing your wife with me.

A special thank you to both my sons, Noah and Zach Lentz. You listen to me ramble on about story plots you don't care about. I call at weird hours of the day and night because I just need to talk out a book idea when no one else wants to listen to me. You and your wonderful wives have given me the greatest blessing on the earth with the gift of grandbabies. They have given me such a different perspective on life. Each day is better because of all of you. I am so proud of you both for the fathers, husbands and sons you have become. I can't wait for the day my grandchildren can read, and they find out what a crazy grandma I really am.

Badar, you opened your home to me and to Ellen. You taught us about the many mystical sides of Oman. Your family is wonderful and gracious. I will never forget your kindness. I welcome you and your family to my home, just as you welcomed me into yours.

Adil, you are the funniest driver in the world. You are a wealth of information, and I can't wait to visit you again in Oman. You truly inspired so much of the book.

Simba, it was because of you that we found all the magic in Zanzibar. I loved how you listened for hours about my fictional Zanzibar wife and her family as if they were real people. You showed me the house you thought Miza and her sister would live in. You took me to the house of the creepy uncle. You found the magic man. You were a great translator and worked hard to help me find everything I needed for the novel.

For my posse of women friends: Ingrid, I love our breakfast times, and discussing so many different ideas for current and future books. It's so much fun. Thank you for being willing to listen and help me purge things from my head. Rene Carlson, you are the best. When I called you in the middle of the night and asked you to go to Dubai and Oman with me, you booked the ticket before morning. I am so glad we shared this great time together. Linda Bine, a friend who is always so willing to lend a critical eye. You were always a big help.

Polly, you are the longest relationship I have ever had. You put up with my endless chattering about the meaning of life.

And I put up with your shedding, hairballs and your litter box. You are the best cat ever.

And what can I say about the amazing people that walk through the doors of Tippy Toes (the little spa by the sea)? You have made Mazatlán the best place on earth to live. Between the staff and the customers, I am surrounded with so much love and friendship. I am honored to call this beautiful seaside city of Mazatlán my home.

Lastly, the people of both Oman and Zanzibar opened their homes and heart to me during my time of research. I gained such insight and respect for you. I so admire these warm and wonderful people who helped populate these pages with so much joy, mystery, and friendship. I will always be grateful to my many new friends in these two beautiful places on this earth.

A Q&A with Deborah Rodriguez
(contains spoilers)

Your first two novels were either fully or partly set in Afghanistan. Why did you choose Oman as a new location for this novel?

I was preparing for a trip to Dubai when I began to wonder why, after so many trips to the Gulf region, I had never visited Oman. That's when I decided to do some research to see if it might be a good holiday spot. Straight away, the country came alive for me. I was drawn in to the amazing history and intriguing geography, and wondered how this country seemed to stay off the radar while so much was happening all around it. That's when the holiday trip became a research trip. My head began to spin ideas of different storylines with the backdrop of Oman. What really sealed the deal for me was when I read that the town of Bahla, in Oman, was named by *National Geographic* as one of the ten most haunted places in the world. I was certain that this country would be the perfect place for a book.

How did Zanzibar come into your story?

On my first visit to Oman my driver kept saying things like, *My father and his Zanzibar wife did this*, or *I can't wait to go to Zanzibar this summer to visit my family and do that*. First, I asked him, "How many wives does your father have in Zanzibar?" His reply was, "Only one, right now."

Next I asked why his family was in Zanzibar. It was then I learned that in 1698 Zanzibar fell under the control of the Sultanate of Oman. So today Zanzibar still is the ancestral home to many Omanis, and the two countries have a very strong connection. I loved how the exotic spice island seemed to be the perfect yin to Oman's majestic yang. The two places are such a good fit, and felt like the perfect combination from which to weave a tale.

Oman and Zanzibar are new settings for you, yet they completely come alive on the page. What research did you undertake to write this novel?

Research can be fun, crazy, and this time a bit out of my comfort zone. I began by searching for the homes that my characters would live in, the roads they would walk on, the foods they would eat, but I also knew that, for this book, I had to search out the magic in both Zanzibar and Oman. It's easy to say, *Yep, doing some research, going to try to find the magic*. But trust me, it's not that easy, and it definitely can't be found in the travel brochures. I tried my hardest to reach out to people online, to try to arrange meetings, but I was either turned away or the email threads came to a halt when I tried to talk about magic.

I think one of the reasons the story feels so real is that much of it is real. I have a difficult time creating a story unless I have experienced the majority of it first-hand. For example, once the basic idea of the book was born, I traveled to Oman to make sure the storyline could actually work in this location. Pages were written, and the book was on its way. Now it was time for the second trip, the trip to get all the important details. I wanted to trace the footsteps of the main characters, so that I could see what they saw, feel what they felt, and possibly understand the fear they faced. I wanted this book to tell a story, but to be as real as it possibly could.

I wasn't in Oman long before I could tell that the book was taking on a life of its own. It honestly felt like something was guiding me, that the story wanted to be told. It's amazing what you can learn when you listen to the universe and follow the clues in front of you. There was definitely something super-natural that happened in Bahla, and I do not have an explanation for it. I wasn't looking for a ghost story—what I did want to understand was what they meant by magic. I have to tell you, there was a moment when I did begin to question myself, and wondered how far I would actually go to get the story.

What was it that you found most surprising about these two places?

With Oman, I think I was surprised most by the incredible natural beauty. Muscat is a wonderful city, but the moment you leave the city and enter the mountain area it's unbelievably stunning. I had also heard that the Omanis were some of the friendliest people on the planet, but thought that was a pretty broad statement. But seriously? OMG. They *are* the kindest, gentlest and friendliest people on the planet.

Zanzibar, what can I say . . . the name sounds exotic, and the place truly is. I loved the flavor of the old spice trade, the ancient seaweed ladies, the clear blue beaches, and the old, winding streets of Stone Town. I felt like I was going back and forth between a holiday postcard and *National Geographic* magazine. I don't say this lightly, but it was one of those places that made me think, *I could live here.*

Are there any personal experiences you had in either of these two places that are reflected in the novel?

There was one experience that happened in Bahla that to this day kind of scares me to think about. My research partner, Ellen, and I were heading off to Bahla, hot on the trail of the magic. I had read that Bahla was the birthplace of the *jinn*, and that a lot of magic happened there. After hitting a lot of dead ends, we were finally told to go to the old souk in the center of the town and talk to the man who has the shop in front of the large tree. *He will be the only one who can assist you*, they said. So off we went and found the man in the small shop in front of the tree. His was the only stall open, as it was nearing lunch time. After introducing ourselves and telling him that we were there doing research on the "folklore" of Bahla, I just blurted out, "Are you the man who does the magic?" He didn't even flinch; he calmly offered us dates, poured us a coffee and said, "Yes." When I asked him if he would answer my questions, he agreed, but insisted we join him and his family for lunch. He politely told our driver to leave, assuring us that his son would make sure we got back to our hotel in Nizwa.

Now, remember, we were in a mountain village in what is considered to be one of the most haunted places in the world. Ellen and I looked at each other, both trying to figure out if we should simply bolt back to the car before our driver disappeared and head back to Nizwa before we both turned into goats or something. But we didn't run. Instead, we went to the magic man's house for lunch.

While eating grapes and apple slices, the man turned his focus on me, and began telling me all these things about myself. He knew of my past marriages, and was certain that someone had performed black magic on me in the past, which was causing me to not sleep and to have vivid dreams. It's true, I don't sleep well and my dreams are like movies. And I had always wondered about a time in Afghanistan when I found a lock of my hair, some nail clippings, and some odd looking writing I did not understand hidden in my salon. When my cleaning ladies found these hidden items in a glasses case, the salon was in an uproar. Water was poured over the writing, and I was taken to some guy who read my palms. I had no idea what he saw, as I didn't have enough command of the language. But I could hear the staff whispering about this for days, and acting as if I were going to drop dead on the spot or burst into flames. I really never thought about it much again until that day with the magic man in Bahla, who seemed to already know about this event. He told me that someone close to me had been trying to harm me and my family. Looking back, maybe I should have taken what happened in Afghanistan more seriously.

After the meal the magic man casually asked if I wanted it removed. I didn't know if "it" meant a *jinn* or what. I didn't know what to think. I looked at Ellen and thought, shit. This is not what I signed up for. It's just a book! How did it get to the point where I was going to have something *removed* from me? At the time it felt like I was going to be donating a kidney or something. I was afraid. Did I really want this? And then I thought that even if I did have a *jinn*, I was very comfortable with it, and we seemed to get along very well, and I really wasn't certain if I believed in all this hocus-pocus, and what have I gotten myself into anyway? Ellen looked at me and said, "Deb, you really don't have to do this." I was definitely not keen on having what sounded like some sort of exorcism ritual being performed on me, but, I reminded myself, this entire trip I'd been looking for the magic, and here it was, right in front of me. How could I pass up the opportunity? So I told Ellen not to leave me alone for one minute, to take notes and pictures. She assured me that she wasn't about to go anywhere, and she stayed to witness the magic, just like Ariana did.

Did something happen to me in the house at the lunch with the magic man? I believe it did. Do I feel any differently since all this took place? Well, I do feel that we should never think we are alone on this earth. I do feel like I was touched by something powerful. Is my life perfect after my big event? No, but who wants a perfect life anyway?

On a totally different note, it appears that you can't go two feet without running into a gigolo in Zanzibar.

Are any of the characters in this story based on people you met in your travels?

No one is safe from being a part of one of my books. When I start taking notes over dinner, you're most likely being auditioned for a part in a book. I think all my characters start out as real people, then morph into a final character who is sometimes someone very different. In this book, Ariana was greatly inspired by one of my dearest friends. I would visit her as often as I could when passing through Dubai. I loved how the real Ariana and I could one minute be shopping in the world's largest mall, and the next minute she'd fling her clothes into my dressing room and say, "I'll be back in seven minutes, I need to pray." I found it impressive that no matter where she was or who she was with, she always took the time to pray. I admired her commitment.

Kanu, now referred to as my favorite gigolo, was very real and did help me find the magic in Zanzibar. Okay, people, minds out of the gutter: not that kind of magic! I paid him to keep his clothes on while in search of voodoo and witch doctors.

My real driver in Oman was as kind and funny as the driver in the book. It was because of him that the book got the title of *The Zanzibar Wife*. And my real-life magic man and Hani's father are one and the same. His family is so incredible. I still text them at least once a week. This guy was one very amazing, and very kind, man.

The strapline on the book cover is 'With a little magic, anything is possible'—have you had any experiences that you can't explain? Do you believe there are forces at work we don't necessarily understand?

I think that miracles are happening around us all the time. I don't think it hurts to believe in a little magic.

Your novels feature women who—despite different backgrounds and cultures—come together to help and understand each other. An important theme, particularly in the world today?

I enjoy different cultures, traditions, and religions, and love how we are all different yet very much the same. Life is so full of color because of these differences. It's all about respect, and realizing that different is good, and we really all need to stick together. It's about every little girl being able to have the right to dream big. I love a quote by Ellen Johnson Sirleaf, the first elected female head of state in Africa. She said, "If your dreams don't scare you, they are not big enough."

Some ideas for your reading group party

Reading group questions

1. When we first meet Rachel and Ariana, they both appear to be stuck at a low point in their lives. How did their attitudes and beliefs seem to change over the ten days they spent in Oman and Zanzibar?

2. What do you think influenced those changes most?

3. How did the two women influence each other?

4. Miza is living the life of a second wife. What are your thoughts on the nature of a polygamous society?

5. Faith and destiny are strong themes in this novel. Discuss.

6. Have you experienced things in your own life that can't be explained?

7. Have you or anyone you know ever sought advice from a non-traditional source, such as a fortune-teller or a healer?

8. Is there anything about the setting of Oman that was surprising to you?

9. The cultural mores in relationships between men and women in these three women's lives vary greatly. Discuss.

10. Imagine the lives of the three women following the close of this story.

Some delicious dishes to share

The 'real' Spice Island spice cake

By Vanessa Arena, *www.olivesandlucinda.com*

To make this cake I have adapted a basic sponge recipe by introducing soft brown sugar in place of a proportion of the usual superfine (caster) sugar. The balance is designed to give the cake a nice, rich and grainy brown-sugar appearance, while still keeping the mixture sponge-like and light in texture. With regards to the amount of spice you might wish to add, the amounts I suggest here give a good flavor, but this is using reasonably fresh spices. If yours have been sitting in the cupboard for a while, perhaps consider using a little more. This cake stores very well, and will taste fresh for up to five days after it is made if kept in an airtight container.

6 ounces (170 grams) butter, cubed and at room temperature
3 ½ ounces (100 grams) soft brown sugar

2 ½ ounces (70 grams) superfine (caster) sugar
3 free-range eggs
6 ounces (170 grams) self-rising (self-raising) flour
2 teaspoons baking powder
1 teaspoon ground cinnamon
½ teaspoon cloves
2 cardamom pods
1 vanilla pod
3 tablespoons of milk

Preheat the oven to 350 degrees Fahrenheit (180 degrees Celsius) and line a loaf tin with baking parchment. I do this by cutting a rectangle just as wide as the base of the tin, but longer than you need to cover the base and long sides, so that there is a parchment overhang of approximately 2 inches (5 centimetres) over each long side of the tin. When you come to lift the cake out, the overhanging sections can serve as handles. Not having to line the ends of the tin with paper saves time and the problem of having to fold or cut the paper to fit—instead, a small amount of butter to grease the exposed ends of the tin will suffice.

Cream together the butter and both sugars in a large bowl using an electric mixer, until pale and fluffy. Add the eggs, one at a time, mixing to fully incorporate after each addition. Sift in the self-rising flour and baking powder. Gently mix everything together until the flour is fully incorporated. (The mixture should be soft but quite thick at this stage.)

Using a mortar and pestle, grind the whole cloves to a fine powder. Remove the cardamom seeds from their pods by splitting the pod open at the bottom and popping the black seeds out. Discard the empty pods and add the seeds to the ground cloves in the mortar and pestle, continuing to grind until these are also reduced to a fine powder. On a clean cutting board, make an incision along the length of the vanilla pod, and, using a small knife, scrape the black seeds from inside the pod. Add the vanilla seeds to the cake batter, along with the ground cloves and cardamom, and the ground cinnamon.

Add the milk to loosen the batter slightly, and mix gently until the spices are distributed and the milk is incorporated.

Pour into the prepared tin, and bake for 35 minutes or until the cake has begun to come away from the tin at the sides.

Cool slightly on a wire rack before serving warm, with some ice cream for dessert, or enjoy with tea in the afternoon.

Ginger beef samosas

By Vanessa Arena, *www.olivesandlucinda.com*

Though I've used the familiar name 'samosas' to describe these meat-filled triangles, in Zanzibar they are more likely to be called 'sambusas', an amalgam of the Arabic term 'sambousek' and the Indian 'samosa'. Either way, the outcome is an entirely addictive little deep-fried parcel of spicy meat that it is almost impossible not to eat too many of.

If my experience is anything to go by, samosas seem to be a bit of a Zanzibari staple. They are available everywhere (with a special commendation to the selection at the airport departures lounge), are offered with an incredible array of fillings, and are usually accompanied by a large choice of sauces. My favorite sauce may have been the hot *pili pili mbuzi*, a local fluoro-green concoction in a Tabasco-style bottle. Lime pickle is also delicious on the side, as is green mango chutney, or, of course, the classic mint yogurt sauce. Each has its own merits, so perhaps it's better not to restrict your options and to set up a little condiment buffet to go with your samosas.

Makes approximately 24 medium-sized samosas

For the samosas:
1 pound 7 ounces (650 grams) ground (minced) beef
4 tablespoons sunflower or canola oil
1 brown onion, finely grated
3 garlic cloves, crushed
1 ¼-inch (3-centimetre) piece of fresh ginger, finely grated
1 teaspoon ground cumin
1 teaspoon garam masala

1 teaspoon of coriander seeds
salt and pepper to taste
juice of 1 small lemon
12-piece packet of frozen parathas (usually available in
    Indian grocery stores)
¼ cup all-purpose (plain) flour
3 tablespoons water

For the yogurt dipping sauce:
8 ½ ounces (250 grams) thick-set natural yogurt
1 small bunch of mint
juice of 1 lime
salt to taste

To deep-fry:
Approximately 60 fluid ounces (1.75 litres) sunflower or canola oil

Begin to prepare the filling by crushing the coriander seeds to a powder using a mortar and pestle. Combine this with the cumin and garam masala, and lightly toast the spices in a dry pan over medium heat for a couple of minutes until they become fragrant. Once sufficiently toasted, set aside.

Next, heat the 4 tablespoons of oil in a large frying pan or shallow casserole dish over medium heat. Fry the grated onion until it has begun to color slightly, before adding the crushed garlic and grated ginger. Stir everything around occasionally, and keep a close eye on things to ensure that the garlic does not begin to stick and burn. When everything has begun to cook and take on a golden color, turn up the heat to high, and add the beef (along with a little extra oil at this stage if the pan has become dry), breaking up the meat with a wooden spoon as you fry. Once the beef has begun to brown, add the toasted spice mixture and continue to fry until the meat is well browned and cooked through—approximately 10 minutes in total.

At this point the mixture should be quite dry and rubbly. If you still have some liquid in the pan, continue to cook until this has evaporated completely. Lastly, add some salt, and a grind of pepper to taste, before turning off the heat and squeezing in the lemon juice. Cover the pan and set aside to cool for 30 minutes.

While the filling is cooling, make the yogurt dipping sauce by blending the mint in a food processor with a few drops of oil until it forms a paste. Add the yogurt and lime juice, then blend for a further few seconds until everything is well combined and you have a nice green-flecked sauce. Add salt and mix through. If you'd like to add a little more lime juice (and think the consistency can stand the extra fluid), feel free to do so at this point. Pour the sauce into a serving bowl, and refrigerate until you are ready to use.

When you are ready to assemble the samosas, take the parathas from the freezer and allow them to thaw for 3 minutes. Meanwhile, heat a dry frying pan over medium heat.

Next, take the first paratha from the packet and lightly brush a small amount of oil over all over its surface using a pastry brush. Then, take a second paratha from the packet, and over one surface of this, use your hand to sprinkle a light dusting of flour. Finally, place the oiled surface of the first paratha directly on top of the floured surface of the second.

When the pan is sufficiently hot, carefully heat the conjoined parathas until they begin to round at the edges, and the edges of the bottom disc seem to lift slightly from the pan. Use a spatula to flip and heat the other side.

When both sides are cooked and lightly golden, remove from the pan and place back on the bench. Carefully peel the two discs apart (the oil and flour should have ensured that they do not stick to each other) and slice each disc in half. What you'll have now is 4 semicircular samosa wrappers ready to be filled.

(By cooking the discs together like this, we are trying to ensure that the outer surfaces will become dry, making the dough-wrapper easy to handle, while the inner surfaces remain uncooked and sticky enough to be helpful in sealing the samosa once the meat is inside.)

To assemble the samosas, combine 3 tablespoons of flour with a little water to make a sticky paste. Place a semicircle of dough uncooked side facing up on your worktop. Position this so that the flat or cut side is facing to the right (that is, inward), and spread a small amount of the flour paste along the bottom half of the rounded edge of the wrapper.

Now fold the top of the wrapper down so that a small triangle extends slightly over the cut edge. Bring the bottom part of the wrapper up to meet it to form a cone shape with two short 'bunny' ears, and then press to join along the seal where you have spread the flour paste.

Fill the cone with the beef mixture, then, to seal, dab a little more flour paste onto the inside of the bunny ears. Fold the ears over to join to the opposite side of the cone and press down to seal. Continue until you have rolled, filled and folded the rest of the samosas.

Next, heat the oil in a deep, heavy-based saucepan. (Note that the oil should not come more than halfway up the saucepan to avoid it bubbling over.) Test the temperature of the oil by dropping in a square of bread or excess samosa wrapper: if the oil immediately forms small bubbles around it, and colors the bread within about 30 seconds, then it is at the right temperature.

Deep-fry the samosas in batches of three until they are golden brown in color. Drain on paper towels and keep warm in a 140 degree Fahrenheit (60 degree Celsius) oven until you have finished frying and are ready to serve them alongside the yogurt dipping sauce, mango chutney, lime pickle, hot *pili pili mbuzi*, or whatever else you've managed to gather up!

Omani halwa

By Jaleela Banu, *www.cookbookjaleela.blogspot.com*

Since 1920, the Omanis have prepared this authentic sweet during feasts and Eid celebrations. Halwa is a fundamental part of daily life in Oman, often served at special occasions like weddings, funerals, or other social gatherings. It is the standard food when greeting guests, regardless of class or social distinction, along with Arabic coffee, which is known as *qahwa*.

Serves 9
1 tablespoon ghee (or butter)
1 ¾ ounces (50 grams) cashew nuts, chopped
1 ounce (25 grams) almonds, chopped
17 fluid ounces (500 millilitres) water
6 ounces (175 grams) sugar
1 ½ teaspoons cardamom powder
3 ½ ounces (100 grams) cornstarch (cornflour)
a few drops of red food coloring
1 ¾ ounces (50 grams) butter
1 tablespoon saffron
3 tablespoons rosewater
1 ounce (25 grams) pistachio flakes

In a wide, nonstick pan, heat the ghee (or butter) and fry the cashew nuts and chopped almonds. Set aside.

Make the sugar syrup by adding the sugar and ½ teaspoon of the cardamom powder to 10 fluid ounces (300 millilitres) of the water in a saucepan, and boiling for 5 minutes.

Put the remaining 7 fluid ounces (200 millilitres) of water into a bowl and add the cornstarch and red coloring, and mix well.

Add the colored cornstarch mixture to the sugar syrup, stirring continuously until there are no lumps.

Then add the butter, saffron, rosewater and 1 teaspoon cardamom powder, and stir continuously until combined.

Finally, add the roasted cashews and almonds, and stir well.

Grease a slice tray with ghee. Pour the halwa into the tray and let it cool. Garnish with pistachio flakes. Cut into desired shapes.

THE LITTLE COFFEE SHOP OF KABUL

Deborah Rodriguez

One little café. Five extraordinary women . . .

In a little coffee shop in one of the most dangerous places on earth, five very different women come together.

Sunny, the proud proprietor, who needs an ingenious plan— and fast—to keep her café and customers safe . . .

Yazmina, a young pregnant woman stolen from her remote village and now abandoned on Kabul's violent streets . . .

Candace, a wealthy American who has finally left her husband for her Afghan lover, the enigmatic Wakil . . .

Isabel, a determined journalist with a secret that might keep her from the biggest story of her life . . .

And **Halajan**, the sixty-year-old den mother, whose long-hidden love affair breaks all the rules.

As these five discover there's more to one another than meets the eye, they form a unique bond that will forever change their lives and the lives of many others.

"The idea behind this book was a beautiful one, and I can say without a doubt that the sheer genius of the idea has come across to the reader through the pages. To write about a warzone, to humanise it for one's readers, give it life and an identity beyond bloodshed is a feat that deserves more appreciation than I could ever articulate into sentences." *Guardian*

AVAILABLE NOW

RETURN TO THE LITTLE COFFEE SHOP OF KABUL

Deborah Rodriguez

*Six women, on opposite sides of the earth,
yet forever joined by a café in Kabul.*

Sunny, its former proprietor and the new owner of the
Screaming Peacock Vineyard in the Pacific Northwest.
But can she handle the challenges of life on her own?

Yazmina, the young mother who now runs the café,
until a terrifying event strikes at the heart of her family,
and business . . .

Layla and **Kat**, two Afghan teenagers in America, both at
war with the cultures that shaped them . . .

Zara, a young woman about to be forced into a marriage with
a man she despises, with devastating consequences for all . . .

These five women are about to learn what **Halajan**, Yazmina's
rebellious mother-in-law, has known all along: that when
the world as you know it disappears, you find a new way
to survive . . .

Reuniting us with many of the compelling characters from
the international bestseller *The Little Coffee Shop of Kabul*,
Deborah Rodriguez offers up an inspiring story of strength
and courage in a world where happily-ever-afters aren't as
simple as they seem.

AVAILABLE NOW

Join us at

The
Little Book
Café

For competitions galore,
exclusive interviews with our lovely
Sphere authors, chat about
all the latest books
and much, much more.

Follow us on Twitter at
@littlebookcafe

Subscribe to our newsletter and
Like us at /thelittlebookcafe

Read. Love. Share.